THE KEEPER'S LEGACY

MEG ANNE

Cover Art by Story Wrappers

Edited by Analisa Denny

Proofread by Dominique Laura

❀ Created with Vellum

Mom, All of this is your fault. ❤
I love you forever.

Kel —
we are all born with
gifts. It's up to us to
discover them.

[signature]

THE KEEPER'S LEGACY

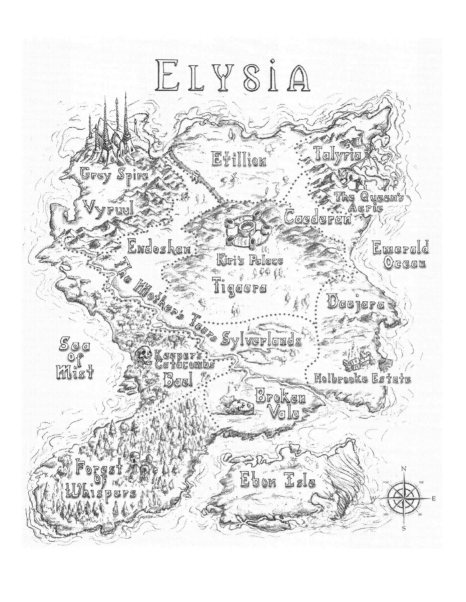

impossible to know which of the three was speaking. Instinct told Effie it was the one in the middle, whom she'd always assumed was the leader, although she would not have been able to explain what gave her that impression.

"I'm not afraid. You merely caught me off guard," Effie lied, taking two more hesitant steps toward the trio.

The trees rustled, and Effie could have sworn it was the Triumvirate's laughter. She would have been insulted if she hadn't been on the brink of bolting back into the tent. Pride be damned. There had to be another way for her to learn how to control and interpret her visions.

A quick glance at the large tent in the center of the camp filled her with resolve. Helena was counting on her.

Pushing her fear into the furthest recesses of her mind, Effie steeled her shoulders and closed the distance between them.

"Well, what are we waiting for?"

After another rustle of branches, all three figures twisted to the side and held out their right arms, gesturing for her to precede them.

Mother's tits, they want me to walk in front of them? How am I supposed to know where we're going? It seemed that there would be no easing into the head games. If this was some sort of test, Effie was desperate not to fail. So rather than giving voice to her question, she obeyed their silent command.

Gulping, she moved forward on shaking legs, taking great care to ensure no part of her touched any part of *them*. If they could pull visions from her mind with a mere touch, Mother only knew what else they could do. She had enough issues dealing with her own visions. No need to risk overseeing any of theirs.

The only sound Effie could hear over her racing heart was the soft brush of her boots over the forest floor. The Triumvirate were utterly silent behind her. If she closed her eyes, she might be able to pretend they weren't even there—if it wasn't for the hair on the back of her neck standing on end to remind her of their presence.

Nothing about the three of them following along behind her

provided any measure of comfort or reassurance. If anything, it only served to make her jumpier.

The crack of a branch had Effie reaching for the small dagger the Commander of the Kiri's army had given her the night before. Ronan's words echoed in her thoughts.

'Remember what I taught you. If you're in danger, stab first and ask questions later. Better to beg forgiveness than risk your life.'

Without any power to protect her, Effie had taken the lesson to heart and had no qualms gutting a man if it meant she or her friends would live to see another day.

The dagger bit into her skin where she held it in a death grip. Realizing what she'd been ready to do, Effie closed her eyes and let out a heartfelt curse. *You simple-minded fool. Don't go stabbing one of the most revered men in all of Elysia in your first handful of minutes together. You'll likely not live to share the tale. What good would you be to Helena then?*

Shame flooded her. She needed to be stronger than this. There was no one left to count on to protect her, save herself. Did she really want to be a timid little mouse for the rest of her life? It seemed like the fastest way to get herself killed.

Swallowing the ball of emotion that had lodged itself in her throat, Effie forced the fingers gripping the handle of her dagger to loosen and fall back down to her side.

"It's not much farther."

"We need only leave the protective barrier of the camp."

Stumbling at the unexpected voices, Effie's arms flew out to catch her balance, but there was nothing to support her. A vise-like grip on the back of her cloak was all that kept her from falling face-first to the ground.

Humiliated, Effie's eyes squeezed shut and a lone tear rolled down her cheek. It hadn't even been a full fifteen minutes since she'd joined them, and she'd already managed to make a complete and utter ass of herself.

"Breathe," one of the spectral voices ordered.

Effie didn't hesitate. Following orders was second nature after years spent in the service of others. She sucked in the pine-scented air, holding it deep in her lungs before it burst back out of her.

"Again."

More controlled this time, Effie took another deep breath. As she let the air out, her heart began to slow back down to something resembling normal—or at least as normal as it could get given her present company.

The hand fell away from her back and Effie braced herself for chastisement, certain that one or all of them would berate her clumsiness. When none came, she slowly turned back to face the trio. They were closer than she'd thought, their misting breaths mingling with her own.

"This is far enough."

Startled, Effie glanced over the right one's shoulder, where she could still clearly see the scattering of tents through the trees. They'd barely gone any distance at all.

"H-here?"

The Triumvirate's synchronized nods were her only answer.

Confusion added itself to the list of emotions spiraling through her. What made this patch of the forest any different than the rest?

As if he could read the question in her eyes, the left figure lifted his hand and let his long fingers unfurl to reveal a glittering purple stone lying in the center of an unfamiliar rune that covered his bone-white palm.

The stone, at least, Effie recognized. It was a Kaelpas stone, and it was the first thing that had made any sort of sense all morning. The small stones were very rare and did much to explain how the Triumvirate always managed to appear as if out of thin air. When activated, the stones allowed the holder, and anyone else that made physical contact with them, to travel anywhere they desired within the realm—so long as they'd been there before. The stronger the stone, the farther one could travel, and the more people that could accompany them.

This was going to be a shorter trip than she'd initially thought. Travel by Kaelpas stone was instantaneous, but also incredibly

7

MEG ANNE

disorientating. Effie prayed that she didn't embarrass herself further by puking on one of the Triumvirate once they arrived . . . wherever it was they were going.

Heavy silence stretched between them before Effie realized the trio was waiting for her to reach out and touch them so that they could be off.

A flicker of annoyance brought a scowl with it. The least they could do was give her a bit more direction instead of letting her fumble around and make an ass of herself. Their mouths might be sealed, but they clearly had no trouble communicating when they wished to. Which only made their silence all the more damning. It was intentional. Meaning this was very much a test.

Effie grit her teeth, not appreciating the realization one bit. She might be a mouse, but she refused to be a plaything.

When her hand lifted, it was steady. Chin tilted high, Effie stared at the central figure, imagining that she was staring him straight in those pits that served for eyes. There was another rustle of branches, but Effie barely had time to note it before her palm made contact with the surprisingly soft fabric of his robe and the ground was yanked from beneath her.

The breath was pulled from her lungs and her body felt like it had been turned inside out. The feeling passed as quickly as it appeared, but even so, Effie was on her hands and knees when the world finally righted itself again. Swallowing back waves of nausea, Effie silently sent up heartfelt thanks that she'd manage to hold onto that small measure of dignity.

An outstretched hand came into her field of vision, and it was all she could do not to flinch. It still took her longer than she would have liked before she could bring herself to willingly touch the inked skin.

"Thank you," she mumbled when the hand closed around hers and pulled her to her feet. For as delicate as those bony fingers looked, their grip on her was strong . . . and warm. Effie frowned at the unexpected discovery. Perhaps there was a smidgeon of humanity to be found in the trio after all.

"Welcome to your new home, Daughter."

Tearing her eyes away from the hand that still held hers, Effie managed to catch a glance at the maw of darkness yawning before her. That was all it took before her final shred of dignity was lost.

In the midst of her blood-curdling screams, Effie couldn't find it in herself to care.

CHAPTER 2

*I*t took all three of them to stop her screaming by turning her slight body away from the horrific sight, but nothing could stop the tremors racking her body. Effie didn't consider herself easily frightened, but then again, she'd never come face-to-face with a skull easily the size of seven grown men.

A skull whose mouth was wide open as if it were about to swallow her whole.

This? This is where the Keepers reside? While massive, it hardly looked like it would make suitable living quarters. Not that Effie's brain was even capable of processing much more than the fact that it was a thrice-damned *skull*.

Currently huddled up against the base of a tree with her head bowed between her knees, Effie struggled to catch her breath. The haunting image continued to assault her even though her eyes were squeezed shut.

Surrounded on the sides by a copse of thick vines and massive trees, the skull had every appearance of a giant breaking through the ground. The early morning darkness emphasized the ghostly white of its surface, making the sinister sentinel all the more terrifying. Its pitted eyes, so like the Triumvirate's, seemed to stare straight through to the heart of her. Despite the toothy grin, its mouth was nothing short of menacing. If it had lips—or a tongue—Effie was certain the skull would be licking them.

The massive snake that wound its way through the nostrils and dangled down the back of the throat in a macabre imitation of a uvula wasn't helping either. If anything, it only made the promise of death more real. If the skull wasn't going to make a meal of her, the snake certainly would.

Overall, there was something unholy about the darkness that emanated from within the skull. As if it were a sentient being in its own right and its purpose was to judge her worth. Unfortunately, Effie had the feeling she'd already been found wanting and that if she made the mistake of stepping foot within its endless depths, she'd never make it out again.

"It is an illusion."

"Cast to keep away all unwelcome guests."

"There's no need to be frightened."

"You didn't think to tone it down for those who were welcome? If this is your idea of welcoming, maybe there's a thing or two I should be teaching you instead."

Her voice sounded weak, even to her own ears. It was hard to sound fierce when you couldn't manage more than a hoarse croak.

"Once you cross the boundary the illusion will fade."

Effie lifted her head and mustered a glare that she hoped conveyed the depths of her growing hatred for them. "The only way I'm setting foot anywhere near that thing is if you drag me in against my will. And the only way you'll manage that is if you disarm, bind, and gag me. I promise, it won't be as easy as you'd think."

The chittering of leaves swelled around her. Effie's scowl deepened.

"If you think I'm kidding, you're welcome to test the theory. The way this morning's been going, I'd love the opportunity to blow off steam by shedding some blood."

There. Even Ronan would be proud of that threat.

"What makes you think you could, Daughter?"

She didn't know where the bravado came from, only that she couldn't afford to lose it. If she had any hope of proving that she would not break, she had to make a stand. While her heart may very well be broken, *she* was not. If anything, her pain had only served to forge her into something new. Something stronger, although perhaps not quite fully formed. At least, not quite yet. Right now, she had an opportunity to define who and what the something new would become.

Effie pushed herself to her feet, using the trunk of the tree behind her to support the bulk of her weight. The dagger she didn't recall grabbing glinted dangerously in her hand.

In answer to their question, she replied in a deadly soft voice she'd heard Ronan and Von use countless times before. "The corpses I've left behind me on the battlefield are more than proof enough. Tell me, *Father*," she spat the word out with every ounce of vitriol she held for her actual sire, "how many men have you killed?"

"More than the number of breaths you'll take in your lifetime, child."

Effie couldn't stop her eyes from flaring wide at the answer. Hoping they didn't notice, she clenched her teeth and stood her ground.

The leftmost figure tilted his head. She assumed it was he who spoke as the spectral voice echoed within her mind.

"Stand down. We are not your enemy."

"Really? You could have fooled me."

"How so? We've done nothing but offer our assistance."

A muscle began to spasm in her jaw. *Assistance? That's what these mind games were supposed to be?*

"Since you snuck up on me this morning, you've done nothing but ensure I'm off-balance and terrified."

"Your terror is your own doing."

Effie glanced between the three motionless figures, her ire spiking. It was infuriating trying to fight with someone when you weren't entirely sure *who* you were fighting with. Was it only one of them or all three?

"I strongly disagree. Sneaking up on a girl in the dead of night—"

"We were waiting for you at the edge of the camp. As promised."

13

"—and then gesturing for her to blindly walk ahead of you without any idea of where she was going—"

"You knew we were bringing you to the citadel."

Effie continued to speak over their mental interruptions. "—not to mention the part where you scare her out of her damn mind with your creepy mind speaking, and then insist on keeping her in the dark with vague half-truths or by not deigning to speak at all—"

"We provide information when it is necessary."

She let her dagger fly, not bothering to check where it landed, knowing it would fly true. "Do better," she hissed.

The central figure's hood dipped as he glanced down to eye the dagger that was still vibrating with the force of her throw. All that was visible was the soft glint of its dark hilt against the scarlet of the Keeper's robe. The blade sunk clean through the damp earth.

Effie allowed herself a small gratified smile when the Keeper tried to tug his robe back. She'd managed to pin it—and him—to the floor.

The leaves rustled, lifting the hair on her arms. Effie's smile faded as the Keeper jerked the cloth once again. The resulting tear should have filled her with satisfaction, but somehow all she felt was childish. Guilt began to eat at her, making her cheeks burn.

Somewhere in the middle of trying to establish her worth, she'd ended up throwing a tantrum.

Things were definitely not going as planned.

In one fluid move, the Keeper bent and pulled her dagger from the ground. Silently he held it out to her.

She eyed the blade and then the hooded figure. Sighing, she stepped forward and reached for the weapon. As her fist closed around the hilt, the Keeper jerked the blade toward his body and pulled Effie forward.

"I will let your unfounded accusations go unpunished this once, because you are scared, and you do not yet know the rules. Be warned, Daughter, that I will not do so again. The measure of a person is defined by the level of respect they are granted by others. You have just lost mine. It will take much for you to earn it back."

He let go of the blade and dropped his arm, further throwing Effie off-balance.

"Moreover, you will step inside the citadel without further comment. If you do not, I will arrange for someone to come get you, and I'm sure they'll simply toss you over their shoulder if you continue to resist. I'd prefer not to have to treat you as a child, although you seem to insist on behaving like one. Every action has a consequence, Daughter. It would serve you well to remember that in the future."

Effie's jaw was hanging at the end of his speech. It was the first time any of the Triumvirate had ever referred to themselves as an individual, and certainly the longest speech she'd ever heard one utter. Even the deep echo of his spectral voice in her mind had altered as he'd spoken. As if it had not been the shared consciousness of the Triumvirate he'd used, but a different, personal timbre. While trying to classify the distinction of the tone, an image of smoke curling up from a blazing fire flared to life in her mind.

Effie took great pride in learning to stay out of sight and not draw any attention to herself. Somehow, in a mere handful of minutes, the Triumvirate had gotten under her skin to the extent that she'd managed to throw away a lifetime of careful habits. That, combined with his damning words, was more than enough to have her mouth slamming closed. She was not surprised he lashed out. She'd earned the rebuke with her impetuous actions. What did surprise her, however, was how deeply his words cut.

Before she could apologize, he spoke again.

"Consider that your first lesson."

Without another word, the trio turned and strode toward the skull. Effie shuddered as she warily eyed the monstrosity, no less averse to it now than she'd been initially. There was no getting around it. She was going to have to step into that gaping mouth and its perfect darkness.

"Mother's heaving tits," she muttered.

A soft breeze blew a few loose curls in her face and Effie distractedly pushed them away with the back of her hand, her conflicted emotions still swirling within her. Fear of the unknown. Fear of failure. Fear of these *creatures* she'd just placed her trust in. Fear wasn't the only emotion that had taken residence in her heart. There was a bubbling anger and endless pool of heartache that had lodged itself deep within her when Darrin died, and it only swelled in size after her grandmother's meaningless death.

It was no wonder her scattered thoughts were all over the place.

Effie's eyes fell closed and she let out a soft sigh.

If this was who she was now, then so be it.

Not eager to test whether the Keeper really would send someone to throw her over a shoulder, Effie hurried after their retreating backs, the scarlet of their cloaks already getting lost in the black of the cavernous mouth. If there was the slightest chance she would run into any of the others whose gift she now shared, Effie would really rather not do it arse first.

CHAPTER 3

*T*he darkness faded between one step and the next. One moment Effie was staring down the face of death, and the next she was blinded, blinking rapidly to adjust as she was bathed in a pool of golden light. Effie had heard whispers of the Keeper's Catacombs hidden somewhere in the middle of Bael, but that's all she knew: whispers and fragments. The reality was . . . breathtaking.

It wasn't a catacomb at all; no underground lair hidden beneath miles of earth and rock, or cave littered with rotting bones. It was a city, and the biggest one she'd ever seen at that. Granted, that wasn't saying much seeing as how she'd barely stepped foot outside of the Holbrooke Estate before a few months ago.

How is this possible? Weren't we just in the middle of the jungle? No remnants of the thick roping vines or humid air was to be found.

Mouth gaping, Effie's eyes hungrily drank in the sight of the sprawling buildings illuminated by hundreds of floating orbs under a dusky lavender, predawn sky. She'd been so sure she'd be greeted by spiderwebs and the putrid stench of death, and instead there was only beauty.

The Corruptor's war had clearly not touched this place. Effie had no doubt that if the impostor-queen, Rowena, knew such a place existed, she would have already tried to lay claim to it.

Towering stone buildings of the palest gray surrounded her. She didn't recognize the stone, but if mist had a solid form, that would certainly be it. At first glance, there was no rhyme or reason to the structures' placement. They simply seemed to crawl out of the city's center—where Effie currently stood—with swerving roads disappearing between them.

Other than the stone, there were no discernable similarities between the buildings. It was as if countless generations of people had found their way to this place and left a little piece of their history by crafting a unique building to stand for all of time. It should have been chaotic, all of the competing styles, but the differences only underscored the beauty of the city as a whole.

Effie spun in a slow circle, her brain desperately trying to relate what she was seeing with what she'd been expecting. She was stunned to find no hint of the darkness they'd left behind. Not so much as a doorway to indicate how they'd arrived here.

"Portal," one of the Keepers said, perhaps in response to the unspoken question on her face.

So, they really had walked into another world. Just like that, everything Effie knew to be true fell away.

"Come." The rightmost figure gestured up ahead to where a circular tower practically disappeared into the clouds.

"Oh," she breathed.

While not demarcated in any notable way, the structure they were leading her to was clearly the city's heart—the citadel.

Shallow steps curved along the front of the building and led to a walkway that wrapped around the outside. Pillars were evenly spaced along the outer rim of the walkway with a half wall that linked them together. It would make a lovely place to curl up with a book on a warm day.

It wasn't until she'd almost walked past the outer wall that she noticed the mosaic along its surface. The tiny tiles were shimmering shades of silver and pearl, all of which blended into the stone seamlessly. Once the sun rose and hit the tiles, the building would glitter. Effie's fingers itched to trace the design in the smooth surface.

Fighting the impulse, she moved up the stairs, stepping out of the soft glow and beneath the arched ceiling that covered the walkway. Glancing up, she noted more mosaic scenes along its length. It was too dim to make out the images, but she was looking forward to returning later.

Her head twisted back to the Triumvirate as the air rippled around her. Two doors, the same deep red as their cloaks, swung open inwardly without a sound. A quick glance at the trio's arms confirmed they were still at rest by their respective sides, which meant that not one of them had done something as obvious as turn a knob. So, how did they open the doors?

Before her mind could chase yet another question, light spilled out of the citadel and down the stairs. Effie lifted a hand to shield her eyes, not prepared for blinding luminescence.

Not waiting to see if she was still following, the trio stepped over the threshold and into the brightly lit room, leaving her with no choice but to hustle after them or get left behind.

Thick scarlet rugs muffled the sounds of her footsteps, giving the room a hushed, reverent feel. It was opulent; bookcases filled with every color tome encircling its walls. In the rare case a shelf was not filled with books, intricate artifacts stood in their place. In the center of the room there was a huge, round table. Its surface was currently empty, but Effie could easily picture a dozen people sitting around with books and parchment scattered before them. She could only imagine what secrets the room held, both within the pages of the books, as well as the walls themselves.

Eyes still bouncing around drinking in every detail, it was a moment before Effie noticed that they weren't alone. Had it been any other day, maybe she would have known better, but in that moment the man with golden hair and piercing green eyes stole the breath from her lungs with more force than a blow to the chest.

Harsh buzzing filled her ears and her surroundings took on a hazy cast. Transfixed, all Effie could see was the man who had been dead for the better part of a year. Her hand lifted, her fingers attempting to touch him even from a distance.

Heart pounding, she struggled to breathe.

"Darrin . . ." The name fell from numb lips as the memory of his charred and bloody corpse superimposed itself over the very alive male standing before her.

"I'm afraid not," a deep, cultured accent replied.

The unfamiliar voice jarred her from her reverie. Disappointment filled her, tasting like ash in her mouth as the man came into focus. She knew it was impossible. Darrin was dead, and had been for a while, but for that split second . . .

The hope hurt almost more than the reality. Heart aching with a wave of fresh grief, Effie shoved the memory of Darrin away.

"I'm sorry," she whispered, her voice croaking around the sudden emotion.

The stranger peeled away from the entryway in which he was standing, allowing her to finally notice the details her distracted mind had initially missed.

"No need to apologize."

He was blond, yes, but where Darrin was sunshine, this man was a deep molten gold that bordered on bronze. While green, his eyes were nothing like the grassy fields she'd always associated with the man who had stolen her heart with his boyish smile. The stranger's eyes were darker, more of a deep sage she'd never seen before, and fringed with dark lashes that further enhanced their unusual color. Full lips, a square jaw, and high cheekbones gave the man a distinctly aristocratic air. But if he was here, then he must be a Keeper, which meant his past station held no relevance.

A knowing smile stretched across his handsome face as she studied him. He walked toward her with slow, prowling steps. "It's a pleasure to finally meet you, Effie."

She flinched at his use of her name. Tracking the movement, his eyes and mouth tightened almost imperceptibly before the emotion cleared and she wondered if she might have imagined it altogether.

Lifting one shoulder in a careless shrug, he explained, "It's a hazard of our position to forget that not everyone knows as much as we do."

It took a moment for her to understand. "Oh, right. The visions."

"Indeed."

Silence swelled between them as he stared at her with an expectancy she didn't understand. Suddenly uncomfortable, she shifted, looking around for the Triumvirate who had stepped back at this man's appearance. *Shouldn't they introduce us or something? What are they waiting for?*

Holding out a hand, palm up, he offered another enigmatic smile. "I'm Kieran." He made the announcement with the smugness of one declaring they'd just won a bet.

She narrowed her eyes suspiciously, not liking the hungry way he was studying her. Since he already knew her name, he must have Seen her in at least one of his visions, but what had he Seen? There was an unwelcome vulnerability that accompanied the revelation.

Falling back on the polite formality that had been engrained into her during childhood, Effie murmured, "Hello, Kieran."

Not wanting to embarrass herself more than she already had that morning, Effie finally offered her hand, shivering slightly when his warm, smooth fingers wrapped around hers. He dipped, his eyes never straying from hers, and pressed his lips to the back of her hand.

Her skin burned where Kieran's lips gently pressed against it. It was chaste and proper by every standard she knew, and yet Effie could not shake the feeling that the action was entirely more meaningful to him than it ought to have been.

"I've been waiting for you."

The weight of the words and the intensity of his stare unnerved her. That, combined with her temporary confusion, had her more than a little eager to put distance between them.

Just what in the Mother's name has he Seen?

"I can't say the same, seeing as how I've no clue who you are." The words were meant to be a dismissal, but he only let out a deep, rolling laugh.

"Fair enough, but I am looking forward to remedying that in the days to come."

"Mmm," she responded evasively, looking pointedly at the three robed figures who were obviously watching this interaction play out.

A little help would be nice.

Knowing better than to assume any response would be forthcoming, she flicked her gaze back up to Kieran's. "I probably shouldn't keep them waiting much longer. See you around, Kieran."

His eyes darkened at her words and a smile curved his full lips. "Yes, you will."

She blinked. *Right, then.* Rushing forward, Effie waited until Kieran was no longer in hearing distance to mutter, "Thanks for nothing."

The middle figure tilted his head in a move that was starting to remind her of Ronan's raised brow.

"You were in no danger."

"That's not the point. The least you could have done was introduce us and save me from the awkward conversation."

For once, none of them had a comeback.

Effie's shoulders sagged. She officially couldn't process anything else. "I find that I am suddenly very tired. Is there a place I could set my bag down and rest for a little while before we continue with the rest of the tour?"

The middle figure dipped his head after a long pause.

"Follow me."

He turned to the left, leaving his counterparts behind. Effie glanced between them in surprise. She'd never known them to be apart. It was disconcerting.

He moved quickly, giving her no chance to steal more than passing glances at the dozens of rooms they passed. The citadel was a maze of countless hallways and floors, and Effie was thoroughly lost. After descending the third flight of stairs and making as many turns, her guide pushed open a door and gestured for her to enter.

"These will be your quarters."

She looked at the barren room. There were no adornments beyond clean linens and the most basic of furniture: bed, desk, bookcase, trunk. It was still nicer than many she'd been in before.

"For how long?" she asked, turning back to him.

"Forever."

Effie blinked.

"This space is yours, anytime you have need of it. Do with it what you will."

He moved to leave, and Effie found herself reaching out to stop him. He froze and her hand fell short of actually making contact with his arm. She flushed and bit the inside of her cheek as her hand fell back to her side.

"I just wanted to say thank you . . . for giving me some time."

He nodded, waiting to see if there was anything else.

Knotting her fingers together, she added, "What should I . . . that is, I was wondering what I'm supposed to call you?"

"We have no names."

"Oh," she said softly, not sure why the answer made her sad.

"We released our identities when we took our vows."

Her brows scrunched together. "But there has to be something that the other Keepers refer to you as beside your joint title. How else do you three know who people are talking to?"

He shrugged, a gesture that looked out of place on his towering frame. *"Does it really matter?"*

"It does to me. There is power in a name, just as there is power in a title."

"Only the power you give it."

"Fine," she agreed, weary and out of patience with his non-answers. "Then I will give you each my own names and you'll be forced to live with them."

She could hear the amusement in his voice. Once again it was not the haunting voice of the Triumvirate, but the deeper and less refined voice he'd slipped into outside. *"And just what do you propose to call me?"*

Asshole, for starters. The thought caused her lips to twitch and she tried to cover it by pressing them together as she scrambled for something suitably disrespectful and yet not entirely offensive.

"You shall be Smoke," she announced as the name popped into her mind.

"Smoke?"

Too embarrassed to explain it had to do with the way his personal voice sounded in her mind, she shrugged and grasped for an explanation. Blurting out the first thing that came to her, Effie said, "You three are nothing but smoke and mirrors. You create the illusions you want others to see and hide behind them, all in an attempt to manipulate the world you try so hard to remain apart from."

"So, if I am Smoke, what shall you call the others?"

"Mirror One and Mirror Two, obviously."

The rustle of his cloak was the only indication he might be laughing. *"And how do you intend to tell them apart?"*

"One is on the left, and Two is on the right."

"What makes you think we are always in the same position?"

"Balls," she muttered, biting her lip. She hadn't thought of that.

Smoke held up a hand. *"The names shall serve. I will let the others know. If you have need of us, just call and one—or all—of us will find you."*

He turned and disappeared back down the hallway, leaving her alone for the first time since she'd left her tent. Grateful for the solitude, Effie quickly shut the door and pressed her back against it.

Her bag fell from her shoulder and her head dropped against the wood with a soft thud. Suddenly too fatigued to stand, she slid down the door until she was sitting on the floor and closed her eyes.

Effie couldn't say when the first of the tears started to fall, or when she curled up in a ball on the floor. It could have been hours or perhaps only minutes later, but eventually she found peace in the silence of her room and her breathing evened out as she drifted off into the sleep of the truly exhausted.

And while she slept, she dreamed.

CHAPTER 4

*K*ieran bit back a growl of frustration as he stalked down another random corridor. He'd lost count of how many years he'd been searching for the girl who'd visited his dreams. It had been at least twenty-five since he left home and joined the Keepers, but when you're one of the long-lived races, twenty-five years may as well be a heartbeat.

Centuries of dreams, of yearning to meet the girl with the cornflower blue eyes, and when it finally happens, she thinks he's someone else.

Kieran sneered. That was a social misstep he'd never experienced in his centuries as a prince. Especially not from women. Prince no longer, Kieran didn't hold the luxury of a title, or any of the inherent fame that went along with it. For once, he would have to be judged solely by his words and actions.

He wasn't sure that was a good thing.

With a sigh, Kieran continued his aimless pacing. He'd been returning a book to the main archive when Effie had crossed the threshold. Kieran had forgotten how to breathe. He'd Seen her in countless dreams over the course of hundreds of years, but when he finally laid eyes on her for real it had been a surprise.

Her wild blonde curls had been tied back in a thick braid, but rebellious strands had sprung free to rest against her cheeks and neck. Her luminous eyes were wide, and her rosebud lips had fallen open in surprise as she eyed the archives with a wonder he'd long since lost. Kieran struggled not to think too long on the shape and curve of her mouth.

She was shorter than he'd realized, the top of her head barely reaching his shoulder, and she looked thinner than usual, as if she'd been more worried lately about feeding others than herself. He knew from his dreams that was entirely plausible. Thin or not, her generous curves were not diminished. If anything, her tight battle leathers only enhanced them, even if they were finely coated with dirt. A few dark smears had even found their way to her milk and honey cheeks.

Kieran let out another deep sigh. Travel stains and all, Effie was even more beautiful in person. It was going to be a constant battle to keep himself from touching her.

He let out a soft chuckle, fully realizing he was laying it on thick, but still too in awe to care. *She* was here. The girl from his dreams. Effie.

Finally.

Excitement coursed through him. After years of searching, his wait was over. Everything he'd given up to find her would now be repaid sevenfold. None of it mattered. Only her.

Too bad she has no clue who you are . . .

The unwanted thought jolted him out of his planning. A frown pulled at his lips. That was an unforeseen problem. Something few of the Keepers ever experienced given their various gifts. All this time, Kieran had been certain she'd dreamed of him as well. Clearly that was not the case.

For all that he knew of Effie and his desperation to finally be with her, he was still a stranger to her. Which meant he'd need patience.

A realm's worth.

Elder's piss in a pot.

Kieran's frown deepened as he recalled the wave of disappointment that crashed into him the moment she whispered someone else's name. It had nearly sent him to his knees.

Stubborn resolved filled him. He'd never met a woman he couldn't win. With a little bit of time, she would be just as eager for his touch as he was for hers. Besides, he'd already waited centuries to hold her. What was a few more days?

Whistling, Kieran rounded the corner and barely avoided crashing into the wall of scowling muscle that went by the name of Lucian.

"Watch where you're going," Kieran snapped.

"Something has your knickers twisted tighter than usual," the Guardian murmured, crossing his arms.

Kieran bit back his annoyance. Verbally sparring with Lucian was one of his favorite pastimes, but he had a seduction to plan and no time to waste with the man that lived to make his life a living hell.

"Miranda's granddaughter has finally arrived," he said instead.

Lucian lifted his brows, clearly unimpressed with the news. "And?"

His years of courtly training were all that kept him from sputtering. "And so it would seem that my purpose is finally about to be realized."

"Lucky you."

Kieran scowled. Only a Guardian could scoff at the notion of a Keeper's prophecy coming to fruition. *Immortal bastard.*

"You have no idea," he gritted out.

Lucian stared at him, unblinking. Realizing the conversation was over, Kieran made to move around the man, who stopped him with a palm to the chest. An able fighter, Kieran could have held his own if he'd been armed, but without a weapon to aid him, he was no match for the warrior's strength. Kieran stumbled back, his stare darkening as he straightened his simple jerkin.

"Did you need something?" Kieran growled, his voice deceptively soft.

"The Triumvirate have summoned you."

Kieran's eyes narrowed. He had no appointment with them, but it wasn't unusual for them to call on him out of the blue either. So why did he get the feeling Lucian was trying to keep him from wandering down the hall? What was the Guardian hiding?

"Did they now? And you know that how?"

Lucian didn't bother to reply. He rarely did.

Kieran studied the man, trying to find a clue to indicate he was bluffing, but he may as well have been studying stone. There was nothing to be found but the mild hint of disdain that always accompanied Lucian's intense gaze.

Nothing to do for it but assume he was telling the truth. Not exactly like the Triumvirate were the sort to keep waiting.

"Very well. Must be about the girl."

Lucian continued to stare him down, offering no comment one way or the other.

"We really should work on your conversation skills, Lucian. It is the one area where I can say with absolute certainty that you are woefully inept." Kieran's voice was carefully solicitous, even if the words were barbed. "You never know when you're going to need to actually talk to someone about something important. Don't want to make an ass out of yourself by being out of practice when the time finally comes. I know how deeply you value your pride."

Ah, there it was. A small muscle in Lucian's jaw ticked, telling Kieran he'd finally struck a nerve.

"No? Some other time, then." Kieran turned on his heel and walked back the way he came, his jaunty whistle echoing loudly down the empty corridor.

CHAPTER 5

*"Y*ou really shouldn't let people talk to you that way."

Effie looked up at the blond man who had fallen into step beside her. Surprise tingled along her spine.

"It's hard to break a lifetime's worth of habits."

Darrin frowned, the golden stubble along his jaw glinting in the soft light of the hallway. "What could you have possibly done to warrant such abuse?"

Effie wasn't certain whether or not the question was rhetorical. On the off chance he was genuinely curious, she answered in a muted voice, "I'm ungifted."

A dark blond brow quirked up in a silent demand for her to elaborate. Is it possible he doesn't know what that means? Flustered at the idea of having to explain, and risk losing the warm comfort of his companionship, she pressed her lips together and stared hard at a crack in the wall.

Darrin stopped her with a brush of his calloused fingers along her arm. "Why should anyone care whether or not you can call on the Mother's power? That has nothing to do with your worth as one of her children."

Pleasure tinged her cheeks a rosy pink. Only one other person had ever told her the same. To hear one of the Kiri's Circle validate her despite her lack of magical ability . . . it was one of the highest compliments she'd ever been granted. Effie risked a glance up at the handsome warrior. His face was twisted into a thoughtful scowl. He didn't have a clue how deeply his words affected her.

"Most people feel that without power, you are not one of the Mother's children—"

"What utter horse shit. That's like saying the Mother didn't create the Daejarans because Von is a rutting bastard."

A surprised snort escaped, and Effie's hand flew up to cover her mouth. His words were practically treason, but if anyone could get away with saying such about the Kiri's Mate, her Shield was certainly the one.

Darrin's lips lifted in a smile and his eyes warmed as he studied her. "Not used to hearing anyone talk that way about Von?"

Effie shook her head.

He lifted a shoulder in a careless shrug. "I've said the same to his face . . . worse actually."

Another helpless laugh bubbled up and a genuine smile stretched across her face. "I can't imagine he took it well."

"No, he didn't." Darrin's eyes had fallen to her lips. "You should smile more often, Effie. It suits you." He lifted his hand and ran a single finger along her cheek. "Your whole face lights up with your joy. It's quite—"

Darrin blinked, cutting off the flow of words that he'd been uttering almost reverently. The tops of his ears and cheeks pinkened and he cleared his throat. Effie desperately wished he would finish saying whatever he'd been thinking. Her wish must have been shining in her eyes because Darrin's gaze sharpened, and his voice had deepened when he finally spoke again.

"Lovely. Your smile is lovely, Effie."

Her breath caught in her throat as butterflies exploded in her belly. "Th-thank you," she stammered, her eyes dropping to the tips of her scuffed boots.

Darrin crooked a finger beneath her chin and tilted her head up until her eyes reluctantly met his again.

"When was the last time someone offered you a compliment?" he asked, his voice barely above a whisper.

Effie shrugged. "Lady Holbrooke complimented my sewing—"

"No," he cut her off with a jerk of his chin. "You. When was the last time someone complimented you?"

Stymied, Effie searched her memory trying to think of a time when someone other than Darrin had offered her a kind word.

A frown pulled at his lips. "If you have to think that hard, it's been too long."

"Aye," she agreed, not sure what else to say.

Darrin's eyes searched her face. After a moment he let out a soft sigh. "I guess I shall have to remedy that for you. The next time someone asks, I don't want you to have to even think about it. You deserve to be reminded daily, Effie. You are a beautiful woman with an even more beautiful heart. No matter what anyone else says or thinks, there are none who are your equal in that regard."

Effie's mouth fell open on a silent gasp. No one—no man—had ever said anything so tender to her before.

"Darrin," an annoyed voice called from the other end of the hall. "Helena's looking for you."

Darrin's hand fell from her chin, and his eyes flicked to where Ronan stood with his arms crossed. "I'll be right there."

"Now!"

With a roll of his eyes, Darrin turned back to her. "I guess this is goodbye for now." His fingers brushed against hers, grasping lightly to lift them to his lips. With the gentlest brush of his lips against the back of her fingers, he released her and smiled. "Until tomorrow, Effie."

Speechless, she gave a limp wave and stared at the direction he'd taken off. She was still staring long after he'd gone.

❧

EFFIE CAME AWAKE SLOWLY. She was still on the floor, her body stiff and cramped for being curled up in such an uncomfortable manner. Even so, a soft smile curved her lips. *Darrin.*

When he'd first passed, he would visit her dreams nightly, or at least her memories of their time together would find her in her sleep. As the days turned to months, the frequency of such dreams had lessened. She hadn't realized how much she'd missed those nightly visits. It couldn't be a coincidence that he'd return now, when she'd been desperate for something normal in a sea of change.

"Thank you," she whispered, tucking away the memory of him back into her heart.

Feeling bolstered, both by the sleep and the dream, Effie pushed off the floor and took in the bare chamber.

She didn't have much in the way of personal belongings, but she'd packed a few things that would make this place feel more like hers. Lifting her pack, Effie got to work making the room feel like a home.

A COUPLE OF HOURS LATER, a brisk knock on the door halted her in the middle of folding up a thick blanket. Effie glanced up and stared at the door as if it would show her who was waiting on the other side. A second knock had her dropping the blanket onto the bed and crossing the short distance to swing it open.

"Wh—" Her words died as she took in the well-dressed man with his hands clasped behind his back. *What is he doing here?*

"Kieran," he supplied with a half-smile, mistaking her blank stare for confusion.

"I remember," she said sharply, her fingers biting into the door. What was it about this man that set her teeth on edge?

His brows arched in surprise at her harsh tone, but he dipped his chin in a nod. "Right, well the Triumvirate sent me to fetch you. I'm to be your guide and tutor while you are here."

"Oh," she said, surprise and something that felt oddly like disappointment coiling in her stomach.

She supposed it made sense that it wasn't one of Triumvirate that would be seeing to the basics of her training. After all, they were sort of important. They probably had a variety of other tasks that required their attention. But still . . . they had promised to see to her training themselves. So why then had they passed it off to him?

Effie eyed Kieran warily. Perhaps she'd misjudged him. She had only known him for about five seconds, she realized. She bit down on the inside of her cheek, feeling foolish. It wasn't his fault he reminded her of Darrin. Nor had he actually done anything worthy of her icy reaction to him. Straightening her shoulders, she resolved to try to judge him fairly.

Taking her change of expression as a good sign, he lifted one of the arms from behind his back. "If you're ready, I would be happy to escort you to the dining hall to grab something to eat before we start our lesson."

Just as she was about to refuse, her stomach gave a loud growl. Pressing his lips together, Kieran politely refrained from commenting, even as his eyes sparkled with mirth.

"Yes, something to eat would be welcome."

Kieran nodded and waited for her to step into the hall and close the door behind her before setting off.

"So, what do you think of the citadel thus far?" he inquired politely.

"It's a lot to take in," she answered honestly.

"What a lukewarm response."

Effie chuckled. "Don't get me wrong, it's a lovely place. I've just seen so little of it. I think it's too soon to form an opinion."

"Mmm."

She risked a glance at him, trying to gauge whether she was imagining the hint of censure in his tone. Seeing nothing, she decided it was simply the niggling of her own conscience.

"I had thought, given the name, that it would be a bit. . ." Effie trailed off, at a loss for words.

"Creepier?" Kieran supplied, startling a laugh out of her.

"Yes, exactly."

Kieran nodded. "I know what you mean. I felt the same way when I arrived. It would be hard not to when they refer to the place as a catacomb."

"It is a bit misleading."

"Intentionally so."

Effie rolled her eyes. "The Keepers do seem to love their mysteries."

"Can you think of a better way to keep people away? With the allure of prophecy and glimpses into the future, they need a way to dissuade the masses from seeking them out."

She was silent as she considered his words.

"The reasoning behind their actions does have a tendency to make it hard to stay annoyed with them," Kieran added.

"Is it that obvious?"

He offered her a lopsided grin that made him appear years younger. Effie looked away, not ready to admit to herself how much she enjoyed looking at it . . . or him.

"It is a common reaction to the Keepers, the Triumvirate especially. They have a habit of infuriating those closest to—"

"Only because they insist on being so damn secretive all the time!" The words exploded from her before she'd realized she'd spoken aloud. "Sorry," she whispered, cheeks burning.

"You simply said what we all think. They know it too. Not that it stops them." Kieran gestured for Effie to turn right, and then paused to open a large red door. "Dining hall is just through here."

Effie stepped past him into a spacious room with high ceilings. Long tables ran along the length of the room. It was big enough to comfortably seat well over a hundred people, but was currently empty.

"Where is everyone?"

Kieran shrugged. "Outside of lessons, we come and go as we please." Effie's confusion must have been written on her face because Kieran continued. "The life of a Keeper is not so structured as you would think. No one is born a Keeper. The gift appears when it will, which means that school in a classic sense is impossible. None of us start in the same place, let alone at the same time. We all must learn as we go, and some learn much faster than others. Such is the nature of our power."

She was frowning by the time he was done. *What a sublimely unhelpful explanation.*

"You're actually the first new Keeper since I arrived twenty-five years ago."

That stopped her dead in her tracks. "Seriously?"

Effie's eyes searched his face. He didn't look much older than she did. *Considering most people confuse you for a twelve-year-old girl, maybe that's not entirely true.* There would be no mistaking Kieran for a child.

He smirked as her eyes roamed his well-muscled body and she jerked them back up to his face.

"How old are you?" she demanded.

"How old do you think I am?"

"Gah, you really are one of them, aren't you?"

He laughed, a deep chuckle that had his eyes crinkling. "I wasn't trying to be vexing. I am truly curious."

Narrowing her eyes, she observed him again before tossing out an answer. "Twenty-seven?"

His lips tilted up in amusement, so she tried again.

"Thirty-two?"

He shook his head.

"Forty?" she asked, throwing her hands up in exasperation. "The least you could do is give me a clue."

"I was forty, two hundred and twenty-six years ago."

"Two hundred and. . ." Effie's knees buckled, and she sat down hard. "But . . . how is that. . ." Mind swirling with questions, she could only gape up at him.

Kieran's smile was filled with more compassion than she would have expected. "It can be a lot to wrap your head around the first time you meet one of the long-lived races. I met a man once who was well over three thousand years old, and I think my expression was somewhere along the lines of yours."

Dumbfounded, she blinked up at him. She couldn't even

comprehend living to be a hundred, let alone three thousand. Pushing the staggering admission aside, she asked, "Are all Keepers as old as you?"

"Part of our gift is an extended life, yes. But no, I am the only one among us who is truly long-lived. Well, aside from the Triumvirate. It is believed those three are actually immortal."

It was hard to breathe. *Extended life? Immortal? Mother's tits. What have I gotten myself into?*

Sitting up, she squinted at him. "Do you have any other shocking tidbits for me? Might as well get them over with now before I try to stand again."

His laughter washed over her. "I'm sure many things you learn in the days to come will be surprising. The limits of your power among them."

Effie made a face at the reminder of her visions. She was not eager to face another. They hit her with the force of a blow to the gut. Finally finding herself in the presence of someone who was familiar with her gift and didn't seem to mind talking about it, she blurted, "When did your visions stop feeling like someone has shoved their fist into your head and scrambled your brains?"

"Is that what it feels like for you?" Kieran asked, his eyebrows pulling together and his eyes widening.

"Yours don't?" Effie asked in dismay. *Am I broken? Is something wrong with me?*

Kieran shook his head.

Effie stood, cursing as her head swam and she fell back onto the bench. "How in the Mother's name is that fair? Am I the only one who foams from the mouth and shakes as if the world was splitting into two beneath me?"

Kieran sputtered. Effie would have laughed if she wasn't so upset.

He studied her for a moment before stating, "You're joking."

"Does it look like I'm joking?" she snapped, angry tears shining in her eyes as frustration overtook her self-pity.

Nameless emotions clouded his gaze. She didn't know him well enough to recognize what was going on in his mind, but he looked conflicted.

"That sounds . . . uncomfortable."

"I would say it's a wee bit more than *uncomfortable*," she choked out around a snort of derision.

With a shake of his head, Kieran took a seat beside her. A muscle twitched in his jaw before he tilted his head to look at her directly.

"Perhaps what you learn here will help with that. Miranda never seemed to suffer from any of those symptoms and one can only assume you inherited your power from her."

The only word she heard was her grandmother's name. She had hoped when she joined the Keepers that she would meet people that knew her, but she never thought to ask Kieran.

"You knew her?" she whispered, her emotions once again oscillating wildly. She was starting to feel unbalanced, but was too interested in his answer to care.

Kieran offered her a soft smile, his eyes kind. "I did. She was my guide when I came here. It's part of the reason I asked to be yours. I was happy to learn that the Triumvirate had granted my request."

"Part of?"

"My dreams were the other."

Oh, right. Those. Despite the heat she could feel crawling up her neck and into her cheeks, Effie forced herself not to look away. *No longer a mouse, remember?*

"Will you tell me about them?"

His smile turned wolfish. "Sometime, perhaps."

She rolled her eyes. Blasted enigmatic Keepers and their secrets. She couldn't wait until she knew something no one else did so she could lord it over them and see how they liked being on the other end of these infuriating mind games.

Companionable silence stretched between them. Knowing Kieran had been acquainted with her grandmother definitely changed her opinion of him. It was almost like her grandmother had gifted his friendship to her. The errant thought made her smile.

"What's that for?" he asked.

"I just realized that if my grandmother taught you, then your teaching me is sort of like her doing so by proxy."

"She really was an amazing woman. I was sorry to hear of her passing."

Grief, swift and fierce, nearly choked her. Unable to speak, Effie nodded her thanks.

Kieran's hand brushed over her knee in a sign of silent comfort.

Her grandmother had been an amazing woman. As a Keeper, she'd rarely been around, but even so, she'd been a constant fixture in Effie's life. One of the only people who'd never made her feel she was less for being born without power. Effie held tight to the memories of their time together. She didn't think she would ever fully get over her death. It was too painful to think that she'd no longer hear the stories of her adventures or be held in her warm embrace.

Needing to distract herself before she lost the fragile hold she still held on her emotions, she changed the subject. "Didn't you promise me something to eat?"

"I did." Standing, Kieran held out a hand.

Effie eyed it for a moment before hesitantly placing her hand in his. As far as signs of trust went, it was a small one, but it was the first she'd shown him. Kieran's growing smile told her he recognized it too.

CHAPTER 6

*O*nce she was able to relax around him, Kieran really was pleasant company. He spent the next few hours asking her thoughtful questions about her past. Better still, he never seemed to pry and always had an amusing story of his own to share in response.

If she didn't know better, Effie might say she was starting to enjoy herself.

Or at least she was until he brought up her visions.

"I have an idea."

"Oh?" she teased. "Is that an uncommon enough occurrence you felt the need to announce it?"

"Hilarious," he replied dryly.

Effie grinned with impish delight. It was rare she felt comfortable enough with someone to willingly provoke them. She quite liked it.

"I want to see if we can induce your visions."

Her smile vanished. "What? Why?"

Kieran held up his hands. "Just hear me out."

Wishing she hadn't had that second helping of stew, Effie waited for him to continue.

"I think it could be really helpful for both of us to work through one of your visions together. It will help you learn the process of breaking it down. And it will have the added benefit of letting me get an idea of where we're starting. In order to be accurate, we need to be able to explore each detail, so an older vision wouldn't work. It needs to be fresh. There's an herb we use sometimes when we are seeking the answer to something, but our visions go quiet. Well, the others use it. It doesn't work with my dreams."

"Why not?"

Kieran shrugged. "We aren't sure. Since my visions manifest themselves through dreams and not in the same manner as the others, our best guess is it's tied to that."

Effie frowned. She wished her visions would come to her in her sleep instead of accosting her while she was awake. Maybe then she could ignore them.

"Why are you special?" she grumbled.

He grinned. "I have a theory about that as well, but we'll save it for another time."

"Figures."

"What was that?"

"Nothing. So, what were you saying about your magic drug giving me visions?"

"Herb, not drug."

"Mind-altering equals drug in my opinion."

"You're a barrel of laughs at parties, aren't you?"

"Who says I was invited to parties?"

"Maybe if you knew how to have some fun . . ."

She stuck her tongue out at him.

Kieran laughed, but it was tinged with melancholy. "You remind me of my sister when you do that."

"Sister?"

He nodded. "Liyah. We were always at each other's throats."

Picking up on the tense, her voice softened. "Were?"

Kieran glanced away, his face slipping back into an impassive mask. "A story for another time."

Resting her chin on her fist, Effie didn't press further. She knew better than most what grief could do to a person's insides.

"So, you want to drug me and send me into a fit of convulsions?"

Kieran jolted. "Elder's sagging sack, when you put it that way it sounds absolutely barbaric."

Effie snickered at the unfamiliar curse. She was definitely saving that one to use later. "Just saying it as I see it, Keeper."

Some of the amusement returned to his face. "Well, I'm hoping it's significantly less exciting than all of that. With a controlled dose, I am hoping that your transition into the vision is less extreme."

Intrigued by the idea of experiencing a vision that didn't completely debilitate her, Effie nodded. "Worth a try, I suppose."

"Excellent." His answering smile radiated approval.

She wasn't sure why it made her feel shy. She covered the emotion by reaching for her glass of water. After swallowing, she asked in what she hoped passed for a casual tone, "When did you want to give it a go?"

"How about now?"

"Now?" she asked, choking a bit on her water. What sounded good in theory was something else entirely when faced with having to act on it.

"No time like the present."

Effie grimaced. "Says the man whose gift has never brought an ounce of pain."

Kieran's expression darkened so suddenly that Effie froze. The storm was over as quickly as it began, but she didn't need him to tell her that his gift, which perhaps lacking side effects, had not always been a source of pleasure for him. It would seem her guide had many stories hidden beneath his mask.

"Fine," she sighed. "Let's get it over with."

Kieran stood and walked toward a shelf filled with various bottles. He sifted through them, their soft clinks filling the room until he found the one he wanted. Grabbing a small silver object, he returned to the table.

"Here?" she asked, startled when he sat back down.

"It's as good as anywhere else."

She wasn't sure she agreed. There was a worrisome lack of padded surfaces to catch her if she fell.

Effie watched as Kieran measured and dumped a mound of fragrant blue leaves into the bottom half of a silver dome. The base was flat, allowing it to sit on top of the table without toppling over. The top half had a dozen tiny circles cut out of it. To release the vapors, she guessed.

Once filled, Kieran took a nearby candle and used the flame to set the leaves on fire. There was a flash as the leaves sparked and began to smolder. Blue smoke made lazy spirals as it drifted up and out of the holes.

"You don't have to stare at it quite so hard, love. It's not going to bite you."

"Just because it doesn't have teeth doesn't mean it can't hurt me."

He quirked a brow. "How exactly do you intend to fend off smoke?"

An image of Effie wrestling with the Triumvirate's leader startled a peal of laughter out of her. Unable to stop once she'd begun, Effie doubled over, gasping as she tried to catch her breath.

"A diverting image to be sure, but not one I'd expect to be quite so amusing," Kieran murmured, eyeing her.

Effie wiped at her eyes, hiccupping as she tried to speak. It was an impossible task. She couldn't contain her laughter long enough to form a single word, let alone a complete sentence. Kieran had no clue that he'd inadvertently used the name she'd picked for the head Keeper. *Fending off Smoke. Priceless.* Effie couldn't wait to see what he thought of that same suggestion the next time she saw him.

Shaking his head, Kieran said, "You are a constant surprise, Effie. I'm starting to think I may never know all there is to you."

"You've known me for less than a day. Of course you couldn't possibly know all of me," she said, her voice still tinged with her amusement.

"Mmm."

Feeling a little light-headed, Effie glanced around for her water. The room swayed as she twisted her neck and she simultaneously felt as if she was underwater and floating. The sensation was enough to send a bolt of panic spearing through her.

"Kieran . . ."

"Are you alright?"

"Something's wrong." The words sounded odd to her ears, as if her lips and tongue had grown too large for her to enunciate clearly.

She watched him hurdle over the table but couldn't make sense of the image. She was too busy gripping onto the table in an effort to remain upright.

The room continued to swing like a pendulum, each new oscillation sharper and more disorienting than the last. Swallowing back a wave of nausea, Effie clenched her eyes shut. It didn't help. She was a rowboat being tossed about the ocean during a storm. She'd lost her tether.

Without an anchor, there was only one way this would end. Gasping, she fought for balance. Invisible hands pulled at her, tugging her down into the inky recesses of her mind. She shoved at the hands, scared of where they wanted to take her. The movement tossed her off balance, and she fell, spiraling down into the dark.

THE WORLD WAS ON FIRE.

Everywhere she looked embers floated through the air like fiery rain. In the middle of the storm, Helena stood, blood dripping off her talons, and huge glittering wings unfurling from her back.

"Helena!" Effie cried.

Tipping her head back, Helena roared, fire billowing from her mouth and into the air. She was the one who'd caused this.

Horror clawed at her and Effie tried to run away, but she was trapped.

Bodies began to fall from the sky, one nearly crashing into her.

Effie screamed. She knew that face. Those tattoos. Von.

"No. No," she sobbed, wanting to close her eyes and unsee the twisted and broken body laying before her. This couldn't be real. Helena would never harm her Mate.

The scene shifted. A castle in ruins replacing the endless destruction. It was all Effie could see in a world of black. Once again, in the center of everything, Helena stood. This time she was a shining beacon of light. Her hair floated on a non-existent breeze and her eyes twinkled with iridescence.

The sounds of death called from the darkness, but Helena looked serene, unconcerned with the battle taking place around her. Turning her head, she stared directly at Effie.

"This is only the beginning."

Ripping down the center, the two images combined. A world on fire and one lost to the dark.

Helena was nowhere to be found.

EFFIE JOLTED AWAKE, gasping for breath.

"I've got you."

Body trembling, Effie's hands fisted into a smooth fabric. She could still see the fire raining from the sky. Tears streamed down her cheeks and she sucked in air, trying to breathe. Trying to remember what was real.

Arms banded about her body, lifting her into a sitting position.

"What did you See?"

Effie shook her head, not ready to utter the words. Unable to make sense of what her heart couldn't believe was true. But visions didn't lie.

Kieran pulled her into his body, tucking her face into his neck and holding her tight.

Any other time she would have fought the unwelcome embrace. He was practically a stranger, but he was all that was holding her up. Right now, she needed him.

One of his hands ran down the length of her braid and over her back. He rocked her gently as he held her. Soon her breathing returned to normal, and Effie pushed away, embarrassed for him to see her come undone.

He let her go without protest, his eyes focused on her face. "What happened?"

"I *hate* these visions. I never asked for this."

Kieran frowned, but remained silent.

"What is the point of Seeing something that doesn't make a damned bit of sense?"

"Perhaps if you would tell me what you Saw, I could help make sense of it."

"But that will make it real," she whispered.

"Effie, it's already real."

The truth of his words destroyed her. She wanted to scream, to hit something. She could at least pretend to be safe while clinging to her denial. Kieran wanted to tear that away. Force her to face the truth. It was what she was here for, after all. As ugly and horrible as her visions were, she couldn't run from them. They were as much a part of her now as her name.

"Tell me what you Saw," he demanded.

Shoulders sagging, she complied. "Death."

Kieran sat back, his shock registering only by a slight widening of his eyes.

Effie snorted. "I take it your visions aren't nearly as exciting."

He shook his head.

"Lucky bastard."

"Who died?"

Taking a deep breath, she stared him straight in the eye. "Everyone."

Kieran's nostrils flared as he sucked in a sharp breath. His eyes narrowed as she continued.

"It was total destruction. Bodies were everywhere. The world was on fire, and Helena," she choked on the name, ". . . Helena was at the center of it all."

"Helena . . . she's the Kiri?"

Effie nodded.

Kieran wiped a hand over his face. Effie watched his jaw work as he sifted through her words searching for possible meanings outside of the obvious.

"Do you think what you saw has to do with the war?"

Effie nodded. "What else could it be about? Helena's preparing to make her last stand. If she fails, it would mean the end for the Chosen."

Kieran's expression was grim. "As I understand it, your premonitions come to you in metaphor. They are a mosaic, pieced together by images and events that hold significant meaning to you. Rarely are they a literal representation of what's to come." His voice was low, as if he was reciting something from memory.

"As you *understand*? Yours are different in that regard too?"

Kieran darted his gaze back down to her. "I watch actual events unfold as if I am there. These events can be past or future, and generally follow people that I know or at least hold some sort of personal significance to me."

"Generally?"

His lips quirked up in a smile. "Well, there's you . . ."

Right. "You think I have personal significance to you."

His eyes flashed, appearing almost gem-like in their radiance. "I do."

Effie lifted a brow, at a total loss of what to do with that new piece of information. "Why aren't all visions like that?"

Kieran shrugged. "I asked the Triumvirate the same when I arrived. They didn't know either."

Effie sighed. *Of course, they didn't.* "Does anyone actually know a damned thing around here?"

He laughed. "Rarely. Or at least not anything they'd willingly share."

Her gaze dropped to her hands. She came here for answers, but it seemed all she was going to find were more questions. Pressure built in the back of her neck and eyes. Effie lifted a hand to squeeze at the bridge of her nose. *Why does everything have to be so damn complicated?*

"Let's decipher your vision. If we can identify the hidden metaphors, I can start to help you catalog the meaning of certain elements—"

Effie held up a hand, cutting off his flow of words. "I'm going to stop you right there. I think doing this was a mistake. I don't have any interest in analyzing the quite literally bloody details of my vision. Experiencing it once was enough."

"But, Effie—"

"I said no, Kieran. Not right now." *Not while my head feels like it's being crushed by a vice.*

"You have a responsibility to understand your vision and share what you've Seen."

"I already told you what I Saw."

"I'm your tutor. I think I know better than you how we should proceed. Just do as I say, and you'll be fine. You'll see."

Effie grit her teeth, his words stirring memories of similar conversations she'd locked away a long time ago. "Can't we do it tomorrow?"

"We need to break it down while the details are fresh."

"I don't *need* to do anything." Effie didn't recognize her voice. It was dripping with disdain; an emotion she didn't recall experiencing before today.

He scoffed. "Don't be such a child, Effie."

Effie's jaw clenched. She didn't think before striking. There was a sharp crack as her hand made contact with his cheek. He jolted back in surprise, a bright pink handprint blooming on his skin. Horrified at what she'd done, but too enraged to stop now, she jumped up, wanting to make use of the height advantage while he was still on the ground.

"Don't you dare call me a child. I may be naïve, but only because this is new to me. Just because I inherited this stupid gift doesn't mean I have to suddenly bend to anyone's will but my own. We'll do this at my pace, when I say I'm ready, or not at all. You may think that you know me, Kieran, and that gives you special rights or access where I'm concerned, but you don't. I'm not your toy or your pet. I don't belong to you and I certainly do not owe you anything, least of all unlimited access to my soul. So, you need to back off and let go of whatever misguided notions you have about me."

A pulse pounded in Kieran's neck, but he gave no other indication that her words were affecting him.

Shaking with anger, Effie bent down until her nose was barely a hairsbreadth from his, her voice dropping to a low hiss. "The next time I tell you no, that is the end of the conversation. I will not be bullied into anything, least of all from you. Is that clear?"

He gave a short nod.

Spinning away, Effie stormed out of the room, echoes of her past tormenting her with each angry step.

"Stupid girl, your mother should have drowned you when she had the chance. If I'd been cursed with an ungifted brat, she'd never lived to see her first name day."

"Look at her. She's practically a child. There's not even a curve on her to make her tolerable to look at. What a waste. There's only one thing she's good for."

"What's the problem, love? You could do worse than spend the night beneath a man like me. Might as well lift that skirt of yours so we can have a bit of fun. Not that I need you to be willing. You're as weak as a child . . . look at those bones, so fragile. I could break you in half before you made it two steps."

Kieran's dismissive rejection of her wishes was entirely too familiar. She'd spent years being told what to think, what she was worth, that her opinions held no value. In a day where everything was new, for *that* to be the one constant was more than she could bear. She'd snapped.

The thought of having to be that girl again when she finally thought she was free . . . it was too much. She'd lashed out like a cornered cat trying to defend itself.

As a child, the only protection she had was to hide. To make herself so small that no one could find her. To be silent, unseen. A ghost instead of a girl. It had taken years for her to find her voice, to feel safe enough to come out of the shadows and try to a claim 'a place for herself in the world.

She didn't want to go back there.

She couldn't.

Not now that she'd gotten a taste of what it meant to truly live. To be loved. To be seen.

She'd never silence herself again. Not for anyone.

CHAPTER 7

"Of all the pigheaded, egotistical . . ."

     Effie's impassioned muttering followed her down yet another hallway. She was lost, but it didn't stop her from slamming doors and venting her anger.

Her emotions had been out of control all day. It was exhausting trying to make sense of why she was sad one moment and angry the next, but of the two, anger was easier.

Making a sharp left at the end of the corridor, Effie found herself back in the main archive. Recognizing the arched doors that would take her back out into the heart of the Keeper's city, Effie beelined straight toward them. She didn't care that she didn't know a single person outside the citadel's walls, or that she had no clue where she was going. The only thing that she cared about right now was getting outside.

Pushing through the doors, she stepped out into the evening. The smell of jasmine greeted her, and Effie paused long enough to close her eyes and breathe it in. Some of her tension ebbed, and her muscles started to relax. As long as she could stand under the sky, she was free.

She was safe.

Soft strains of music floated to her on the breeze and Effie was moving toward the sound before consciously realizing she wanted to. The city was mostly deserted. She saw a few people weaving through the streets, but no one paid her any attention. Effie followed suit, intent only on finding the source of the melody.

She came to a surprised stop across the street from a small pub. Its doors were thrown wide open to accommodate the overflow of guests inside. Those that didn't fit inside were scattered around the tables placed just outside. Both within and without, patrons were puffing on pipes or drinking deeply from wooden steins.

"I guess we know where everyone's been hiding," Effie muttered

A sign hung from the roof, swaying gently in the evening breeze. Effie shifted position so she could make out the gilded letters. *The Pickled Piper.* A slow smile lifted her lips. *That explains the music . . . and the crowd.*

The song concluded and roars of approval and applause filled the air. Mind made up, Effie crossed the street so she could go inside. For once, she was grateful she was small; it made squeezing in that much easier.

Three men stood on a lifted platform in the back corner. One held some kind of flute, another a stringed instrument that looked like a lute, although its body was shorter and wider than any she'd seen before. The last of them had a simple drum held between his legs that he used to keep time as he sang.

Effie had rarely been allowed to go into the village since there was always work to do at the Holbrooke's Estate, unless it was some sort of feast day. But her love for music and storytelling had been born there all the same. Bards and musicians would wander into town, sharing their songs and their stories and Effie would hum them for days— sometimes weeks—after, eagerly awaiting their next visit.

A waitress with a tray filled with sloshing drinks shouldered past and Effie eyed the mugs with envy. She didn't have a coin on her.

"Here, lass. First one's on the house," a bartender called, filling one of the steins with an amber liquid and passing it to her.

Effie grinned at the bearded man but didn't have time to so much as thank him before she was bumped out of the way by another thirsty customer. She lifted the surprisingly heavy mug in a salute and made her way over to one of the windows so that she could better see the performers.

She came to a halt beside a table full of rowdy patrons who snagged her attention with a loud chorus of boos. There were six chairs encircling the table, five of which were filled. Two of the five men were playing a card game she didn't immediately recognize, the other three making bets based on the cards the players laid on the table. Feet tapping in time to the music, Effie watched, trying to learn the rules.

"Want to play, sweetheart?" one of the men asked, taking notice.

Effie quickly shook her head. "No thanks, I don't know how."

"Oh, it's easy, lovey. 'Ere, take a seat," said the man closest to her, his wide smile missing more teeth than not.

For a city that was supposed to be filled only by Keepers, it certainly seemed to have its share of characters. Not wanting to risk offense, Effie sat herself down into the empty seat.

He pointed at the man on her left whose red hair was pulled into a topknot that made her think of Ronan.

"Tomas there is the guard. His job is to keep Davis from storming the castle."

As her new friend spoke, Effie was making out the faded images drawn on the cards. There were castles, wolves, archers, and figures that were clearly Chosen wielding their various elements. It was a strategy game. Each player holding a deck that—depending on what order their cards were drawn—would allow them to protect or overtake the castle, which was a pile of coins that the betting men were building in the center of the table.

"Seems easy enough," she murmured. "But what's in it for you?"

The men around her chuckled. "The side bets can be just as lucrative as the castle. For instance, Nile"—her friend pointed to the heavyset man with bright blue eyes sitting across from her—"believes that Tomas will go undefeated. He's got an entire purse up for grabs if he's wrong."

Effie nodded, understanding how the game would be a lure for spectators and players alike. She gulped the amber liquid, sputtering a little at its strength. She'd drank ale and mead often enough, but this was more potent in flavor.

The men chuckled again, Tomas sparing her only a passing glance before laying down a card that had his opponent groaning and the other three cheering. Squinting Effie leaned in, trying to get a better look at the card. It was a woman robed in purple. Effie didn't need anyone to tell her who that was supposed to be.

"The Kiri," she murmured.

The man beside her nodded. "Most powerful card in the game. Davis is doomed."

Effie smirked. Helena would have loved that.

It didn't take long for Effie to get lost in the game, shouting out her own words of encouragement and making ridiculous wagers of her own. She had nothing to gamble with, but her new friends didn't seem to mind. They only egged her on, ensuring her cup was filled and convincing her that it was finally time for her to take a turn storming the castle.

Effie, giggling with laughter and having the time of her life, couldn't think of anything she'd rather do.

CHAPTER 8

*L*ucian strode into the dining hall, stopping short when he saw Kieran slumped over one of the tables. The Eatonian was obnoxious at the best of times, but something about the defeated slump of his shoulders gave Lucian pause.

"Contemplating your dinner options?" Lucian called dryly, making his way to the buffet table that was kept filled throughout the day.

Kieran swung his head up, his eyes shooting daggers at Lucian before he schooled his face back into his usual bored expression. "Something like that."

Lucian noted the purple blotches that formed a very distinct pattern on Kieran's face. "You going to tell me what happened?"

"My, aren't you feeling chatty all of a sudden."

Lucian continued to pile food onto his plate. "Last I heard you were working with the girl. What'd you do to her?"

Anger shone in Kieran's eyes, the dangerous glint a warning to tread lightly. "My job," he gritted out.

Raising a brow, Lucian asked, "Teaching her the laws of the Keepers led to her feeling the need to hit you in the face? I'm familiar enough with the urge myself, but I find it odd that she would be so inclined."

Color bloomed in Kieran's cheeks. Outright hostility Lucian was used to, expected even, but an outward sign of regret from the once prince was unusual enough that Lucian stopped what he was doing.

"That was what you were told to do, wasn't it? Teach her the ways of the Keepers?"

Kieran gave a terse nod.

"So, what's the problem?"

Lucian watched Kieran work his jaw and narrowed his eyes with growing suspicion. A familiar scent tickled his nose and Lucian breathed it in, understanding dawning. *Halus bane.*

"What did you do?" he demanded, stalking over to the other man.

Kieran flinched, but faced him head-on. "What needed to be done."

Lucian grasped him by the collar and pulled him to his feet. Shaking him slightly he growled, "Halus bane, Kieran? Are you really as stupid as you look? Do you have any idea how dangerous that is for a novice?"

Kieran slapped at the hand still gripping his tunic, but Lucian only held tighter, pulling the man up on the tips of his toes.

"In a controlled environment—"

Lucian shoved Kieran away. "You damned fool. Do you even know what you've done? The herb will be in her system for hours. She shouldn't be left alone—" Fuming, Lucian shook his head, cutting off the flood of words. "Where is she?"

Kieran shrugged, the color in his cheeks deepening.

"You just let her go?" Lucian roared.

"She stormed off. What was I supposed to do?"

"Go after her, you mopey piece of shit! I knew you were dumb, but I didn't realize you were fucking useless."

Food forgotten, Lucian spun around.

"How do you intend to find a girl you've never met?" Kieran called after him.

Lucian didn't bother to reply. He was a seasoned hunter, there wasn't a creature in this realm he couldn't track. One way or the other, he'd find her.

CHAPTER 9

*E*ffie's opponent looked up from his cards long enough to throw her a smug grin. "You should have given up, sweetheart."

It didn't take the men long to realize Effie was far from a skilled gambler. A fact they were quick to press to their advantage. What had started off as a fun game between friends had taken a sharp turn somewhere along the way, and most of Effie's pleasant buzz was starting to fade as a bead of sweat snaked its way along her back.

Swallowing, Effie shrugged. "I still have my tunic and pants." But that was all she had. When the few coins she'd won through her side bets were gone, the men told her she could barter her finely crafted garments in their stead.

"Not for much longer," he crowed, throwing down his last two cards.

Effie stared at the Kiri card in dismay. Game over. She was either walking out of here without a shirt or without her pants. Neither one sounded like a good time.

Licking her lips, Effie reached for her mug, draining it in the hopes the extra time would provide her with a third option.

"That's enough stallin', sweetheart. Pay up."

There was nothing friendly about the men's leers as they stared at her. Standing slowly, hoping the shaking of her legs wasn't too obvious, Effie's fingers moved to the ties at her waist. Her tunic fell to the tops of her thighs, so it seemed the safest bet if she had any hope of maintaining some of her modesty. At worst, she'd only be exposed in the brief time it took her to pull the leather over her hips. She only saw a flash of black on her right before a grip like iron tore her fingers from her pants. A sharp tug sent her tumbling to the side.

"The lady is finished for the evening," a growling voice declared.

The men started to argue, and Effie glanced up at the stranger who'd dared to intercede. He towered over her. *Mother's tits, he's a giant.*

She craned her neck up in an attempt to make out his face. Once she did, she wished she hadn't. It was twisted in a dangerous scowl. His lips pulled back in a snarl, the white of his teeth a shocking contrast to the dark scruff of his beard. It was hard to make out the color of his eyes, narrowed as they were under the slash of his brows, but she guessed they were a brown so dark they were all but black. His hair was long, windblown, the dark curls tangling together where they fell just below his shoulders.

All in all, her rescuer was terrifying, and Effie wasn't so sure he was the safer of her options.

Hoping he was too focused on them to notice her, she started to tug her wrist back. His grip tightened, pulling a timid squeak from her. *So much for not being a mouse.* She glanced down at the hand that held her in place, blinking when she realized it was easily the size of both of hers together. No wonder she couldn't pull from his grasp. His hand easily spanned the better half of her forearm. She followed the arm up, gulping back her fear as she tried to process the sheer amount of muscle he possessed. *He can snap me in two.*

"Fair's fair. The lady owes us a debt."

A heavy bag fell onto the table, the weight of it causing it to topple. Greedy hands snatched the bag up before it could fall and spill its contents over the grimy floor.

"Debt's been paid."

"Who the 'ell you think you are?" the redhead with the topknot demanded, pushing to his feet.

Her rescuer turned toward Tomas, leveling him with an angry glare.

A frightened voice whispered behind him, "'E's one of them Guardians."

The color leeched from Tomas' face, and the men began to back away from the table. Holding up his hands, Tomas stuttered, "Didn't mean no trouble."

Effie thought she heard her rescuer growl.

A wet stain grew in Tomas' pants as he stumbled away from the table and began to run for the door.

Terrified, Effie stared up at the man the others were so afraid of. Feeling her eyes on him, he turned that scowl on her for the first time. If it was possible, he seemed to grow even angrier.

"Grab your things," he ordered.

Flinching, Effie picked up her boots and cloak from where they'd fallen on the floor. She wasn't sure who he was, or why he felt entitled to boss her around, but self-preservation beat out fear.

"Let's go."

Effie blinked up at him. "G-go where?"

"I'm taking you back to the citadel."

Relief made her knees weak. If he was taking her back there, then he couldn't mean her any harm. She scurried to the door, not needing to look to know that he was on her heels.

"I know the way from here," she called over her shoulder, hoping he might leave her to make the trip on her own.

All she got in return was another glower.

They walked in silence: her steps quick and uneven, his soundless. If it weren't for the sheer force of his presence, she would have thought she was alone. Shivering in the dark, Effie stumbled. A hand shot out and kept her from falling forward. Apparently, she wasn't entirely sober just yet.

Manners warred with pride.

Manners won.

"Thank you," she whispered, trying to pry one of his fingers off of her arm. It didn't budge.

"Watch where you're going."

The not-so-gentle rebuke had her shoulders lifting defensively. So much for manners. "The ground is uneven."

One long, slow glance down at the perfectly smooth walkway was his only response.

"I don't even know your name." She tried to keep her voice steady. She wasn't sure she succeeded.

One beat of silence, and then another. Effie sighed, convinced he was only going to ignore her again.

"Lucian."

She looked over in shock. He stood just between two of the street's lamps, but his face was somehow cast in shadows. Not being able to see his expression almost made it easier to talk to him. "I'm Effie."

"I know."

Riiiiight. She couldn't shake the feeling that he'd already judged her and found her wanting. The thought was like an itch just out of reach, and she squirmed uncomfortably under the weight of it.

"I had everything under control, you know."

A pointed glance at the boots she still carried told her what he thought.

"I didn't need you to rescue me," she insisted, stopping to turn and face him. "I can take care of myself."

"I beg to differ."

Boots and cloak falling to the ground, Effie balled her hands into fists. "You don't even know me."

He took a step toward her, and Effie stepped back. He kept coming, and she matched him step for step, until her back was pressed against the wall. Lucian closed the distance between them, leaning down so she could see his eyes glittering in the soft light.

"I know all that I need to know about you."

The words, so filled with arrogant conviction, ignited that part of her that was tired of being not good enough. For the third time in the course of the day, Effie found herself facing off with a man twice—or in this case maybe thrice—her size.

She shoved at his chest, and the force of it zinged up her arms. Unimpressed, Lucian continued to crowd her.

Effie's voice dropped to a deadly whisper. "If you don't step back, my dagger is going to find a new sheath."

"You don't have your dagger."

Her fingers grazed the spot where it had been strapped to her leg only to come up empty.

Lucian held it up so that its sharp edge glinted. "Not much of a threat when you're so easily disarmed."

Frustration burned in the back of her throat, but she wouldn't back down. Whether it was the warm buzz of alcohol that still flowed through her, or an inner strength she was just now discovering, Effie was fearless. For once, she would not be the one to walk away.

"It's not the only weapon in my arsenal," she spat.

Lucian anticipated her move at the last second, dodging just in time for her knee to slam into his thigh.

"That's enough."

"It's enough when I say it is," she sneered, lunging at him. He blocked her blows easily, although a few grunts were enough to let her know some of them still landed with considerable force.

Grasping both her wrists in one of his hands, he pressed her arms up over her head and into the wall. "Control yourself."

With a cry that was more animal than human, Effie twisted her hand and sank her teeth into his forearm.

Lucian grunted as the metallic tang of blood filled her mouth. His other hand snaking into the base of her braid, he forcibly pulled her head away. She bit down harder, but she was no match for his brute strength.

"Stop it, before you hurt yourself."

"You're the one that's bleeding." Her grin must have looked savage with his blood smeared down her chin.

Lucian muttered something she didn't quite catch. It sounded like hell's bane.

"What did you just call me?"

Turning back to her, he shook his head. "There's no reasoning with you when you're like this."

"Like what?"

"Out of control," he growled, letting go of her wrists so suddenly she was too surprised to react.

Dipping, Lucian wrapped an arm around her thighs and stood, taking her with him. The unexpected shift in altitude threw her off balance and she fell forward, landing over his shoulder. The wind was knocked out of her with a whoosh. Lucian didn't bother to see if she was alright; he just started walking.

Once she regained her breath, she began to struggle in earnest. "Hey . . . put me down! What do you think you're doing? My boots!"

The change in gravity tugged her hair free of its braid and her hair spilled over like a waterfall, completely obscuring her view of everything except his back. She pounded against the muscled surface, but Lucian was done talking. He didn't stop until they reached the citadel, where he dropped her without a word just inside the archive's doors.

Fuming, ready to go another round with him, Effie shoved her hair out of her face. But instead of Lucian, she was face-to-face with two familiar scarlet robes.

Elder's sagging sack.

CHAPTER 10

*D*irty, embarrassed, and still more drunk than not, Effie stared at the hooded men in silence. That resolution lasted all of three seconds.

"I'm sorry I left, I just needed—"

"You are not a prisoner here."

"You are free to come and go as you please."

"Although, it would have been best if you let someone know so they may escort you."

"If I'm not a prisoner, why do I require an escort?"

"To ensure you are safe while you become familiar with your new surroundings."

Effie huffed, annoyed that they chose now to be completely reasonable. Folding her arms, she asked one of the questions that had been eating at her. "Who were those people I met tonight?"

"Just like any city, we have need of local craftsmen to make and sell the goods we use."

Oh. That did make sense. "So, they weren't Keepers?"

Mirror One shrugged. *"A few of the patrons may have been, but not all."*

Somehow Effie doubted her gambling buddies held the gift of prophecy.

"About Kieran . . ."

Effie's gaze sharpened at the mention of her tutor.

"He should have never used the halus bane without permission."

Halus bane . . . that must have been the blue herb, she thought.

"For a first-time user especially, it is crucial that certain guidelines are followed to ensure their well-being."

"The herb is potent, and its side effects unpredictable."

Side effects? Effie straightened. "What do you mean?"

There was a beat of silence before they responded, and Effie had the feeling they were choosing their next words with care.

"In small doses, the herb—"

"Induces visions, I know."

"It also lowers our protective instincts."

That sounded less good.

"Moreover, it is our belief that some visions are kept from us because of the message they contain."

The image of bloody talons floated through her mind.

"The herb allows us to access such visions because our minds are no longer able to fully protect themselves against it."

"By lowering our guard, we are also more prone to making decisions that might not be in our best interest."

Heat flooded her face as Effie recalled her evening. They were putting it mildly.

"So, you're saying tonight was a result of the halus bane?"

They dipped their hoods in unison.

Rolling her lips together, Effie stared past them at the hall that would lead to her room. So not even her little display of independence was really her own. An exhaustion unlike any other pulled at her limbs.

"He should not have let you go off on your own without protection."

"It will not happen again."

Her gaze snapped back to them. "What are you saying?"

"We are assigning you one of our Guardians."

"You will not be alone outside of these walls again."

The man from the pub's words came back to her. *"E's one of them Guardians.'*

"No. No way," she protested, shaking her head vehemently. "I don't need a nursemaid."

"It is for your safety."

"I am perfectly safe here."

Their silence was deafening. She thought she heard the creaking of a gate snapping closed in this distance. So much for this not being her prison.

"Absolutely not."

"Lucian, or one of his brothers, will accompany you from now on."

Lucian. Effie shivered, her arms breaking out in goosebumps. The thought of the dark-haired Guardian following her around did not exactly invoke warm and fuzzy feelings. *Liar.* Effie ignored the little voice.

"We'll kill each other inside of a day."

Mirror Two shrugged. *"Do not give him a reason."*

"Me?" she sputtered.

There was a rustle that sounded suspiciously like a snicker.

"Oh, for the love of—are you serious?"

"The Guardians have always been the Keepers' protectors."

"Such an assignment is not unusual."

"Why would Keepers need protection?"

"Desperation is a great motivator."

"Many would give anything to know that which comes to us."

Sighing, Effie looked at her bare toes. She was familiar enough with stubborn men to recognize that this was a fight she wasn't going to win. "Fine."

They never asked for her permission, but granting it anyway provided her the illusion of choice.

"Are we done here?"

Two more nods.

"Great."

Effie stalked past them, heading down the hallway that Smoke had used to take her to her room. She'd find her own way back . . . eventually. Maybe she'd even find a bathing chamber along the way.

~

HEAD POUNDING, Effie rubbed her bleary eyes and wondered what woke her. Two dull thuds on the door answered the question.

Swinging her legs over the side of the bed, she stood with a groan. Everything hurt. Her body felt like she'd spent the previous day training with Ronan and his men. Slowly, memories of the night before returned to her and Effie groaned again. Kieran, her vision, Lucian. . .

"Mother's tits," she moaned, pressing the heels of her hands into her eyes. *Did you really have to bite him, you fool?*

There was another knock and Effie eyed the door with suspicion. There was one of three men waiting for her on the other side of that door, and she wasn't eager to see any of them.

Wrapping a soft blue robe around herself, she swung the door open. "What do you want?"

Blond brows lifted over smoky green eyes. "Not much of a morning person, I take it?"

Scowling, she snapped, "Good morning. Now what do you want?"

Kieran chuckled. "It's time for your lessons."

"Planning on drugging me again today?"

He had the grace to look embarrassed. Rubbing a hand along the back of his neck, he said, "I'm sorry about that. I didn't anticipate your reaction, to your vision or to the herb. When you're ready to try again, I'll make sure we're both better prepared."

She studied him. He seemed sincere enough and she was terrible at holding a grudge. "So, if we're not going to analyze my visions, what's are we doing?"

"Why don't you get dressed and I'll show you?"

It took everything in her not to glance down and make sure it wasn't obvious her robe was the only thing covering her body. Last night she'd barely had enough energy to tug off the few pieces of clothing she still had on and leave them in a haphazard pile on the floor—something she'd never do if she was in her right mind. Just to be safe and add another layer between them, Effie pulled her hair over her shoulder—under the guise of braiding it—and gave him a short nod.

"Give me five minutes."

"Is that all? My sister took hours to get ready in the morning."

Effie lifted a shoulder. "Pants, tunic, cloak, boots. Not a whole lot of effort tying up some strings." *Or untying them.* Heat flooded her cheeks as more of the previous night returned. She turned away from Kieran, hoping he didn't notice, and slammed the door closed with her foot.

"I'll just wait right here, then," he called through the thick wood.

"You do that," she muttered, lifting the lid to her trunk and rifling through the handful of garments within.

A thick cream tunic with long-sleeves and dark brown leather pants in hand, Effie pulled them on and then went to grab her boots. It didn't take more than a cursory scan for her to realize she wasn't going to find them.

Groaning, Effie stomped back to the door and pulled it open.

Kieran spun around with a smile. "All set?"

"Do I look ready?"

His eyes roamed over her body, his eyebrows lifting when he reached her feet. "No shoes?"

"It would seem they have been misplaced."

If her casual assessment seemed odd to him, he gave no hint of it. "I'm sure we can find something for you to wear. Will you be alright without them in the meantime?"

With no other choice, Effie gave a sharp nod.

"I guess we will begin our morning with a tour then."

They made it three steps down the hall when Lucian rounded the corner, a familiar navy cloak hanging over his arm and her missing footwear in hand. Effie noticed him first, stopping dead as he continued to make his way toward them.

Seeing her wide-eyed stare, Kieran followed it, a scowl marring his handsome face when he discovered their visitor.

Without preamble, Lucian held the items out to her. "You left these."

Effie could feel Kieran's eyes boring a hole into her, demanding an explanation for why Lucian had her clothes. Blushing, she snatched them from his grasp, but Lucian didn't let go. Momentum stunted, Effie stumbled forward.

"Well, are you going to give them to me or not?"

"You should take better care of your things."

"You should be less of an antagonistic prick."

Kieran snorted, one of his hands lifting to hide his smile.

Lucian scowled and shoved her things into her arms. "I'll see you later."

"Can't wait," she called to his retreating back. She frowned in confusion as she eyed her things. They should have been caked with dirt after being dumped in the mud yesterday, but they were pristine. Someone had cleaned them. Surely not Lucian . . . She was having trouble picturing the hulking brute performing such a mundane task.

"I see you've met Lucian."

Sitting down in the hallway, Effie pulled on her boots and grunted, "Unfortunately."

Effie wasn't sure if he was amused by her antics or her answer, but he was grinning as he asked, "Not a fan?"

Effie sighed. Technically Lucian *had* rescued her, or at the very least kept her from having to walk back to the citadel mostly naked. If nothing else, she owed him a sincere thank you for allowing her to maintain her dignity. And an apology for biting him.

Boots on, Effie stood up and shook her head. "I'm not sure what to make of him, but so far he seems like he'll be a joy to have around."

Kieran nodded. "Lucian does tend to suck the fun out of a room. His brothers are better, but not by much. Have you met the other Guardians?"

Effie shook her head. "No, not yet."

"Nord and Kael. It's rare that the three of them are all together."

"Why's that?"

"They're bound to the Triumvirate. One immortal guard for each of them. The Triumvirate sends them off when they need answers about something, since they rarely leave the citadel themselves, but at least one of them is always nearby lurking in the background."

Effie stopped Kieran with a hand on the arm. "Wait, the Guardians belong to the Triumvirate?"

Kieran nodded.

"Are there more than the three of them?"

"Not in the citadel, although it's rumored that the Brotherhood of the Guardians is vast."

Confused, Effie frowned. "Then why did they assign one of their personal guards to me?"

Kieran shrugged. "I have no idea. I'm guessing it has something to do with the fact that Lucian had your missing boots."

Effie ignored the less than subtle request for information. "So it would seem," she murmured, still feeling as though she was missing a crucial detail.

"You really aren't going to tell me what happened last night?" Kieran asked as they started up a flight of stairs.

"Nope."

Kieran shook his head. "I guess I deserve that since it's probably my fault in the first place."

Learning what she had about the halus bane, Effie wasn't of a mind to disagree. Deciding now was a perfect time to change the subject, Effie asked, "Are you still taking me on that tour?" She smiled when he rolled his eyes.

"Might as well. At the rate you're going, who knows when you'll need to find a spare pair of pants."

Effie shoved his arm, and Kieran laughed. A second later, Effie joined in.

CHAPTER 11

*A*fter introducing her to a handful of the other residents whose names she'd already forgotten, Kieran had led her around the citadel, showing her all five of the libraries, two of the closest supply rooms (in case she needed anything for her chamber, or found herself missing more random items of clothing), all thirty-seven meditation rooms, seven bathing chambers, the four additional archives, and one non-descript black door that led to the Hall of Prophecy. When she asked if they were going to look inside, Kieran had given her a curt shake of the head.

"Triumvirate only."

"Then what's the point of showing me the door?" she asked, staring at it with growing interest as they'd passed.

"So that you know which door *not* to open."

"I'm pretty sure piquing someone's interest is the exact opposite thing you're supposed to do if you want them to stay away from something."

Kieran shrugged. "Better that you know to avoid it then find yourself there on accident."

She threw him a glance over her shoulder. "If you say so."

"Trust me on this one. There's all sorts of wards down there to protect what's hidden inside. You don't want to find yourself on the other end of that."

Now even more curious, Effie twisted back to catch another glimpse at the door. *What in the Mother's name was down there?* With a name like Hall of Prophecy, she could hazard a guess. But even if it was some sort of room that housed various prophecies, why all the extra secrecy and precaution?

"Ah, we're here."

Looking around at yet another twisting hallway, she asked, "Where's here, exactly?"

Kieran gave her an enigmatic grin. "See for yourself."

He pushed open a door, revealing a dark, glittering hallway. The walls were made of some kind of reflective stone, and the small orbs of light that floated above shimmered on their surface. It reminded Effie of a sky filled with stars.

Entranced, she stepped past Kieran into the hallway, her fingertips lightly brushing against the cool stone, and she followed it down to where it opened into a chamber full of steam. Effie had no real idea how big the chamber was; it seemed endless. If Kieran had told her they stepped through a portal and now walked amongst the night sky, she would have believed him.

"Hot spring," Kieran said, coming up alongside her.

That was when she noticed the soft slap of water as it hit the rock. Focusing, she could just make out the edge of the steaming liquid.

"It's beautiful," she breathed, taking a tentative step toward the water.

"I come here a lot when I need to think. Something about this place helps me put things into perspective."

Their voices echoed around the chamber, as Effie knelt down and dipped her fingers into the pool. The water was warm and inviting. She was already planning to come back once she was alone and go for a swim.

"Want to test it out?" Kieran asked, his eyes twinkling in the relative darkness.

Blushing, Effie abruptly stood. "If this was just some play to get me to take my clothes off—"

Kieran held up his hands. "Can't blame a guy for trying."

She narrowed her eyes on his handsome face. "Yes, I can."

"Ah, well. Worth it, if only to see your cheeks heat up like that."

Effie's stomach gave a little dip and she blinked at him in surprise. His eyes were hooded, and his golden hair hung loose about his shoulders. His smile grew as she studied him, and Effie gulped audibly. The last time she'd gone for a swim with a man, he'd kissed her. If Kieran's intent expression was any indication, he had something similar in mind.

That was not exactly what she'd pictured when he told her it was time for lessons. Scowling, she turned away. He was entirely too charming by half and she was not here to play such games. She came to the Keepers to learn about her visions—specifically how to control and interpret them—and then return to her friends. She didn't have time to fool around with some roguish, albeit handsome, tutor.

Crossing her arms, she stared into the water with a frown. She could just barely make out her distorted reflection in the undulating surface. Kieran's reflection joined hers.

"I didn't mean to upset you."

Effie shrugged. "I'm not upset."

"Clearly."

She watched as he began to tie up his hair.

"Listen, I just thought after yesterday you would want to relax a bit. The water's known for its restorative properties, especially after a night of indulgence." He smirked.

The persistent pounding in her temples begged her to consider his offer, but Effie's eyes grew wide as Kieran's fingers moved to the buttons at his neck.

"What are you doing?" she squeaked.

"It's your prerogative if you want to refuse out of some weird sense of principle, but I don't have the same aversion to fun as you. So, I'm going in."

He said all this while peeling off layers of his clothes. Effie gaped when his shirt flew at her but was too afraid to pull the garment off of her face before she heard the tale-tell splash as he dove into the water.

Kieran was a walking distraction; one she could not afford. She should go find Smoke and ask that he assign her a different tutor— one whose spicy scent didn't still fill her nostrils.

Mind made up, Effie started to turn away, but something about the playful smile curving his lips, and the burnished gold of his hair sending drops of water sliding down his sculpted chest kept her feet rooted to the ground.

Her breath hitched as the feeling of déjà vu crashed into her. Between one ragged breath and the next, Effie fell into the memory of the last time a man had looked at her that way.

"STOP WORRYING what everyone will think. Come for a swim with me," Darrin cajoled, his green eyes pleading.

"But you're the Shield and I'm a noth—"

He pressed his fingers to her lips, cutting off the flow of words. "What did I tell you about talking about yourself that way?" He pulled his fingers away, grasping her hand. "I'm not taking no for an answer."

"You're too stubborn for your own good," she muttered, smiling as she trailed after him through the dense patch of trees.

He flashed her a quick grin over his shoulder. "I got what I wanted, didn't I?"

Effie scrunched her face up and he laughed, but the racing of her heart betrayed her. She wanted this . . . with him.

All of the men in the Kiri's Circle were so much more than their titles, but none of them had surprised her as much as Darrin. Playful one moment and intensively protective the next, she never quite knew what to expect from him. He was a bit like a puppy. One she desperately wanted to cuddle. Lost in the metaphor, her nose crinkled as she hoped that his kisses would be less slobbery than those of a canine.

Her eyes darted to his back as heat crept up her neck. It wasn't the first time she'd tried to imagine what it would feel like if he pressed his lips to hers. The thought had become more frequent as they increased the amount of time they spent together.

She sighed, glancing down at their interwoven fingers. It was all wishful thinking on her part anyway. Nothing could happen between them. He'd already taken his vows. She needed to rein in these feelings, and fast. Only disappointment waited for her down that road.

The rush of water grew louder as they stepped out of the forest. It was a beautiful day; the sun was warm in the sky and the water sparkled beneath its happy glow.

Darrin pulled off his boots, dumping them on top of a smooth rock. His weapons followed and then his shirt. He purposefully never turned back to look at her, giving her privacy to undress as he walked into the center of the stream.

Effie only warred with herself for one half-hearted second. There may not be a future for them, but she'd always have this stolen moment. Tugging off her boots and a few of her outer layers, Effie tossed them on top of his and then took a running leap into the water.

"Mother's tits, it's cold!" she hollered, popping up.

Laughing, Darrin splashed her. "Swim around a bit. It will warm you up."

Rolling her eyes, Effie did as he suggested. It helped, but the icy bite of the water never fully went away.

Something brushed against her foot and Effie shrieked, spinning around as best she could half-submerged as she tried to locate the source.

Darrin's laughter was the only answer she needed.

"You ass!" she chided, splashing him. "You scared me half to death."

"Ah, I'm sorry, sweetheart," he murmured, his face instantly contrite.

Effie didn't buy it for a second. "Just you wait, Shield. I'll get you back when you least expect it."

"Is that so?"

"Count on it. I have access to your tent and *your meals."*

"You want to sneak around in my tent?" he asked, lifting his brow.

Effie's cheeks burned. Damn it, he always managed to turn things back around on her. She hadn't realized how close he'd gotten while they'd been talking. She could make out each of the freckles dotting the bridge of his nose, and the spikes of his lashes as water dripped down his face.

Her heart stuttered as he lifted a hand and brushed a few wet strands of hair off of her face.

"You are so beautiful, Effie. Damn near takes my breath away to look at you."

His words were reverent, and she went still, afraid that anything she said would only break the moment.

"I can't stop thinking about you," he confessed, his hands closing around her waist and pulling her that last inch forward until their bodies all but touched.

The heat of his hands over her wet clothes made her shiver.

"Cold?" he asked.

She shook her head, never once looking away from him. She'd freeze to death before risking anything that would cause him to let her go and leave this moment.

His gaze roamed over her face, pausing on her lips before lifting back up to her eyes. There was a question in his own, a request for permission. She tilted her chin up, hoping that was the only answer he required. She didn't think she could form coherent words; her heart was beating so fast she could feel it in her throat.

He moved slowly, giving her every opportunity to stop him. She would have laughed if it wasn't so heart-wrenchingly sweet. If he only knew how desperately she wanted him to kiss her.

Maybe he did.

His breath fanned over her lips before finally brushing against hers. It was the barest hint of a touch, a butterfly landing on her cheek would have been more aggressive, but her heart exploded all the same.

Lifting her hands to his shoulders, she pressed her lips against his.

Darrin groaned, one of his hands lifting to cup her cheek while the other held her body against his.

"EFFIE? ARE YOU ALRIGHT?"

The voice pulled her back to the present, and she blinked back tears, refusing to let them fall.

It had been her first kiss. A perfect moment that was forever imprinted on her heart, and one she'd refused to let herself remember in the days after Darrin's passing. It just hurt too much.

"Effie?"

She looked to Kieran as he swam toward her, frowning with concern. Holding up a hand, she stopped him before he could step out of the water.

"I'm fine."

"You don't look fine."

"It's rude of you to say so."

Kieran groaned. "Oh, come on. I should be allowed to comment on the fact that you look about one heartbeat away from sobbing."

Crossing her arms, Effie glared at him.

"Are you going to at least tell me what has you so upset?"

"Absolutely not."

He rolled his eyes. Standing there in the water, he looked so much like her lost love that it hurt to breathe.

"I . . . I have to go," she stammered, spinning away and practically running to the exit.

"Effie, wait!"

She heard the splash of water as he tried to follow her. No longer trying to hold on to pretense, Effie ran.

She didn't stop until her legs were shaking and she was gasping for air.

CHAPTER 12

*S*he fell to her knees in the jungle with absolutely no clue how she'd arrived there. After fleeing from the hot spring, she'd blindly ran through the halls, aware of nothing except her overwhelming need to get away.

Effie sucked in breath after breath, her shaking limbs unable to do more than crawl over to the base of a nearby tree. She slumped against it, using it for support while she tried to slow her breathing. There was only one possible explanation she could find to explain how she'd ended up here: she'd stumbled through a portal during her flight.

It wasn't until her heart slowed and inhaling no longer felt like tiny knives scraping against her throat that she realized how much trouble she was in. Alone in the jungle, with no clue how to get back to the citadel and no weapons to speak of. Rowena and her army may not have made their way to Bael, but that hardly meant it was safe.

"Great job, Effie," she scolded herself. "You're really making a name for yourself here. At the rate you're going, it's not going to take more than a few days for the Keepers to realize you're more trouble than your worth and send you back to Helena in disgrace."

Closing her eyes, Effie continued her tirade in silence. She couldn't seem to go more than five minutes at a time without humiliating herself.

Gauging the sun, she estimated it was just after midday. *Good, that gives me at least a few hours of light.*

Not quite ready to stand, she scanned the jungle, making note of her surroundings. Huge trees with heavy vines hanging between them, and massive flowers with blooms easily the size of her face ranged as far as she could see. The low hum of insects filled the air, but that was it—until a branch snapped.

Effie's body went rigid. She pressed back into the trunk of her tree, hoping it concealed most of her body, regardless of the fact that her cream tunic must have stood out like a beacon in the otherwise verdant colors of the jungle.

She peered around the tree searching for the source of the noise. There was nothing there. Only slightly mollified, she started to turn back around until one of the shadows on the floor rippled.

Fear shot through her body, but outwardly she remained calm. She'd held her own in enough battles to know how to deal with an enemy. *Yeah, but here I am without a weapon, like a fool.* Crouching low, Effie kept her eyes on the shadow while her hands moved over the dirt nearby searching for something she could use to protect herself.

She found and discarded a couple of branches. They were unlikely to cause any significant damage. After a few more frantic swipes, Effie's hand smacked into a heavy rock. It took both hands for her to lift it, which didn't make it an ideal weapon, but if she could heave it at an opponent's head, it should buy her the time she needed to run like hell.

Her heart thumped erratically in her chest as she waited. Just when she thought she might have imagined it, the shadow moved again, this time peeling away from the darkness.

Effie's mouth dropped as a horrified gasp escaped. The sound of her terror seemed to encourage the monster. Its scaled body crept closer, two forelegs dragging the rest of it into the light. She scooted back, trying to keep the distance between them. The rustle of her movements brought its head twisting toward her.

She fought a scream as she searched for a place to strike. The creature was easily the size of two men, but there was nothing human about it. If anything, it seemed reptilian, but Effie had never seen anything like it before. Its scales were the color of night and thick like armor, so any kind of body shot would be useless. She had to aim for its head, although the rock that had felt like it was half a boulder now seemed like a piece of flint. Gulping, she scanned its face. Its eyes were two red slits set above a wide mouth filled with what had to have been hundreds of needle-like teeth.

How in the Mother's name am I supposed to fight this?

Ronan had always told her that every enemy had a weakness, you just had to find it. But standing here in the dappled sunlight with a monster bearing down on her, she knew he was wrong.

A grim acceptance worked its way through her, numbing some of her terror. If she was going to die, she wasn't going to make it easy.

Springing to her feet, Effie pulled the rock back before hurling it at the monster's head. It flew wide, landing to the far left of the creature's body with a thud.

Fuck.

The beast snarled, its head tracking the movement of the rock while Effie darted back to her tree and started to climb. The rustle behind her was the only proof she needed that it was coming after her. Palms slick with blood from the rough bark, Effie didn't stop pulling herself up the tree, using the vines for leverage as she scooted higher.

What am I going to do? Think, Effie.

If she'd been one of the Chosen, she could make quick work of this creature with her magic, but she wasn't. Once again, her gift was utterly useless. The only thing she had at her disposal was her wit, for all the good that would do her when fighting this threat.

Effie watched the beast push against the base of her tree, causing it to tremble beneath her hold. Her head smacked into the wood as she struggled not to fall. She hissed in pain as something wet and warm started to trickle down her face. *Blood.* But that was the least of her worries. A few more powerful hits and the tree was going to break.

I'll never survive the fall, unless. . .

A plan clicked into place.

She started to tug at one of the nearby branches, nearly toppling out of the tree as the creature below slammed into the tree trunk a second time. *Just a little bit further*, she chanted, her arm burning as she stretched it to get a better grasp on a sharp piece of bark.

The monster rammed the tree a third time, and the responding crack was Effie's only warning before the tree began to tip. It was more than she needed. Angling her body, Effie prayed her plan would work.

As the tree fell, the monster's mouth gaped open, eagerly anticipating its dinner.

"Sorry to disappoint you," Effie growled, swinging her feet up before letting go of the branch and flying through the air. She landed on the monster's back hard enough that her teeth clanged together. The impact was more intense than she'd imagined, and for one terrifying moment she forgot to hold on.

She started to slide down its back, its scales shredding what remained of her sweater. Effie threw her free hand out, grasping onto one of them with a cry. The edges were razor sharp, but she only needed to hold on long enough to twist her body around.

Beneath her, the beast roared, trying to dislodge her, but Effie clung to its back, working her fingers beneath its scales to help her climb up to its neck. One wrong move and she'd slice herself open before the beast could eat her. *Not necessarily an improvement.*

Mercifully, Effie managed to hold onto the branch she'd pried off of the tree on her way down.

There was a snap and then a loud curse.

"Why can't you ever do as you're bloody told?"

Effie's head shot up, her eyes flying wide as she spied Lucian bursting out of the trees, sword drawn.

His shout provided the opening she needed. The monster twisted its head toward the newcomer, and Effie wasted no time slashing her makeshift spear down into one of its glowing eyes.

Its shriek of agony was deafening, and it began tossing its head left and right in an attempt to dislodge the piece of wood.

Guess it had a weakness, after all, she thought with a savage grin. But the moment was short-lived. The frantic movements beneath her had broken her hold and Effie started to fall.

"Effie!" Lucian roared.

Airborne, her arms windmilled as she was thrown off the monster's back, trying to catch hold of something that would keep her from hitting the ground, but it seemed that her luck had finally run out. With nothing else to do, Effie closed her eyes and prayed.

She landed arm first, the small bones shattering with a sickening crack as the rest of her body followed. She didn't stop once she hit the ground, the momentum sending her tumbling across the jungle debris. White-hot pain burst through her, nearly rendering her unconscious with its intensity. Screaming, Effie skidded, finally coming to a full stop when she slammed into another tree.

Spots danced behind her eyes, further clouding her vision. She tried to push herself up and failed. With a whimper, she watched Lucian hack at the beast. Everywhere his weapon made contact with the monster's body, black blood sprayed out.

Effie blinked, trying to clear the oncoming haze. Something had happened to his sword, and she was certain it was just her addled mind playing tricks on her. It looked like smoke was wafting out of the black hilt. She knew that didn't make any sense. Swords couldn't be made of smoke. Her thoughts grew sluggish and it was a battle just to keep her eyes open.

"Don't you dare," Lucian barked at her. "You stay awake, damnit."

"Ass," she muttered, but if his white-knuckled grip was any indication, she sounded less than threatening.

With a roar that rivaled the beast's, Lucian flung his weapon high. It arced through the sky, the foggy tendrils looking like a million daggers, before sliding across the monster's elongated neck. With a gurgle, head separated from body, the beast fell.

Lucian grabbed his weapon, which looked like a standard sword again. Effie blinked at it curiously, wondering which of the Mother's Branches he controlled. She'd never seen any of the Chosen do anything like that with their power.

Wiping the blade along his leg, Lucian didn't stop walking until he was kneeling beside her.

He cataloged her injuries before returning his dark glare to her face. "I thought you were told not to go anywhere without a guard."

"Wasn't intentional," she gasped, his harsh words helping her think through the pain.

Instead of lessening his anger, her words only seemed to enrage him further.

"I'm going to have to carry you," he declared, looking thoroughly put out.

"Sorry for the inconvenience."

His lips flattened. "It's going to hurt."

"What's a little pain amongst friends?"

His brow quirked. "Friends?"

"You saved my life."

There was no response. Lucian slid an arm beneath her legs, and another beneath her back. Effie didn't know if he'd even bothered trying to be gentle. It hurt almost as bad as the fall itself.

"Hold on," he growled above her.

Effie snickered at the absurdity of his order. With her arm shattered, there was no way she would be able to hold onto him.

"Just don't fall," he amended.

Too late, she thought with another snicker. *Apparently, Lucian is a barrel of laughs when I'm suffering from blood loss.*

"How did you even find the portal?"

"Accident."

"Why weren't you armed?"

"Rough morning," she wheezed, her eyes fluttering closed.

"Effie," he snapped.

Her eyes flew open, finding his intense gaze on her face. If he was relieved she was still conscious, he didn't show it.

"Why did you flee?"

"I didn't."

He shook his head, jaw hard. "The citadel," he clarified.

Even if she was capable of forming the words, she wasn't about to tell him about *that*. "None of your business."

He looked like he wanted to shake her; thankfully, he didn't.

"How did you find me?" Effie asked, interjecting before he could question her further.

"Wasn't hard."

How underwhelming.

"How?" she pressed.

"The two of you were making enough noise that anyone would have been drawn to you."

Anyone with a death wish, maybe.

"What was that thing?" Her voice was thin; her words barely audible.

Lucian must have had excellent hearing because he still caught her question. "Angcerta."

"Ang-what?"

"Certa."

The combination of syllables didn't make any more sense the second time.

"Right," she murmured, resting her head against his shoulder.

Lucian's arms tightened and the added pressure made her squeak in protest.

"Sorry."

"The Guardian apologized. I must be dreaming," Effie murmured.

Not breaking his stride, Lucian glanced down at her. "Fucked up dream."

A laugh burbled up and the side of Lucian's lips twitched in the hint of a smile.

"Definitely dreaming," she decided, the fingers on her mostly uninjured arm lifting to touch the side of his mouth.

This time when her eyes closed, not even he could bring her back.

CHAPTER 13

"*Effie, my sweet girl, where are you hiding now?*"

Hearing her grandmother's voice, Effie thrust the heavy curtain aside and clambered down from the window seat, her joy making her clumsy as she awkwardly scrambled off the ledge.

"There's my girl." Miranda's smile grew, her dark sapphire eyes glowing with pleasure. "What were you doing up there?"

Effie shrugged, not wanting to tell her grandmother that she'd been hiding from the other children.

Miranda's shrewd gazed missed nothing. Kneeling down, she tilted Effie's chin up, brushing back the heavy wave of curls that hung around her face.

Effie tried to pull away, but her grandmother's grip, while gentle, was unyielding.

"How did you get that bruise?" she asked, her voice sounding like quiet thunder.

She recognized that voice. It was the one her grandmother used when telling the grown-ups her important stories. Effie knew better than to lie if her grandmother was using her special voice.

"B-Ben . . . threw his book at me," she whispered.

"Why would the Olivesters' son do that?"

Effie's eyes prickled with tears as she recalled the hateful words he'd hurled at her. "He . . . he said that a waste of space nothing girl like me had no right to read about the history of his people. That I-I wasn't good enough to be taking lessons with them."

"Is that so?" her grandmother asked, her voice hard.

Effie swallowed and nodded once.

Sighing, Miranda sat back on her heels. "Effie, look at me."

She lifted her eyes.

"Do not let their ugliness cloud your kind heart, darling. There will come a day when this is behind you. When the short-sided pettiness of others can no longer touch you."

Effie's disbelief must have shown because Miranda gripped her hands hard.

"I mean it. All of the realms will be open to you. Your destiny does not lie within these four walls. When the time comes, do not stray from the hard path. You will discover wonders you never even dreamed of, if only you have the courage to follow your heart."

"You sound like you're telling me one of your stories."

Miranda smiled. "There is truth in all of my stories. This is no different."

"But, Gran, no one is going to let me go on any adventures—"

"Who says you need permission? The Mother will show you the way when the time comes."

"The Mother didn't choose me," Effie whispered, her young voice breaking.

"Oh, my sweet girl, how hard this must be for you to understand," Miranda said, pulling Effie's small body into her arms. "The Mother has not forsaken you. She has a plan, and you will play a very special part. I promise. Do not lose faith."

Pressing a kiss to Effie's forehead, Miranda brushed a gentle finger over the bruise along the top of her cheek. "And give that Olivester boy not a single thought. He wouldn't recognize true power if it smacked him in the arse."

Effie giggled.

"Ah, that's better. Now, shall I tell you a story before I have to go?"

"Can't I go with you, Gran? I promise I won't get in the way."

"How I wish you could, my sweet girl. One day we will be together, but not just yet."

Effie nodded, trying not to let her disappointment ruin the short time they had.

"Now, what story would you like to hear?"

There was only one answer to that question. "Tell me about the Talyrians, Gran."

Chuckling, Miranda scooped Effie up and carried her over to a chair sitting beside the window. "I should have known. The Talyrians are all you ever ask for."

Effie couldn't imagine anything more wonderful that climbing atop one of the massive winged felines. No one would risk saying another unkind thing to her if she had a Talyrian of her own. She'd have them burnt to a crisp if they dared.

"Wouldn't it be wonderful to fly?" Effie asked, closing her eyes and trying to imagine what it would be like to soar high above the clouds. "Think of everything you'd be able to see."

Resting her cheek on top of her granddaughter's head, Miranda hugged her tight. "There are many ways to see the world, darling. And in your own way, you'll grow wings of your own and see it all. I promise."

Clearing her throat, Miranda loosened her hold, but only slightly. "Now, then. Where to begin . . ."

WHEN EFFIE CAME TO, she was lying in an unfamiliar bed, the medicinal smell of herbs filling her nose and the memory of her grandmother fresh in her mind. For one blissful second, Effie forgot she was dead, that she'd never hear that soothing voice tell her about the wonders of Elysia ever again. Reality came crashing down when her eyes landed on the robed figure standing beside her bed.

"Welcome back."

"Which one are you?" she croaked.

"Smoke."

The thread of amusement in the spectral voice wasn't lost on her. If he was amused, then perhaps she wasn't in a steaming heap of trouble. Although, it was more likely that almost dying must have granted her some leniency.

Glancing at her bandaged arm, Effie made her fingers twitch, surprised when they responded. Her body ached, but the small movements didn't send bolts of pain shooting through her, so she assumed someone in the citadel must have healing abilities.

"How long was I out?"

"Six days."

Effie swallowed. If she'd been out that long, then her arm hadn't been the worst of her injuries. "How bad was it?"

The Keeper didn't immediately reply. Somehow, Effie felt like that was answer enough.

"That bad, huh?"

"You should make a full recovery."

Guilt pulled at her. She hadn't meant to run off and put not only herself but one of their Guardians in danger. That was the second time in as many days Lucian had come to her rescue, and she hadn't even gotten around to thanking him for the first. Effie groaned. What was worse, she now owed Lucian two apologies.

"I didn't mean to run away."

An inquisitive head tilt was her only response.

"I just . . . everything just got to be too much. Between the visions and the memories," Effie sighed, shaking her head and staring up at the ceiling. "I don't know whether I'm coming or going anymore."

"You will learn to manage the visions in time."

She gave a small nod. Right now, her visions were the least of her worries.

"The memories, well . . . time has a way of softening their blow."

"So, you're basically telling me I need to be patient."

His scarlet hood dipped in a nod.

"I used to think I was very patient. Lately, I'm not so sure."

Something about his unobtrusive presence, or perhaps it was being on the other side of almost dying, gave her the strength to admit something she hadn't even admitted to herself.

"I'm afraid of them."

"The visions?"

Biting her lip, she nodded.

"I see."

The Keeper folded himself into a chair by the foot of her bed. Effie blinked in surprise, not anticipating a member of the Triumvirate would do something so human.

"They are mere images. Suggestions of potential futures. They only hold importance if you let them."

"How can you, of all people, possibly believe that? I mean, look at what happened to Helena and her prophecy. She was hidden away because an entire realm was afraid of it coming true."

"Yes, but it was centuries later that we learned our interpretation of it had been flawed the entire time. For all that we See, we are not omnipotent. Our visions are limited by our understanding of them. How often do we see the truth and refuse to accept it?"

Effie frowned. "Then why give them any weight at all?"

"We cannot ignore our gifts."

"You're speaking in circles. First you tell me they only hold weight if we let them, then you tell me they can't be ignored. Which is it?"

"That's something you must decide."

"Mother's tits, you're impossible."

"With enough practice, you will learn the difference. You will know when to listen and when to wait."

"How?"

Smoke shrugged.

"You're going to induce more visions, aren't you?" It was hard to fully keep the petulance from her tone.

"Most likely. What better way to help you learn how not to fear them?"

"What about the visions that come on their own?"

"What about them?"

"When will the side effects go away?"

"When you stop fighting them."

Effie frowned, the answer catching her off guard. She wasn't aware she even had the ability to fight against her visions.

There was the brush of a hand against her leg and Effie tensed beneath her blanket, the spindly fingers still unnerving her.

"Get some rest for now. Kieran will return in the morning to continue your lessons."

The Keeper stood and made his way for the door.

"Why him?" she asked, unable to keep the question from flying out.

Smoke paused and turned back to face her.

"Why is Kieran training me, instead of you or one of the others?"

"Would you rather someone else train you?"

"I mean, he's fine, I just . . ."

There was a beat of silence before he spoke again. *"The time will come when you are ready for what we have to share. For now, learn from one who has recently gone through what you are experiencing."*

"You think that's Kieran . . . even though his visions come through dreams?"

"There are always things to learn, Effie."

She nodded, having expected the non-answer. If they really thought it was best for her, she would accept their decision, for now. She wasn't exactly in the best condition to fight them on it anyway.

Smoke opened the door.

Effie called after him. "When will I know I'm ready to begin my training with you?"

He answered without turning around, *"We will come for you when it's time."*

The door softly clicked shut behind him, and Effie stared back up at the ceiling. If she was going to take on the title of Keeper, then she was going to need to learn the art of answering a question without saying anything remotely helpful.

Effie was still smiling at the thought when her eyes fell closed and she drifted off to sleep.

CHAPTER 14

*S*moke was wrong about one thing. When the morning arrived, Kieran did not come for her. Although, that was only because Effie refused to remain in the sterile healing chamber for one more minute.

It was hard to keep track of time in a room without windows, until Effie noticed that the orbs of light would dim or brighten accordingly. As soon as the ones in her room had begun the transition from a dull shine to soft radiance, her feet were over the side of the bed and she was moving to the door.

Effie had never been a good patient. While she was used to taking orders in every other aspect of her life, there was something about being told to stay in bed with only her thoughts for company that sent her screaming for something to do. Her mind was not a quiet place. Nor did it offer any kind of solace, especially these days.

It didn't take Effie long to realize that while the worst of her injuries might have been healed, she was far from a full recovery. Light-headed and legs feeling as supportive as feather pillows, Effie propped her unbandaged arm against the wall, resting her head against the hard surface.

"Maybe if you did what you were told, you wouldn't find yourself in these situations," a deep voice grumbled.

Effie opened one bleary eye and stared at a scowling Lucian. "You're going to pick a fight with me while I'm still injured, Guardian?"

His frown deepened and his eyes roamed over her body. "If you are in pain, you should be in bed. I will send for Kerrie to check your wounds."

He'd already started walking past her, but Effie stopped him with a brush of her hand against his arm. His forearm felt like a slab of granite underneath her fingers. The muscles beneath her flexed, and Effie dropped her arm as if she'd been burned.

"Please don't. I'm fine. Just readjusting to being vertical."

Lucian's eyes had tracked the movement of her hand. He looked up slowly. They'd never been this close while Effie was in full control of her faculties. The first time she'd been too drunk to sense the danger, and the second time, well . . . she'd been on the brink of death. What could he have done that wasn't about to happen anyway? But there were no such excuses now.

Her breath caught in her throat as she stared up at him. She should have been cowed by his size, but she wasn't. The only worry she had in that suspended fragment of time was that she'd been wrong. His eyes weren't black, as she'd originally thought. They were the deepest umber, with tiny bronze flecks around the pupils. As she stared, the flecks seemed to glow, giving his gaze a predatory heat that made her shiver.

"There you are!"

Lucian jerked, his head twisting to the side and a silent snarl curling his upper lip.

Effie felt like a hand had been removed from her lungs and she was able to breathe freely again. She followed Lucian's gaze to where Kieran was striding down the hall. Her tutor was smiling, but there was nothing friendly about it. He glanced between her and Lucian—at the lack of space between them—and Effie squirmed.

There was no reason she should feel guilty; she hadn't done anything wrong. Unless you counted her not being in her room.

"I was just coming to find you," she lied with a wide grin.

Kieran eyed her, his expression softening. "You shouldn't be up and about yet."

Effie rolled her eyes. "I'm fine. A little exercise is good for a healing body." Whether that was true or not, she had no idea. It sounded reasonable though, so she was sticking with it.

"Come, let us get you settled. I'll find something for you to nibble on while we have our history lesson today." Kieran held out an arm for her.

"Wait. Before we go, there's something I need to do." She turned back to Lucian whose brow lifted in surprise. "I owe you my thanks, and an apology. Two actually."

"I'm sure he deserved whatever harsh words—"

Effie scowled at Kieran. "This is hard enough without you adding your unwelcome commentary."

Lucian smirked as Kieran's cheeks turned pink.

Taking a deep breath, she continued, "I wouldn't be standing here if you hadn't found me. I owe you my life, quite literally. Thank you."

Lucian dipped his head. "It's my duty."

The words chaffed. "Be that as it may. I'll try not to make it a third time."

"That would be wise."

So much for trying to make nice. "Right, well. Thanks." She started to turn away from him when his voice stopped her.

"Kael will be your guard today. I have other business to attend to. Make sure he accompanies you wherever you go."

Effie frowned as an unfamiliar tension filled her, warning her against letting this happen. She didn't know what exactly the Guardian had said to raise off her instinctual alarm, but she couldn't ignore it.

"I don't need a guard today. I'm not leaving the citadel."

"You've proven you can't be trusted to keep that promise. Twice now you've fled the safety of the citadel."

"I just apologized for that."

Lucian shrugged. "You will have a guard at all times."

"This is a pile of wolf shit and you know it."

Effie wasn't a troublemaker—usually—and she wasn't in any danger if she was inside the citadel's walls. This decree of his didn't add up. Then again, neither did the intense urge to fight him on it. What did it matter if a guy stood outside her room while she studied?

"Triumvirate's orders," he replied, as if that excused everything. Perhaps it did.

"Why can't Kieran be my guard?" she asked, crossing her arms and wincing when the bandage snagged. As soon as the question left her lips, the tension swelled, sitting heavy in her chest.

Lucian's voice went flinty. "He's not a Guardian."

"I'm more than happy to accompany—"

Lucian silenced Kieran with a look. "No."

"You're being unreasonable," Effie insisted.

"Says the little girl who can't follow an order to save her life," Lucian snarled.

Effie's back went rigid and she stepped forward, chin tilted up defiantly. "I am *not* a little girl. And I have no problem following orders when they are sensible."

Lucian's nostrils flared and his eyes went so dark Effie could no longer make out the tiny metallic flecks in the center.

"Kael will accompany you." His voice was whisper soft, but all the more menacing because of it.

The weight of the pressure building inside her was getting worse.

"I don't know Kael," she said, her voice tight from discomfort.

"Then I'll introduce you."

Frustrated, both with Lucian's stubborn resolve and her inability to understand what was happening to her, Effie shoved his chest, a throb of pain pulsing through her recently healed arm. She might as well have smacked a wall for all the good it did her.

"If following me around is so damned important, then why don't you do it yourself?" she snapped, not sure what was wrong with her. She didn't actually want Lucian following her either, but that niggling voice wouldn't shut up and now the foreign instinct was overriding her reason.

"I told you, I have business—"

The tension peaked, the weight of it practically suffocating her, forcing her to act. This. Couldn't. Happen.

"Your business is whatever the Triumvirate dictates, and for now they've assigned you to me. So do your damned job."

There was a tick in his jaw, the only outward expression she'd struck a nerve. He dipped down until his eyes were level with hers. "You want me, little girl, fine. But we'll play by my rules. See you later."

He stalked away before Effie could reply. It didn't matter. As soon as he'd agreed, the odd tension began to dissipate, the last of it vanishing entirely once he turned the corner. Relief surged through her in its absence.

"And I thought I liked to push his buttons," Kieran murmured, studying her with a thoughtful expression.

"Something about him makes me act like I'm two years old again," she muttered, her mind still trying to work out what had just happened. Why she'd just fought so hard for something that should have been a non-issue.

"Lucian has that effect on people."

The only other time she'd ever felt a buzzing awareness anywhere close to what she'd just experienced were in the seconds right before a vision.

Eyebrows scrunched together with confusion, Effie looked at her tutor. "Kieran, do Keepers ever get premonitions outside of actual visions?"

"Not that I know of. What makes you ask?"

Effie shook her head, looking once more down the hall where Lucian had vanished. The warning bells started when he said he was going to be away and didn't abate until he promised to stay. The potency of her relief when he'd finally agreed not to go were certainly a confirmation that the two were linked.

This was different than the times she'd reacted over being told she needed minding, like a child. There was something more to this. She'd been worried about him. Whatever mission the Triumvirate wanted to send him on, it wasn't safe.

There was no explanation for how she'd known it, but there was no denying that's what had been building inside of her. *Maybe Smoke will know more about it.*

Kieran held out his arm once more, and Effie wound hers through it, her mind leaving the puzzle alone for now.

They started back the way Kieran had come, their steps unhurried.

"You might not believe it, but I was perfectly reasonable—amiable even—before I got here."

Kieran's half-grin was teasing. "Sure you were."

"Don't you start. I only have enough energy to verbally spar with one egotistical male this morning."

He lifted his free hand in a sign of surrender. "I'm still recovering from your last tongue lashing."

Grimacing, Effie looked up at him. "I guess I owe you an apology as well."

Kieran shook his head. "I think you've suffered enough already. Besides, there's nothing to apologize for."

Effie appreciated that he was letting her off the hook, but she owed him an explanation. Sane people didn't tend to run pell-mell out of a room as a means of ending an unwanted conversation.

"You just remind me so much of him."

Kieran's brow furrowed as he tried to follow her shift in topic. "Darrin," he said, not quite meeting her gaze.

She nodded, staring unseeingly at the wall before them.

"It must be tough watching the one you love die right in front of you."

Tears burned in her throat, but Effie pushed them away. "Agonizing," she whispered. "Wait." Her head shot up. "How did you know about that?"

He shrugged apologetically. "None of us can choose what we See."

"Oh." They walked a bit farther in silence before Effie continued,

"Well, anyway. That day in the water . . . it brought back a memory I wasn't prepared for."

"You don't owe me an explanation."

Effie snorted. "Yes, I do. You were just being friendly, and honestly, I could use a friend. I'll try to be less of a mess from now on."

The ghost of a frown crossed Kieran's face, but he flashed her a quick grin and patted the hand that held onto his arm. "You're not a mess."

They walked the rest of the way in silence, stopping before one of the meditation rooms Kieran had shown her the day before. "We're in here today. You get settled and I'll be right back with something to eat."

The room looked like a miniature library. There was a bookcase that filled one of the walls, a small desk, and two overstuffed armchairs. The walk had taken a lot out of her, not that she'd admit it to anyone, so she sunk gratefully into one of the chairs. With the way her morning was going, Effie could only imagine what else was in store for her. She fervently hoped today's lesson would be less exciting than the last two.

At least she'd be sitting down in comfort this time. That was a definite improvement. Lips twitching in a smile, she folded her hands in her lap and waited for Kieran to return.

KIERAN LOADED up a plate with cheese, bread, and a few pieces of fruit.

"A friend," he muttered, frustration sinking its claws deep into him. "If I'd have known she would still be half-in-love with him when I met her, I'd—"

Kieran stopped mid-rant, sighing as he set the plate down and squeezed the bridge of his nose. *You'd have what? Stayed in Eatos? Rotted in a prison while your family forgot about you? You would have done the same thing.*

Shaking his head, he picked up the plate and headed for the door, his thoughts racing, each one darker and more irritating than the last.

It was damn near impossible to seduce someone who he could hardly get alone for more than five uninterrupted minutes at a time. How was he supposed to convince Effie to see him as more than a potential friend when she wouldn't sit still long enough for him to actually talk to her? And what was going on with Lucian? He might be Effie's guard, but he was showing entirely too much interest in her for one who's normally so aloof.

If he didn't know better, Kieran would say Lucian was interested in Effie himself, but that was laughable. The Guardians didn't do romance. They were warriors, through and through. The only thing they cared about was their mission, so it was an understatement to say that they took their duty to the Triumvirate seriously. If Lucian was interested in Effie, it was tied to her role as a Keeper.

Kieran continued to mull the thought over, only slightly relieved that he'd at least come up with some valid explanation for what was going on. Not that it helped him any. Potential suitor or not, if Lucian was going to be Effie's guard, that was only going to make it even harder for Kieran to get Effie's attention. He needed a plan, and fast, or it would be another twenty-five years before they'd be together. There was no way he'd let that happen. He could only be expected to remain patient for so long.

Determined, Kieran made his way back to Effie. One way or the other, she'd be his.

He'd Seen it.

CHAPTER 15

a soft nudge at her knee jolted her awake. Effie could feel a telltale wetness on her chin. Blushing furiously, she wiped at her face.

"Sorry, I must have dozed off."

Kieran smiled, his green eyes dancing with laughter. "It's to be expected. You've been through a bit."

Spying the plate in his hand, her stomach gave a loud growl. Kieran laughed as he handed it to her and took a seat in the chair beside her.

She gave him a thankful grin. "So, what do you have in store for me today?"

"Nothing too exciting. I was given strict orders that its theoretical studies only."

"So, no halus bane?"

"No halus bane," he confirmed.

The depth of her relief stunned her. As much as she told herself she was ready to face her visions, she was in no hurry to do so again. Controlled setting or not.

"I promise not to fall asleep while you talk," Effie said, biting into a piece of cheese.

Kieran grinned. "I promise not to be offended if you do."

Swallowing another bite, Effie gestured for him to start talking.

"So, what exactly do you know about the Keepers?"

"Only what everyone knows, I expect. That they are gifted with prophecy, and that they are the advisors of the Chosen because of it."

Kieran nodded. "That's the gist of it, certainly. And we've already chatted about how the visions are symbolic, rooted in metaphors and images that would make sense to the receiver."

"Yes, you did mention that."

"So, what happens if two Keepers have the same vision, but interpret it differently?" he asked.

Effie blinked at him. "Is that possible?"

"You tell me. If the images are personal and left open to the interpretation of the individual, it seems to stand that they would have two very different interpretations based on their own unique experiences and understandings of the world, right?"

"Right, but if all of that is true, is such a thing as an identical vision even possible?"

Kieran's smile was smug. "No."

Effie dropped the cracker she'd been holding back onto her plate. "Then why ask me in the first place?"

"To make sure you understood why no two visions are ever the same."

She rolled her eyes. "So, you're saying the same prophecy cannot be granted to more than one Keeper."

"I did *not* say that."

"You literally just said—"

"That no two visions are the same. I said nothing of the prophecies themselves."

"I'm not following," Effie admitted.

"What a Keeper Sees is unique, but the message hidden within is not."

"So, it's not the vision itself that matters, it's the message?"

"Exactly."

"But how do you know that multiple people are Seeing the same thing?" Effie asked, brows scrunched together in confusion. "Do we all get together and share them at some kind of gathering?"

Considering she'd come across maybe seven Keepers since coming to the citadel, not including the Triumvirate or her tutor, that seemed unlikely.

"No, not quite. With the majority of us scattered throughout the realm, gathering en masse is impossible. The Keepers have a responsibility to make a record of each of their visions. Once the message has been discerned, they share it with the Triumvirate who check for a pattern. It's the entire purpose of the Hall of Prophecy."

"That's where the Keeper's transcriptions are kept?" she asked.

Kieran nodded. "Sometimes a prophecy will first take shape centuries before it comes into being. The Hall is how the Triumvirate ensures they never miss a pattern, or the fruition of a prophecy."

"And they are the only ones with access?"

"Yes. Keepers cannot afford to color their interpretation of their visions with what others have already Seen. It muddies the message, so to speak. People could start to draw correlations that simply do not exist."

"So, if only the Triumvirate know when there's been multiple references to a certain prophecy, how are the rest of us supposed to know when a prophecy is coming true?"

"They tell us."

Something about that didn't sit right with her. If the visions came to her, were hers to interpret and understand, why should she have to rely upon anyone else to tell her whether they were important or tied to something bigger?

Leaving it for another time, Effie asked, "How do we know if we are interpreting our visions correctly? Isn't it possible to get it wrong?"

"Absolutely. It happens all the time. There's nuance upon nuance within our visions—well, your visions. I See what will be or what has been. They are possibilities, but they are not wrapped in metaphor. Often they are echoes of the truth or a glimpse at what will come to be if certain events occur."

"I'm really starting to hate you," Effie sighed.

Kieran winked at her. "You don't mean that. I bring you cheese."

She eyed her nearly empty plate. "You bribe me. It's not the same as outright adoration."

Kieran laughed. "I suppose not, but I'll take it all the same."

"It's hardly fair that your visions are so straightforward. How is that even possible?"

He looked away from her, his easy smile fading as shadows darkened his eyes. "The Triumvirate say that since my gift was diluted over time that it evolved."

"I don't understand."

"Have you ever heard of the gates?"

Effie shook her head.

"Millennia ago, in an age long since forgotten—"

"You're telling me children's tales now?"

"Do you want me to answer your question or not?" Kieran asked, his voice sharp with censure. Whatever he was about to tell her was not something he shared easily.

"Sorry," she murmured. "I won't interrupt you again."

Kieran snorted. "I doubt that. Anyway, as I was saying. Once there were gates, portals that spanned and connected innumerable realms. The Gatekeepers were the only ones who knew the secrets of these gates and could open and close them as they saw fit. They were revered for this power. Over time, men wandered, testing their destinies in these new worlds, seeking adventure or fortune, or perhaps simply a fresh start. My people refer to this as the Seeding of Worlds."

Effie lifted a brow, but pressed her lips together to contain the questions that fought to be asked.

Kieran's eyes danced as if he could tell how difficult it was for her to remain quiet. "Centuries ago, the Eatonians decided to close the gates into our land. We cut ourselves off from the rest of the realms, and soon the gates became nothing more than stories. Something everyone knew of, but no one really believed in."

What in the Mother's name does this have to do with visions?

"Did you know there is such a gate here, in Elysia?"

Effie's eyes widened and she shook her head.

"It's true. It's a ruin now, broken and inaccessible from this side, but its counterpart in Eatos is still active. It's how I arrived here."

"Inaccessible?" Effie blurted, no longer able to keep quiet. "Then how will you ever get back?"

"I can't," he said flatly. The tick in his jaw was the only hint that he was suppressing a deeply painful emotion.

"Did you know that? When you came here?" she asked.

Kieran gave one brisk nod.

Sadness washed over her. *He must be so lonely.* "And your family just let you go?"

His answering bark of laughter was harsh and wholly without humor. "Let me? That's one way of putting it."

She wanted to press him, but this line of questioning was clearly painful, and it felt like an intrusion. "Where's the gate?" she asked instead.

"I believe it lies in what the Chosen refer to as the Broken Vale."

Effie nodded. That made sense, especially if the gate was a ruin, as he'd he said.

"So, what brought you here?"

"My visions. An elder in the castle recognized my symptoms and was able to tell me what was happening. He'd met a Keeper once, before the gates were closed. He was able to get a message to them, and they came for me."

At his reference to the elder, Kieran's expression softened, losing some of the tension around his mouth and eyes.

"Castle?" Effie asked.

He gave her a self-deprecating smile. "Don't get too excited, love. I renounced my title."

"Title? What were you, the court jester?" Effie teased.

Kieran snorted with laughter. "I may as well've been for all the good being the prince did me in the end."

Her brows lifted, but the bite of anger in his voice warned her away from prying further. It really wasn't much of a surprise to find that Kieran had been raised a royal.

"Your grandmother was the one that came for me," he said after a moment, glancing at her.

Effie gasped. "She was?"

"She was the first Keeper that I met."

The revelation shocked her. What were the odds of that? Him a prince from a different realm, and her barely more than a servant, both discovering gifts that send them here. And with her grandmother tied to both of them. She couldn't help but feel connected to him now, like a force bigger than either of them had brought them together. Kindred spirits.

Effie studied Kieran discretely. His eyes were far away, lost to whatever memories surfaced at the mention of his family. She couldn't even imagine what it must have been like for him, to make that decision knowing he'd never see anyone he'd known ever again. To discover the people his gift stemmed from, only to forever be branded an outcast because of the differences that separated his gift from theirs.

Feeling guilty for wishing her gift was like his, Effie looked down at her hands, thinking of her grandmother as she said, "I can't even imagine how hard that must have been. To leave your family behind."

"Actually, it was one of the easiest decisions I've ever made."

"Seriously?" she asked, her gaze shooting to his.

His eyes seared into her. "I wasn't running away from something, Effie. I was running to something."

The breath left her in a whoosh. He was talking about her. She knew it with a bone-deep certainty she couldn't explain. And it made absolutely no sense.

She squirmed under the intensity of his stare and tried to move the conversation back to safer territory, not ready to explore that new bit of information too closely.

"So, they believe that your gift evolved because it was diluted?"

"That's what they told me."

"Diluted how?"

Kieran shrugged. "Who knows? The best answer I could come up with is that the Keepers' gifts are linked in some way to Elysia and her people. When the gates closed, we were separated from both, so the gift was forced to evolve, seeking its power from a new source and thereby turning into something new itself. But that's just my theory."

"Hmm," she murmured, looking away from him.

Silence stretched between them and Effie fiddled with the hem of her tunic. She could feel him staring at her, willing her to acknowledge what he'd hinted at. But she couldn't. There were strings attached to such an admission, and she didn't want to accept the responsibility that came along with it.

"Will you tell me about her?" she asked eventually, once the silence got to be too much.

"Who? Miranda?"

Effie nodded.

"She was your grandmother, what could I possibly . . ." Kieran trailed off, his eyes warming as he understood. "Of course," he said, his voice soft. "I'd be happy to. What would you like to know about?"

"Your time together. What she taught you. Anything, really."

Kieran shifted in his chair, getting more comfortable before he started sharing his memories with her. The words soon poured out of him and Effie propped her chin in her hand, eager to hear the stories that made her feel closer to the woman she'd lost. With each new story the tension between them faded until they were once again just two companions fondly reminiscing about their mentor.

Effie didn't know when she'd laid her head on her arms, or when she'd fallen asleep. It wasn't until she saw Kieran's face hovering above hers, his golden hair creating a curtain around both of them, that she even realized what happened.

"Shh. Rest now. I've got you," he murmured, scooping her up into his arms.

Too tired to argue, she snuggled into him, letting her eyelids flutter closed as he carried her to her room.

CHAPTER 16

he next morning, Effie found her way to the dining hall unescorted, which was notable only because it was the first time she'd moved around the citadel on her own—if you weren't counting her mad dashes headlong into danger, which she wasn't.

Proud of herself for only making one wrong turn along the way, Effie breezed into the room and faltered in surprise to find it wasn't empty. The frequent emptiness she'd experienced to this point had led to the assumption she'd have the place to herself.

Men and women were scattered throughout the room, some rifling through books while they ate by themselves, others grouped together chatting in low voices. A few curious glances were cast her way, meaning it was too late for a hasty retreat. Returning a polite smile with one of her own, Effie walked over to the buffet table and filled her plate without paying attention to what she grabbed.

After scanning the room for an empty table, Effie spotted one in the far corner, but before she could claim it, a voice stopped her.

"Are they starving you as well as hiding you?"

A peek at her plate explained the woman's question. "Mother's tits," she muttered under her breath, already turning to put back some of the food.

In her haste, she hadn't realized she'd grabbed an entire loaf of bread instead of just the slice she'd thought, or the jar of honeyed jam and container of creamed butter that were meant to remain at the food station.

"I think maybe I should start with some tea. It would seem I'm not quite awake," Effie said, blushing furiously.

"I dunno. I was rather impressed with your selection and wondering where you were going to put it all," the redheaded woman replied with a wide grin that revealed a gap-toothed smile.

"Is it too late to put it back?" Effie asked, eyes darting from side to side to see if anyone else was watching them.

"I think you're safe, not that anyone cares. Tuck it under your tunic and go have a picnic if that's what tickles your fancy," the woman replied in her conspiratorial whisper.

Effie snickered. "As if they'd give me a day to do something like that."

The woman lifted a sculpted brow. "They?"

"Kieran and Lucian. Between the two of them, I can never seem to find time to sneeze let alone wander off by myself." *The last time you wandered off you were almost eaten by a giant snake monster. Better not forget the reason why you're even alive to humiliate yourself right now.*

"Oh, you poor thing. You must join us and tell us all about being held captive by those two delectable . . ." Catching Effie's face, the woman laughed and corrected herself. "I mean *deplorable* male specimens. I'm Josephine," she announced holding out a hand. "But you can call me Jo."

Effie shifted her plate to one hand to shake Jo's outstretched one. "Effie, but um, you can call me Effie."

Grinning, Jo gestured to two other women seated to the right of the door. "Come on, then, Effie, who knows how long we'll get you to ourselves before they find you and whisk you away."

No kidding.

Jo moved fast, snaking through the tables so quickly that her cloak was airborne. Effie struggled to keep up, her much shorter legs requiring her to practically run to stay behind the other woman. It wasn't a far walk by any means, but Effie's heart raced just the same.

"Ladies, this is Effie. Effie, allow me to introduce Tess and Kait." Jo gestured to each woman in kind.

Tess was stunning, her chocolatey skin, warm amber eyes, and shorn curls lending an exotic elegance to her looks that Effie could never hope to match. Kait was also remarkable, and not just because of her beauty. Her silvery hair fell over her shoulder like a waterfall, and her lush lips were tilted up in laughter. But it was her eyes that captivated Effie. One a deep sapphire and the other a blue so icy it was almost white. A thin, practically translucent scar bisected her eyebrow, coming to a stop at the top of her cheekbone where it forked like a bolt of lightning.

"Welcome to the citadel, Effie," Tess said in a melodically husky voice.

"How are your studies coming?" Kait politely inquired before taking a bite of her warm oats.

Effie bit her lip, not sure how much she could freely admit to these women, no matter how kind they seemed.

"That well, huh?" Jo asked with a laugh. "It's always rough at first. Are you still getting the headaches after your visions?"

"So, it's not just me?" Effie blurted, her relief at learning she wasn't the only one to experience side effects leaving her light-headed.

"Mother no, it was the better part of a year before I woke up from a vision without bruises," Tess replied.

"Once you learn how to ride the vision instead of being overtaken by it, the side effects should pass," Jo informed her.

Pausing mid-bite, Kait asked, "Didn't your tutor go over any of this with you?"

"Kieran's gift works differently than ours. He has no experience with the side effects."

"Ah, yes. The dreamer," she said, her dual-colored eyes taking on a hazy, faraway cast.

"Is he as capable as he looks?" Tess asked, arching a sculpted brow as she licked a bit of cream off her spoon.

Effie's cheeks heated at the innuendo and she shrugged. "I guess so?"

The ladies laughed.

"Careful, let's try not to scare her away in the first ten minutes," Jo chided with a quick wink to Effie.

Tess shrugged, wholly unapologetic. "You can't blame me for asking. That man is more elusive than a damned Talyrian and looks like he'd be just as fun to ride."

"Tess!" Jo exclaimed with a cackle. "You're hopeless."

Having witnessed one of the mythical winged cats in flight, Effie wasn't sure she'd agree. There was nothing fun about the relentless way the massive beasts dipped and swooped as they raced after their prey. Furthermore, Effie liked nothing about Kieran's comparison to one. Especially when it was clear she was the prey.

Effie took a large bite of her bread, hoping it would save her from having to comment on Kieran's rideability.

With a pout and a shrug, Tess turned her attention back to her food. "Spoilsport," she muttered.

"So, Effie. How are you enjoying the citadel so far?" Kait asked.

Effie looked up with panicked eyes, still trying to chew what suddenly felt like a fist-sized bite. Reaching for her cup, she gulped some of her tea to help wash it down. "F-fine," she sputtered.

"Really? I was terrified when my parents dropped me off," Jo announced, wrinkling her freckled nose. "One of the Triumvirate was waiting for me and I about pissed my pants when he reached for my hand."

Effie gave a sympathetic chuckle. "Well, those three certainly take some getting used to, although they don't seem to be around all that much. None of the Keepers do."

"We go where the visions take us," Kait said matter-of-factly.

"It's rare for many of us to be at the citadel for any extended amount of time," Jo agreed.

"So, what brings you here now?" Effie asked, her eyes scanning each of the women's faces.

"We just finished with an assignment in Etillion."

Effie's familiarity with the northern realm was limited only to the two delegates she'd met a few months back. There was a certain allure to knowing that one day, once her training was complete, she too would be traveling throughout Elysia and discovering all its secrets.

"It must be nice to come and go as you choose," Effie murmured.

Jo shrugged, her expression one of indifference. "It gets old, never having a place to call home or a family to come home to. We travel because we must, and the novelty wears off rather quickly."

Effie frowned, some of her excitement fading with Jo's words.

Kait must have caught her expression because she quickly added, "It is nice, though, to be able to see so much of the realm. That is a gift rarely given to the Mother's daughters."

"Especially these days," Tess murmured, her eyes darting to Effie's freshly healed arm.

The unspoken message was unmistakable. The realm was a dangerous place to roam, especially for a woman on her own. Guilt and shame turned the food in Effie's belly to lead. Her behavior could have gotten her killed. She had been a complete fool, fleeing from the safety of the citadel without any awareness of her surroundings. Worse still, it seemed that everyone knew about it. Once again Effie felt she was the butt of the joke. Just a stupid girl who lacked even the most basic sense.

Her eyes fell to her plate as a lifetime's worth of insecurities ate away at her.

Jo's hand covered her own, jarring Effie from the dark direction of her thoughts.

"We heard that you outsmarted the angcerta," she murmured, her voice and smile kind.

Effie shrugged. "I climbed a tree."

"It's more than I would have done. I'd have tried to run, and been killed because of it," Jo said.

"And you were smart enough to blind it so you could gain the upper hand," Tess added.

A small smile tugged at her lips. These women had just met her but were doing their best to alleviate the sting of her mistake. One they could tell she was clearly still suffering from, even if her injuries had been healed. It was a kindness she would not forget.

"How did an angcerta get so close to the portal?" Kait asked, her brows furrowed. "Usually they're repelled by the magic and stick to the outskirts of the jungle."

"I was wondering that as well," Tess said. "It's not even the right time of the year for them to be out of hibernation."

"It's unnatural, if you ask me," Jo said, making a sign with her fingers to ward off evil.

Tess and Kait followed suit.

Unease skittered along Effie's spine. Before her attack, she'd never even heard of an angcerta, and her grandmother had always made a point to tell her stories about the creatures of Elysia. For the angcerta to go unmentioned . . . they must be rare indeed. Could it be a coincidence that she'd stumbled across one now, or was there something more sinister at play here?

"No matter," Jo said, her voice brisk. "If there was something to worry about the Triumvirate would let us know. Their silence can only mean it's business as usual."

Kait and Tess nodded their agreement, but Effie wasn't as easily convinced. She made a mental note to ask Smoke about it the next time she saw him.

The table fell quiet as all four women returned to their plates, but it wasn't long before a low cough cut through the silence. Effie's shoulders were already lifting defensively as she looked up into her Guardian's scowling face.

"What?" she snapped.

Lucian's scowl darkened. "You were not in your room."

"Am I not allowed to break my fast without your permission now?"

"You were given an order."

Effie rolled her eyes. "I've already told you I only follow the ones that are reasonable. Now go away, I will find you when I'm done. You're ruining my appetite."

Jo sucked in a breath and Tess gave a shocked laugh. Kait just watched her with an unreadable expression.

"You will come with me now," he said, unfazed by her attempt at defiance.

Effie grit her teeth, not appreciating him making her look like an unruly child in front of her new friends. Especially not after learning they already knew about her incident in the jungle. She didn't need any help making herself look like an incompetent fool.

Effie's eyes darted around the table, surprised to see the women were so subdued by Lucian's mere presence. *Great. Even they fear him.* It looked like she was on her own. No one else was going to help her stand up to him.

In a low, measured voice, she replied, "No, I am going to finish my meal."

"It's not a request."

"I don't take orders from *you*," she snarled, her eyes narrowed on his.

Lucian crossed his arms and stared down at her, his eyes practically black. "You were the one who insisted I guard you. I told you we'd be playing by my rules." He leaned down until his breath fanned her face. "Now get your spoiled ass up."

Effie's mouth fell open. No one had ever accused her of being spoiled before. The absurdity of the comment had her torn between laughter and indignance.

Indignance won.

There was another shocked hiss of indrawn breath, but Effie didn't risk looking at the others as she set her utensils down and got to her feet. She moved slowly, aware that every eye in the room was on her. *Good. Let them watch.*

She shoved her finger into his granite-like chest, not caring that her chin was practically vertical so she could look up at his face. "I don't care who you are, Guardian, you will not speak to me that way."

Lucian's brows lifted in surprise as he glanced from her finger to her face. "Respect goes both ways, fledgling."

The term rankled, even if it was accurate.

"Maybe if you'd try asking me once in a while instead of always bossing me around, you'd find me more agreeable to your requests."

A muscle in his jaw twitched as his brows sunk even lower. "I need to speak with you. Would you join me in the hall?"

Effie was sorely tempted to tell him no, just to piss him off, but he was listening to her and that couldn't be ignored.

"Please," he added, looking pained.

She couldn't have been more stunned if he'd dropped his pants and waved his bare ass around the room. Words were practically impossible to form so she simply nodded.

"I'll wait for you outside." With that he turned and stalked from the room, the door closing behind him with a loud bang.

"You must have balls of steel," Tess breathed, her amber eyes wide.

Effie turned back to the table and shrugged. "I don't appreciate being told what to do. No one owns me." *Not anymore.*

"But he's a *Guardian*," Jo whispered in awe as she stared up at Effie.

"So what? That doesn't give him the right to walk around with a giant stick up his ass."

Jo shook her head as a smile stretched across her face and caused her eyes to crinkle. "Ladies, I think we have a live one."

Kait snorted. "The girl's been here a week and already she's turning the place upside down."

"Can we keep her?" Tess asked, her eyes shining with laughter.

Effie grinned, feeling like she truly belonged for the first time since finding out about her gift.

"I'd better go before he decides he's waited long enough," Effie said with a sigh. "It was nice meeting you."

"You too, Effie. Feel free to join us anytime. We'll be here for at least another week."

Her smile fell hearing that they could be leaving so soon, but she tried not to let her disappointment show. "Looking forward to it."

With a little wave, Effie turned and made her way out of the dining hall and toward the brooding warrior who awaited her.

CHAPTER 17

*T*rue to his word, Lucian waited for her in the hall, his booted foot resting against the wall as he stared down at the floor. He looked up as she stepped out of the door and for a second his expression was entirely unguarded.

Effie's breath caught in her throat as she struggled to remember why she was always so annoyed with him.

"Took you long enough."

That answers that.

Effie rolled her eyes. "What was so important you had to hunt me down and take me away from my meal?" she asked.

Lucian started walking in the direction of her room. He checked his pace when he realized she was struggling to keep up with him. Glancing down at her, he said, "I'm going to be gone for a couple of days."

Just like the last time he told her he was going away, that crushing pressure took hold of her insides. Knowing that she wouldn't be able to convince him to stay a second time, Effie tried a different tact.

"Where are we going?"

"I don't recall saying we."

Effie shrugged, trying to keep her voice light despite her growing sense of unease. "You're stuck with me whether you like it or not. If you won't stay here with me, I'll go with you."

Lucian shook his head, not in the mood for her antics. "You're staying here. Kael will be your guard while I'm away."

"You keep trying to foist me off on men I don't know."

"Not men. A Guardian; singular."

Effie made a face. "Same difference."

"Not even remotely. And as for the second part of your complaint, where do you think I'm taking you?"

She didn't have a comeback for that. "Where are you going?"

"None of your business."

Effie sighed. It would be easier talking to a wall. Maybe she could delay his leaving long enough that the creeping sense of foreboding building inside of her would pass.

Rubbing at her arms to alleviate some of the discomfort, she asked, "Why do you have to leave so quickly?"

"Unlike you, I don't balk at my orders. I do what I'm told."

Effie stopped short, hands on her hips, ready to defend herself.

Lucian pivoted around to face her, holding up his hand. "At ease, fledgling. I don't have time for another one of your verbal sparring matches. I'm behind schedule as is." With a long-suffering sigh, he answered her previous question. "The Triumvirate are sending me on a scouting mission. They have Seen something and need me to investigate. As much as you believe otherwise, babysitting you is not my only job."

Effie barely heard the insult as the pressure crushed her chest and a harsh buzzing filled her ears. Before she could cry out, the world tilted and disappeared.

BLOOD DRIPPED *down the walls of the cavern, the crimson tears soon filling the small space until she was standing in a pool up to her knees. Effie tried to run, to outdistance the surge of gore that chased her, but it was hopeless.*

Gasping, she fell as a tidal wave crested and crashed into her. The

116

liquid poured into her mouth as she cried out. She rushed to expel it, sucking in a final mouthful of air before she was fully submerged.

Lungs burning, Effie tried to swim up to the surface, but something clung to her leg and tugged her down further into the ruby depths. The harder she fought to get free the more tangled she became.

Help! Help! *But her soundless screams did no good without anyone to save her.*

Deeper and deeper she fell, the red substance thicker and darker the further down she went, until she was soon drowning in a sea of shadows.

Effie covered her mouth as skeletal fingers swam up beneath her, but there was no stopping her screams of terror once the first of the bloated bodies brushed against her.

One after another, the dead floated past until she was surrounded by over a dozen.

Choking, drowning on blood, Effie couldn't escape.

Not when one of the corpses opened its cloudy eyes and stared directly at her.

Not when it opened its mouth and started to speak.

And not when its jaw unhinged, and it swallowed her whole.

"EFFIE . . . EFFIE, STOP. YOU'RE SAFE."

Effie flailed, her thrashing arms and legs smacking against something warm and hard in an attempt to escape the monsters from her vision.

"Ouch! I said stop, damn you," a deep voice growled in her ear as her arms were yanked down and pinned to the ground.

"No," she wailed, her voice nearly gone from screaming.

Eyes flying open, Effie's body went still. She wasn't being eaten by a corpse or drowning in a sea of blood. She was lying on the ground with Lucian scowling down at her.

Mouth dry, Effie licked her lips and swallowed. "You can, um, let me go now."

He released her and pushed back, sitting beside her on the ground. "Care to explain what that was?"

"A vision, I think. I've never had one where I was part of it before," she murmured, wincing as she sat up. Her head ached like she'd been beaten. Noticing the smear of red beside her, she gingerly touched her forehead.

"You smacked it when you fell."

She nodded. It wasn't the only place that hurt. Her knees and ribcage also felt bruised. When the vision claimed her, it was instantaneous. She hadn't even had a chance to brace herself before it overtook her.

"And Keepers do not have visions about themselves," Lucian informed her, his dark eyes guarded.

She narrowed hers on his face. "Then explain to me why I was being chased by a river of blood and attacked by a sea of corpses."

His expression didn't change. "Were you experiencing these acts as a participant? Or as a witness?"

"A participant, I guess," she croaked.

Lucian nodded, his right hand dropping to untie something at his belt before he held out his hip flask for her to take.

She accepted it greedily, chugging back the cool liquid until the flask was empty.

"Sorry," she murmured, handing the flask back to him.

He shrugged and retied it to his belt.

"Why does it matter if I was a participant or a witness?" she asked, returning to his question.

He flattened his lips, looking over her shoulder as if weighing whether or not he was going to answer. "You should ask your tutor."

"I'm asking you."

"Keepers are witnesses. Witnesses to the future and all its various possibilities. However, they are blind to their own future, as to know would influence important decisions. Therefore, when a Keeper has a vision, it is never of themselves. Not directly. You were affected by the elements of your vision, but not the main subject. There's a difference."

Effie stared at him, frowning. "You mean to tell me that no Keeper in the history of all Keepers has ever witnessed a vision about themselves personally?"

"Never."

"So, the blood and the drowning and the cannibal corpses, those had nothing to do with me?"

Lucian's lips twitched. "No."

Effie huffed. "Elder's sagging sack."

Her Guardian raised a brow. "Come again?"

She peeked over at him and grinned. "I stole it from Kieran. Has a nice ring to it, huh?"

Lucian shook his head. "Speaking of your tutor, he really is the one you should be speaking to about deciphering your visions."

"Why does it matter who helps me?" she asked.

"It's his job."

"And? You're here, he's not."

"So, I'm the only one you expect to do the job they were assigned?" he challenged, peering down at her.

"No, but . . ." she sighed. "Never mind. Why are you still here, anyway? I thought you were in a rush to go on your special mission."

"How about you just say thank you and be glad that I am?"

The terror of her vision still simmered within her, and Effie realized that she was glad he'd been there. He'd distracted her from the vision itself and helped her from being completely lost to it.

"Thank you," she murmured.

"You're welcome."

They were sitting beside each other, their backs pressed against the wall. She pulled her knees up to her chest and wrapped her arms around them. Lucian's legs were sprawled out, easily filling the distance between the walls. She felt tiny beside him but was no longer threatened by his size. He'd come to her rescue often enough that she knew she was safe with him. Perhaps that's why she found it so easy to mouth off around him.

Resting her cheek on her arms, she looked up at his face. "So, if the

119

vision wasn't about me, and I didn't recognize anyone else in it, how do I know who it was about?"

"Effie," he growled her name in warning.

"You might as well talk me through it, Lucian. You clearly know more about these visions than I do."

"I can't say. It was your vision. Which means your subconscious chooses the images. You're the only one that can decide what it means."

Effie frowned.

With a sigh, Lucian tilted his head back and stared up at the ceiling. "If I were you, I would concentrate on what each element made you feel. The feelings should lead you to the real-life counterparts."

"I was terrified and dying, Lucian. That doesn't really help me narrow it down."

"You weren't dying, you were drowning. At no point did you actually die. Did you?" he asked, twisting his head to look down at her.

"Not unless you count the part where the corpse came to life and ate me."

Lucian stopped her with a hand. "Maybe you should back up and start at the beginning."

For once, Effie was eager to share the vision, to purge herself of some of the fear lingering inside of her. If anyone could handle her monsters, real or metaphorical, Lucian could.

Starting from the beginning, Effie told him what she'd Seen. The metallic flecks in his eyes were glowing by the time she'd finished.

"Out of all of the things that you just told me, which words stand out the most when you think about your vision?"

Effie let her eyes fall closed as she pictured it.

"The blood, the bodies, the shadows . . ." she trailed off as her eyes flew back open. She stared at him, horror and excitement making her already strained voice breathless. "It wasn't a sea of shadows, Lucian. It was a sea of *Shadows*. They were the reanimated bodies that were trying to attack and why there was so much blood."

She shuddered at the memory of the Shadows, the mindless and grotesque creatures that the Corruptor Rowena had created in an attempt to retake Helena's throne. If she was having premonitions about them, then the message was definitely tied to the war that continued to rage in the world outside of the citadel. The war she was supposed to be helping Helena end.

He smiled at her, but it was grim. "It sounds like you've found your answers, Keeper."

"Mmm," she hummed, not sure if it was an answer, but it was certainly a path. One she needed to follow until it led her to the truth it concealed. "I wish I could remember what they said at the end."

"That reminds me," Lucian said, shifting to dig something out of the pack that was on the floor beside him. "I have something for you."

He held out a small leather-bound journal, a thick cord wrapped around its cover. Flowers in all states of bloom had been tooled into its tanned surface, and it didn't take more than a passing glance to tell it was a true work of art.

"We've been chatting for the better part of an hour and you just now remember?" she teased even as her heart gave a little lurch. The only other person who'd ever taken the time to give her a present had been her grandmother.

Lucian rolled his eyes. "If someone wouldn't have insisted on being such a brat this morning, you might have gotten it earlier."

Effie caressed the top of the supple leather longingly before pushing the journal back at him. "Lucian, it's stunning . . . but I-I can't possibly accept such an expensive gift."

His face, which had only just lost some of its glower, scowled at her. "It's not a gift. It's a Keeper's journal. *Your* journal. Take it, fledgling."

Only a second ago I was Keeper. Now I'm fledgling *again.*

Wordlessly, she took the book out of his hand before unwinding the leather string holding it closed and letting it fall open in her lap. Its cream pages were uneven along the edges and made out of expensive parchment, and the inside of the cover was the softest suede. She'd never owned anything so fine in her life.

"Thank you," she mumbled, still stunned by the generosity of the gift.

Standing, Lucian held out a hand to help her up. "You should probably write your vision down before you forget it. That's what the journal is for, after all. If you have any others before your next lesson with Kieran, make sure you add it in as well." With a sigh, Lucian glanced down the hall. "I don't have time to take you to meet Kael. I need to get going if I hope to make it before dark. I'll send him to you. Try not to get yourself killed while I'm gone."

Effie stuck out her tongue and Lucian shook his head, turning away and leaving her without another word. She stared after him, unsettled by his quicksilver moods. He went from intolerable brute to concerned friend in less than a heartbeat. The first she could handle, the latter . . . not so much.

It took longer than she'd care to admit before Effie felt steady enough to make the unaccompanied journey back to her room. The fall she'd taken at the onset of her vision had done a number on her, and the arm that had finally stopped aching yesterday was starting to throb.

Head pounding, Effie let the journal fall open on her desk. Her fingers trailed over the blank pages as unexpected wistfulness filled her. Another time, another place, this journal could have been a beautiful and thoughtful gift from a man who might one day be more than just a friend. But as Lucian reminded her, it was not a gift. It was a Keeper's journal. A tool to be used to fulfill her purpose.

Separated as she was from the rest of the world, it was easy to forget what was happening out there. She'd let herself become distracted. Distracted by her grief, by her aversion to the horror contained within her visions, by the men that surrounded her. But the time for that was over.

It had to be.

They were in the middle of a war. One they could so easily lose. How could she waste time thinking about silly things like a man who wanted to pursue her, or one whose intense gazes made her stomach twist in knots? People were counting on her. There was a chance her visions could contain the answers that would save them.

She owed it to them—to herself—to not lose focus. She couldn't afford to be selfish. Not until Helena defeated the Corruptor once and for all. Lucian wasn't the only one with a job to do. Which meant there was no room for distraction. Not a green-eyed one, and definitely not one with eyes flecked with bronze.

With a groan, Effie eased herself into a chair and began recounting her vision for the second time that morning. Already the details were starting to fade, and she understood the importance of the journal. From now on, the book would accompany her wherever she went. It was as vital a tool as her dagger, and potentially just as useful.

Words could be weapons as powerful as those forged from metal. Stronger even, if they became the clues that would reveal how to defeat their enemies. Effie only hoped that when the time came, she would not miss their signal.

CHAPTER 18

"*Y*ou should have come to me immediately," Kieran insisted, his arms folded across his chest.

Effie rubbed her temples, the headache from her vision lingering even though it had been over ten hours since it claimed her.

"It's not like I have any say over when they come to me, Kieran. Besides, Lucian was there, so what's the difference?"

At the mention of her Guardian's name, Kieran's eyes darkened and his upper lip curled in a snarl. "As if a Guardian knows anything about dealing with prophecy."

Irritation flared to life at his misplaced indignation. *After several lifetimes of working beside and for the Triumvirate, he likely knows more than you.*

She leveled him with a glare. "He knew enough to give me my Keeper's journal."

"He *what*?" Kieran asked, his voice dropping to just above a whisper.

Effie pulled the book out of the small pack she'd tied around her hips. "He talked to me about the importance of writing down my visions so that I could go over them with *you*."

Kieran looked slightly mollified. "It still wasn't his place," he muttered, taking a seat at the small desk.

Effie threw up her hands in exasperation. "Are we going to waste more time debating the point, or can we get to the deciphering of visions part of the lesson?"

He waved a hand. "By all means."

"Finally."

Flipping to the first page, which was now underlined and had circles around or arrows connecting the words or elements she felt were most important, Effie described what she had Seen.

"And you think that your vision was in reference to the Shadow army?" Kieran summarized once she was finished.

Effie nodded. "Unless you know of any other bloodthirsty cannibals currently wandering the realm?"

"Take it from me, Effie. Time has no relevance when it comes to prophecy. You can See things that will not come to be for centuries. A person could lose a lifetime waiting for them to come to pass."

His eyes were glowing with an intensity she was starting to recognize. He always had that particular gleam in his eye when he was referring to his dreams of her.

"This didn't feel like some distant unknown future. There was an immediacy to it," she insisted, focusing on the feelings of terror that had her trying to flee the cave in the first place. "And it didn't feel like a particular event as much as a warning. Something's coming . . ."

Kieran didn't seem moved by her revelation. "Something's always coming."

Frustration simmered within her. His dismissal felt oddly familiar, and not in a comforting way. When were people going to start taking her seriously? *Maybe once you do . . .*

"I don't know when, and I don't know where, but the Shadows are coming, and soon."

Kieran studied her, leaning back in his chair as he stared into her eyes. Effie tried not to squirm under the scrutiny, and she sat on her hands to keep from pulling her hair over her face. Her curls had always been a shield she could hide behind, a physical barrier she could place between herself and those that judged—or pitied—her.

"Let us assume that your interpretation is correct. You've just said yourself you cannot identify any details that would allude to a certain place or time. What then do you suggest we do with the information?"

"Tell the Triumvirate? Let them weigh the information against what they already know is coming, or perhaps what is stored in the Hall."

A smile ghosted across her tutor's face. "A common assumption, but a Keeper cannot go running to them every time they have a vision. The Triumvirate would never get anything done."

Effie was thankful she still sat on her hands. Her palm itched to slap the smile off his face. Why ask her what she thought if he was just going to laugh at her answer? Even if he had a point.

"So, when *do* we bring our visions to their attention?" she asked, her voice brittle with the effort it required to keep her frustration from leaking through.

"When they ask."

"That seems irresponsible, not to mention dangerous. What if we miss something because they waited too long to ask?"

Kieran shrugged. "One has to assume that they know what they are doing. They do have access to centuries worth of warnings."

"You just ridiculed me for such an assumption. At the end of the day, they are still men. Men can make mistakes."

"Are they?" Kieran asked with a lift of his brow. "Now that's an interesting thought."

Effie sighed. This conversation was not nearly as helpful as the one she'd had with Lucian in the hall. Once again, she was left wondering why in the Mother's name Smoke and the Mirrors had insisted on placing her under Kieran's tutelage.

"I'm not purposely trying to irritate you," Kieran said softly, placing a warm hand on her knee. "You've done an exceptional job fleshing out the symbols hidden within your vision, but you are still learning. If your path is similar to the rest of the Keepers, then you will likely experience the same vision multiple times, each new occurrence revealing new details. Those details could change the course of your interpretation entirely. We must wait until we can know for sure that you have drawn the correct conclusion."

She sat back in her chair with a humph. "This is another reason you induce visions, isn't it? So that you don't have to wait around for the lightning to strike on its own."

Kieran nodded.

"So, what are you waiting for?"

"We do not use the halus bane on the same day as a natural vision."

"Who makes up these ridiculous rules?"

His head tilted to the side. "Even you must admit that you're in no condition to experience another vision so soon."

Effie's eyes dropped to the floor. She was running off of pure adrenaline right now. Another vision could render her completely useless. Head and body aches were not the sort of thing one summoned a healer for. Their gift was too valuable to be used on something so minor.

"But if it could help . . ." she started.

Kieran shook his head. "No, Effie. Nothing is so crucial that I would put your health at risk. I know that it is easy to believe each one of your visions is vitally important, but I promise you, with time you will come to learn that they are not. We will not rush this. Not after what happened last time. Trust me."

He sounded so sure, but the need to be useful—to prove herself— warred within her.

"Think of it this way," he said, standing and holding out a hand to her, "you get the rest of the evening off. How would you like to spend it?"

Effie placed her hand in his and allowed him to pull her to her feet. She had no answer for him.

At the Holbrooke's Estate, free time was a luxury she'd never had. There was always something to do or someone to take care of. From dawn to dusk she stayed busy, until it was time to fall asleep, so she could start all over again the next day.

It wasn't until she joined the Kiri and her Circle that she learned how to enjoy the quiet hours of early evening. But even then, it was never really her *choice* on how to pass the time. The decision was made by one of the Circle, and they would have spent the free time sparring or telling stories around the fire.

Effie looked up at Kieran's puzzled face and shrugged. "I don't know."

"How can you not know?"

"No one's ever asked me before. I don't even know what my options are."

"We can do whatever you want."

Effie gave him a pointed glance.

Kieran laughed. "Come on, you can't mean to tell me you truly want to deal with visions all night. There has to be something else. We could go into the town or—"

"I want to train," Effie interjected.

"Train?" Kieran sputtered, incredulously. "That's neither fun nor relaxing."

"You asked what I wanted, and I told you. Why ask if you're just going to tell me why I shouldn't want it or can't do it?"

Kieran folded his arms, his face impassive. "So be it. Will you permit me to ask why that's how you want to spend the evening?"

"Does it matter?"

"No . . . I just find it a peculiar request."

Effie took a deep breath, looking everywhere but at his face as she considered her answer. "I don't want to have to rely on anyone else to save me. I've already lost too many people in this war, and as it stands, I barely made it out of that jungle alive. If it hadn't been for what I'd learned from Ronan's drills, I probably wouldn't be standing here right now."

Kieran went very still as she continued.

"And if I'm being honest, I *like* training. Maybe not the fighting part specifically, but there's a certain sort of peace in the ritual. My mind grows quiet and all the voices telling me—" she cut herself off realizing what she'd be about to admit. It was a confession she'd never made aloud, and one she didn't intend to share now. She didn't want this man's pity, or anyone's for that matter. Shrugging, she finally allowed herself to meet his gaze. "It probably sounds silly to you."

Kieran regarded her with a look so filled with anguish that Effie's breath caught in her chest.

He shook his head. "No, it doesn't. It's not silly at all, Effie. I know exactly what you mean. I spent many nights battling the demons in my mind while in a sparring room. Sometimes it's the only way you can fight the monsters."

Without conscious thought, Effie reached for his hand, squeezing hard as his fingers wove through hers. She may not know him very well, or at all, but no one could fake that kind of pain. Whatever Kieran had lived through left its mark. She knew better than to ask— some hurts were too personal to share—but she could still offer comfort.

She stared into his eyes and something shifted within her, settling into place and recognizing him once more as a kindred spirit. Perhaps Kieran was the perfect tutor, after all.

Smiling softly, she asked, "So you'll train with me, then?"

"Of course. If it would not be an intrusion."

The polite formality of the response hinted at the prince he'd once been, and Effie's smile grew.

"Not an intrusion at all. It will be a nice challenge having someone new to practice with."

They started walking out of the room and into the hall.

"I should probably warn you, I'm an excellent swordsman. I was trained by the most skilled warriors in Eatos. I'll not go easy on you."

Smirking, she replied, "Good. I hate being underestimated."

He stopped her with a brush of his hand against her elbow. "I've never underestimated you."

Effie swallowed, her stomach swooping before a flutter moved up into her chest. "I wish I could say the same."

Her words were purposely vague, and Kieran's answering smile told her he knew it. Lifting a hand, he traced his thumb along her jaw.

"Come on, then. Let's go get sweaty." He moved away with a wink.

Effie's laughter rang through the hallway, following them the entire way to the training room.

THEY'D BEEN at it for hours and her arms were screaming in protest. She'd hardly been at her peak to begin with, but lungs burning, Effie circled her partner, refusing to admit defeat.

Kieran spun his sword in his hand, gracefully sliding his front leg forward as he slashed out and tapped the tip of the blade against her upper arm. He was toying with her now. Showing her that he could end this anytime he wanted.

Effie blew a piece of damp hair off her forehead and tightened her hold on her own blunted blade. She was starting to pick up on his tells. He was an aggressive fighter, showering her in an explosion of moves that made it hard to predict which way his blade would swing next. Effie could understand why it was an effective strategy. She was often too busy reacting to get in any strikes of her own.

However, the men Kieran had fought were clearly much taller than she was. Otherwise, they would have noticed that by being constantly on the attack, the right side of his body was frequently unprotected. At least to someone at her eye level. For once, her height—or lack thereof —was a boon. Taller men would have to slash down or around Kieran's sword arm to get to his exposed ribs, which did not make them much of a target. But for Effie, she only needed to swing up to land her blow.

If she could distract him long enough to strike first.

Ronan had taught her to pay attention to her opponent. To watch the barely discernable shifts of weight or direction of their eyes. It was a lesson that had come in handy more than once on the battlefield. Effie was not exactly what she would call a skilled fighter, not compared to the warriors she'd fought beside, but she was an excellent student, and she knew how to use a blade.

She continued to mirror Kieran's steps, blocking what she could of his attacks when it happened: a minute shift of his hips as he changed

MEG ANNE

his weight. Effie didn't wait. She swung hard and fast, slamming the flat side of her sword into the space just above his ribcage.

Kieran grunted, surprise flaring his eyes wide as he lost his grip on his sword. It fell to the floor with a clatter and Effie lunged, ready to unleash her killing blow. Kieran was lightning fast, ducking and spinning around her in a flash of golden hair.

Pain flared up her arms as he knocked the sword from her hand and pulled her arms back and up behind her body.

Momentarily stunned, it took Effie a heartbeat to register what happened. Kieran's body was pressed against her back, and the heat of his breath tickled her ear.

"Submit and I'll let you go."

With a laugh, Effie lifted her foot and Kieran thrust her away, bending over in a ninety-degree angle in an attempt to protect his manhood.

"Dirty trick," he panted.

Effie turned to face him with a shrug. "It worked, didn't it?"

He looked up at her through long strands of golden hair that had fallen free from his braid. "So it did."

He lunged, hitting her with his shoulder low in the belly and knocking her to the floor.

She hit the ground with an *oomph*, the air whooshing out of her lungs. Tiny stars exploded behind her eyes and she blinked rapidly trying to clear them. Effie lifted her hips, intending to buck Kieran off of her, but he was faster.

Grabbing her wrists, he pinned them to the ground on either side of her body, settling on top of her body and bending down until his eyes were the only things she could see.

"Submit," he growled.

Goosebumps erupted all over her skin as she realized the erotic way her body cradled his. *Not the time, Effie.* But it was too late. Once the thought was recognized, Effie couldn't help but notice the full weight of him pressed up against her.

Her hips shifted, rocking up into his and Kieran groaned low in his throat, his eyes flashing a bright green.

132

"That better not be another of your tricks. It won't work."

Licking her lips, Effie gave a quick shake of her head.

Kieran's eyes dropped to her mouth, tracking the movement of her tongue.

"Tease," he murmured, his husky voice wrapping itself around her.

Effie shivered again, not sure how to navigate this unexpected turn of events. She'd never had a sparring match turn into . . . this. Whatever *this* was.

The change in energy between them was palpable. It was charged, like the feeling of a thunderstorm before the first drop of rain broke free from the angry clouds. The tiny hairs along the length of her arms and neck stood on end, waiting for the storm to be unleashed.

More of Kieran's hair slipped free, surrounding them both in a golden curtain. Her heart thundered in her chest, although with the way he was pressed against her, it could have very well been his. Silence swelled around them until all she could hear was the harsh panting of her breath mingling with his.

Kieran's hooded eyes lifted to hers and the heat in them seared her. No one had ever looked at her that way. Like they were ready to devour her whole.

His hands loosened on her wrists and slid up until his fingers curled against hers. The intimacy of the move, the slip of skin against skin, sent off new sparks along her body. Heat pooled low in her belly. She was stunned by the sudden need for him to shift the angle of his hips and press them into her. How could something so simple cause such a reaction within her?

Sliding his nose down hers, his head dipped, his mouth hovering just above her own.

"Wait," she whispered. The word closed the hairsbreadth between them so that her lips brushed against his.

"Why?" he groaned, his voice tortured.

"We shouldn't do this."

"I disagree," he purred, this time pushing up enough to look at her. "We should most definitely do this."

Temptation swirled within her, and for a second Effie wanted to give in, to submit, but she couldn't ignore the warning bells clanging in her mind. "Please," she whispered, not sure if she was begging him to kiss her or take mercy on her and let her go.

Kieran's eyes glazed as he held himself suspended above her. "For now, little one, I will let you run from me."

Relief turned her muscles to liquid and Effie melted into the floor. Her relief didn't last long.

"But only because I know the day will come when you are the one chasing me."

Effie gulped. *Mother have mercy on me. Is* that *what he's Seen? No wonder he's been relentless. He thinks we're inevitable.*

Kieran turned his head until his lips moved against her ear. "When you're begging me not to stop, but to finish what we started."

Her eyes fluttered closed and Kieran kissed the skin were her neck and jaw met.

"Run, little one, but know that eventually I will catch you, and I won't even need to chase you. You will come willingly. And when you do, there is no turning back."

Dazed, Effie remained motionless, not trusting herself to respond in case the words that came out of her mouth were surrender.

With a sigh, Kieran let go of her hands, his fingers trailing over the skin of her forearms and inner elbows.

The crash of metal against wood broke the heated moment, and as one Effie and Kieran's heads twisted to the door. All she could make out was the ripple of a black cloak as a man exited the room.

Effie blanched, horrified that someone had been watching her and Kieran. She hadn't heard the door open, had no clue they were no longer alone. She'd probably been too shocked by Kieran's words to hear anything but his voice as he delivered his warning against her lips. But it didn't matter that she hadn't seen who was there.

Effie didn't need to see the man's face to know who had returned.

CHAPTER 19

"*M*other's tits," Effie swore.

Kieran smirked in amusement at the vehement curse. "Seems that your Guardian has found his way back."

Effie looked up at him, panic making her eyes appear wild. "Get off me," she snapped.

Pushing to his feet, Kieran held out a hand for her, but she slapped it away, choosing to stand on her own.

"Now look what you've done," she groaned.

"What *I've* done?" Kieran asked, lifting a brow. "Pray tell, little one, what exactly did I do?"

Cheeks still flushed with desire, Effie was damn near irresistible. It had taken more control than he knew he possessed to resist taking her then and there. Only the knowledge of what awaited them allowed him to rein himself back in. But only just. Need still pulsed through him, urging him to close the distance between them and carry her off to his room.

Her eyes were a tempest as they met his. "We'd only just started to get along. Now he's going to think I'm some strumpet and stop treating me like an actual person." Effie frowned, biting down on her full bottom lip.

Kieran used her distraction to discretely adjust himself. *Elder's sagging sack. This is getting ridiculous.* "Stop," he groaned.

She blinked up at him. "Stop what?"

He chuckled, shaking his head at her utter obliviousness. She hadn't the foggiest clue what she did to him. "Your Guardian will not think you are a strumpet." He struggled not to laugh as he used her word. "You're a woman, Effie. It's natural for you to experience desire, to take a lover if that is your choice. He has no say in the matter."

Effie's cheeks turned crimson. Her voice was high when she snapped, "I'm not taking a lover."

Kieran couldn't resist baiting her. "Not yet."

Eyes wide, Effie shook her head. "You're impossible."

Needing to touch her, Kieran stretched out his arm, running his finger along the bottom of her chin. "Admit it; you love me."

It was the wrong thing to say.

Effie's eyes narrowed and she scowled, jerking away from his touch. "You wouldn't know the first thing about love."

"Come on, you know I didn't mean anything by it."

"Maybe that's the problem, Kieran," she said, side-stepping his attempt to grab her arm. "You never really *mean* anything."

"What in the hell is that supposed to mean?" he asked, annoyance eating away any remaining desire.

Her voice was low and cutting as she answered. "Everything is about you. You couldn't care less about who you hurt in your efforts to get what you want. Did you ever stop to think about how your selfish actions affect others? Do you have any idea how important being here is to me? What a distraction you are to my purpose?"

Kieran's mouth fell open in shock. All he'd done since he left home was think about her. He'd changed the entire course of his life to find her. How dare she accuse him of being self-centered. Before he could defend himself, she continued.

"You're so focused on claiming me, like I'm some sort of prize. I'm not a possession, Kieran, I'm a person. It's going to take more than a few sexy words to fool me into giving you my heart. And I promise you, no matter what you think you've Seen, I will *never* beg you for anything."

With a final scathing glance, she shouldered past him.

"Wait just a damn minute," he said, grabbing her wrist and pulling her around. "You don't get to say all that and not give me a chance to defend myself."

She pulled her arm out of his grasp. "Words are cheap, Kieran. You want to prove me wrong? Do it with actions."

Kieran watched her walk away, stunned at how quickly things had turned around on him. One second, she's practically writhing beneath him, and the next she's hurling accusations at him.

He ran a hand over his head, staring at the door as he tried to make sense of the last few minutes.

"What just happened?" he asked, his voice echoing around the empty room.

EFFIE STORMED DOWN THE HALL, her emotions a maelstrom within her. No matter how fast she walked, she couldn't outrun them. Guilt, shame, remorse: each one tore at her.

Whether there was truth in her words or not, Kieran hadn't done anything to deserve what she'd said to him. Not really. It was wrong of her to lash out at him because she felt guilty for wanting what he offered.

It was so easy to forget with him. That she wasn't just here to learn, but that she had an obligation to the Kiri and her Circle. That her heart was freshly broken.

Darrin.

The reminder gutted her, and Effie fought back a sob, throwing out an arm to catch herself as her knees gave out.

How could she do this to him? What did it say about her that she was already entertaining ideas of another man so soon after losing him? It had been almost six months since he died, but her heart shouldn't know the difference.

Darrin had loved her, had *died* to save her. That was true love. Not whatever pale imitation Kieran thought he offered with his seductive caresses. He wouldn't know real love if it bit him in the ass.

"Daughter?"

Effie stiffened at the familiar spectral voice. She looked up at the robed figure standing at the other end of the hall. Wiping her cheeks, she pushed herself away from the wall. "Hello, Smoke."

"Why are you crying? Are you hurt?"

A laugh bubbled up. Yes, she hurt, but not in the way that he meant. "I'm fine."

The hooded head tilted, disbelief evident in the action.

"I just got a little overwhelmed. I'll be fine."

"Would you like to accompany me?"

The offer surprised her. Any other time she would have jumped at the opportunity to learn more about what the Triumvirate did, but right now she just wanted a hot bath and to curl up in her bed and forget everything about the last few hours.

"Next time?" she asked, hoping it wasn't rude of her to decline.

The hood dipped in what she assumed was a nod of assent.

"At least allow me to escort you back to your room."

The distraction from her thoughts would be a welcome reprieve. Even if it only lasted for a few minutes.

"Okay."

He waited as she made her way toward him.

"You were training."

It was not a question, but Effie felt compelled to answer anyway. "I was."

"With your tutor?"

Effie eyed Smoke. "Was I not supposed to?"

"Physical exercise is good for the mind. It can help put things in perspective."

Ah, more vague non-answers. It was comforting that some things stayed the same.

"You might find that the Guardians make for apt partners. They are skilled in such things."

"As opposed to Kieran?"

Smoke shrugged. *"Merely a suggestion, depending on what you hope to learn."*

Her shoulders sagged at the thought of Lucian and what he'd seen. "I don't think my Guardian will have any interest in training with me."

"Have you asked?"

"No, but—"

"Then you cannot know."

Effie frowned. "I guess not. But he said he would be busy with some errand you'd given him." She knew it was probably a futile attempt to get more information.

"He's not the only Guardian."

"True, but he's the only one I've met."

Smoke stopped and turned to face her. *"Kael was supposed to be assigned to you."*

Effie shrugged. "I guess I'm not the only one who's been busy."

"Ah, yes. The vision. Have you succeeded in deciphering it?"

"I think so. Should I tell you about it?"

"There's no need."

Her brows furrowed. "Why not?"

"Your Guardian told us what you Saw."

"Oh."

Apparently, Lucian thought it was important enough to pass on even if Kieran didn't. At least someone believed her. The thought bolstered her some.

"Here we are."

Effie had been so distracted by their conversation that she hadn't realized they were already back to her room.

"Oh, well. Thanks for walking with me."

Smoke dipped into a shallow bow. *"My pleasure."*

Somehow, she doubted that, but appreciated the platitude all the same. "I'll see you soon?"

"Only the Mother knows."

Of course his answer wouldn't be as simple as yes or no. Effie shook her head, laughing to herself as he walked away.

Still smiling, Effie grabbed what she needed and made her way to the shower, her earlier grief forgotten.

～

TOWEL DRYING HER HAIR, Effie stopped short as her eyes landed on the dimpled grin of a stranger.

"I didn't mean to startle you."

Effie eyed the man whose ebony skin had a subtle sheen under the soft lights of the hallway. His head was shaved but his jaw was shadowed with a well-maintained, close-cropped beard. He was leaning against the wall opposite the door she'd just left, his position relaxed, but she assumed that was part deception. His crossed arms rippled with muscles and his thighs were easily three times the size of her own. This was no bookish scholar. But his eyes shone with secret amusement and his smile was open and friendly.

Effie slowly resumed drying her hair. "Then maybe you should try not standing directly outside of the women's bathing chamber."

His smile grew, causing his twin dimples to deepen. "Practical advice."

Something about the man set her at ease and Effie allowed her body to relax. "If you're waiting for someone, you should probably know that there was no one else in there."

"I was waiting for you."

The admission should have frightened her, but instead only piqued her curiosity. "For me? Why? Have we met?"

She knew that she didn't remember meeting him, but she had also been unconscious for the better part of a week, so there was no saying for certain.

The handsome stranger hid his smile behind his hand and straightened, pushing off of the wall he'd been reclining against. "No, much to my chagrin. I'm Kael."

That explains it.

"So, you're the one my Guardian keeps trying to pass me off to? I

140

should warn you, I'm a bit of a pain. You might have been better off continuing to avoid me."

Kael's dark green eyes crinkled around the edges. "So I've heard."

Effie scowled. "Of course, you have."

He tilted his head. "It's okay for you to warn me you're a handful, but not Lucian?"

"Exactly."

Kael's answering laugh was warm and deep. Effie liked him immediately.

"I am sorry if I startled you. It was brought to my attention that I had been derelict in my duties. I sought to remedy that as quickly as possible."

"Brought to your attention? By whom?"

His enigmatic smile told her all she needed to know.

"But if Lucian is back, why bother giving you grief at all? Aren't I still his responsibility?"

The first hint of seriousness crossed Kael's face. "It was my duty to look after your well-being in his absence. I failed."

Effie's brows furrowed. "How is that remotely possible? I spent the afternoon with my tutor. I hardly consider that as the type of situation that requires a guard."

Kael lifted a shoulder. "Be that as it may. Lucian left word for me to come to you, but I was finishing up with other matters and the day got away from me. I apologize, Effie. I will not let it happen again."

All trace of his smile had vanished during his earnest speech, and his eyes bore into hers. Effie noticed the flecks of emerald that ringed his pupils, and while the colors were different, she couldn't help but be reminded of the metallic flecks in Lucian's eyes.

"While I appreciate the apology, none is necessary," she assured him, not liking the idea of this man carrying any guilt on her behalf.

His lips twitched. "I respectfully disagree."

"Oh, well as long as it's respectful I suppose I'll allow it."

They shared a smile.

"I didn't mean to keep you from your evening," he said.

Effie shook her head. "You're not. The only thing waiting for me is my bed and a book."

"In that case, would you like me to walk back with you?"

What is it with these men and trying to escort me everywhere?

"Only if you tell me something scandalous about Lucian."

"Planning on blackmailing him?"

"One never knows when such information may come in handy," she responded primly, but ruined her feigned disinterest by grinning wickedly.

Kael laughed, his dimples flashing. "Remind me to stay in your good graces, Effie."

"Don't be a stubborn, pig-headed bully and we won't have any problems."

He chuckled some more as they began the short walk back to her room.

"He's really not that bad you know."

"He has his moments," Effie agreed, only slightly disappointed Kael wasn't going to share something juicy. As Lucian's brother-in-arms, she didn't really expect him to divulge anything to begin with.

"I was told you were interested in resuming your daily weapons training in addition to your studies with your tutor."

Effie threw him a startled glance, his choice of topic and knowledge of her admission unexpected. "I might have mentioned it."

"I guess I'll see you in the morning, then."

His smile was playful, and Effie found herself returning it with one of her own. "I guess you will."

They came to a stop at the end of her hallway.

"I trust you can find your way from here?" he teased with a lift of his brow.

Effie glanced at her bedroom door, which was clearly visible from where they stood. "Your belief in me is overwhelming."

He lifted his hand in a wave. "Until tomorrow."

"Good night," she called after him.

Alone once more, Effie puzzled over why Smoke would have made a point to tell Kael about their earlier conversation. Had he been the one to chastise Kael for not introducing himself earlier? It didn't seem like something one of the Triumvirate would bother themselves with, but it definitely explained why the handsome Guardian had made a point of seeking her out.

With a shrug, Effie decided it didn't really matter. After what had almost happened with Kieran earlier, it was probably better if the two of them avoided participating in any physical activities together.

Grimacing at the reminder, Effie hung up her damp towel and climbed into her bed. That was a problem she'd deal with tomorrow. For now, all she wanted to do was pretend it never happened and try to get some sleep.

Yawning, she rolled over and closed her eyes.

CHAPTER 20

*E*ffie whimpered as she fought to lace her boot. Ronan could learn a thing or two from Kael. The Guardian had held nothing back as he trained her that morning, making her perform a series of drills with and without various weapons to test her strength and current ability.

It wasn't pretty. For all that Effie thought she'd learned over the last year, it was clear she was still a novice. The only time she felt remotely proud of herself was when she'd managed to sink her dagger deep into the wooden target on her first try. Kael gave her a nod of approval and then demanded she do it again. She wasn't as lucky the second time, or the fifteenth. Having his steady gaze watching and evaluating her threw off her concentration and her aim never made a full recovery.

Every muscle in her body ached and the thought of walking anywhere was intimidating enough that she briefly considered spending the rest of the day in bed.

Not that anyone would let her.

As it was, she had maybe another twenty minutes before someone came pounding on her door wondering what was keeping her.

Tying off her shoe, Effie stood with another tortured groan. It was going to be a long day.

Her hand had just closed around the knob when the knock came. *I didn't even make it five minutes without one of them coming for me.*

She pulled the door open mid-knock, startling Lucian whose hand was still poised in the air.

"I've already been tortured by a Guardian this morning," she warned him.

Lucian raised a brow and lowered his hand. "Tortured?"

"What else should I call what Kael did to me?"

He smirked. "Training."

"Not uh, no way. I've trained before, whatever that was," she said, gesturing vaguely, "was sadistic and cruel."

"I very much doubt it."

Sighing, Effie moved out of the doorway and closed her door. "Speaking of sadistic and cruel, what do you have planned for me today?"

It lasted less than a second, but Effie caught the smile that tugged at his lips.

"I came to tell you that you'd be spending the day with Kael."

As it had the last two times, news of Lucian's departure from the citadel brought with it a wave of foreboding. The accompanying tension settled in the back of her neck, the weight of it impossible to ignore. After her vision, she had no intention of doing so. Whatever was waiting for them out there, she needed to see it. To understand the threat so that she could warn the others.

This was her purpose. Why she was here in the first place. It was never really just about learning how to decipher her visions, but to help her friends find the answers that would save them all. That was going to require her to do more than hide in the citadel and wait for the answers to come to her. If she wanted them, she needed to seek them out herself.

"Scouting again so soon?"

Lucian nodded.

"I want to go with you," Effie said neutrally, bracing herself for a fight

There was no way Lucian was going to readily agree to her request. It would go against his very nature to willingly put her in harm's way. Luckily, she had some practice in that regard. Fighting with Lucian was like second nature at this point. One could argue she was starting to enjoy it, not that she'd ever admit it.

He glanced down at her as she tried—and failed—not to wince with each shuffling step.

"You can hardly walk."

"I'll be fine."

"The answer is no."

"I don't remember asking you a question," she pointed out.

He let out a frustrated breath. "Effie, it's not safe."

The pressure built, knotting the muscles in her neck and spurring her on.

"I'll be with you. Are you telling me you can't keep me safe?" she taunted, knowing that his massive ego would not allow him to say otherwise. It was a cheap shot, but she needed to go with him. She knew it as certainly as she knew her name.

Lucian scowled at her. "I can't do what I need to do and have to watch out for you at the same time."

"So, bring Kael along."

He crossed his arms, studying her. "Why are you so adamant about this? Your place is here, learning how to better deal with and interpret your visions. Not out scouting for potential threats."

"First of all, I'm not a prisoner here, so my place is wherever I decide it is. Second, my visions are based on my knowledge of the world. Going with you can only help me to better understand them."

But that was only partially true, and not the real answer to his question. The expression on Lucian's chiseled face told her he knew it too. If she was going to convince him, she needed to lay everything out on the table.

"I think . . ." Effie trailed off, not sure how to explain the instinct that was currently guiding her.

"Say it," he demanded.

"I think . . . no," she paused to correct herself, "I *know* this is something I need to do."

His eyes were inscrutable as he stared at her. "I don't like it."

Effie shrugged as more pressure settled into her chest. It was a warning not to back down when he was so close to caving. "I don't care."

"You're a brat."

"Deal with it."

"Were you always this mouthy with the Kiri? I can't imagine Helena and her Circle tolerated this level of constant disrespect."

Effie blushed. The short answer was no, absolutely not. It wasn't until she came to the citadel and had to start dealing with the Keepers that she'd developed the habit. But a certain Guardian definitely brought it out of her more than others.

"Some people value my opinion," she muttered.

"Hmm."

She peeked up at him. *Maybe if I appeal to his constant need to be in control . . .* "What if I promise to behave and do whatever you say?"

He let out a bark of laughter. "You wouldn't last a second."

"I will, I promise."

"Fine, let's test it. Stay here."

Her dismay must have shown on her face because Lucian's smug smile slipped.

"*If* I agree to this, I want to make one thing very clear. I will not make a habit of letting a fledgling boss me around. I do not take my orders from you. In fact, out there, I am in charge. Disobeying me could get us all killed. Do you understand?"

Some of the tightness in her chest eased, but for the first time it didn't leave entirely. That was a warning in itself. Effie nodded, afraid that if she said anything else right now, he might change his mind and leave without her.

He studied her for a long moment before sighing. "Fine. But we leave in an hour. You should tell your tutor that you will miss your lesson today."

Effie made a face.

Lucian pinned her with his gaze, missing nothing. "Why does the thought of speaking to him upset you?"

"It doesn't."

A muscle twitched in his jaw.

Effie held up both of her hands. "I promise. It's nothing. I will take care of it. Where should I meet you?"

"Kael and I will meet you in the portal room."

"Portal room?" she asked, her eyes growing wide. How come she was just hearing about this now?

Lucian shook his head. "Never mind. Meet us in the central archive. I don't have time to waste hunting for you when you get lost."

He turned and walked away. Effie made a face at his retreating back.

Her body still hurt, but a flood of adrenaline numbed her to it. She made her way through the citadel quickly, waving when Jo and Tess called out to her, but not slowing down to chat. She wanted to get this over with.

After two sharp raps on the door of what had become her and Kieran's unofficial study room, Effie pushed it open to find him already waiting for her.

"I wasn't sure I was going to see you this morning after what you said yesterday," he admitted, relief flickering in his eyes before his expressionless mask dropped back in place.

Effie leaned against the doorway. "I'm just here to let you know I'm going out with Lucian today."

Kieran stood and walked over to her, his expression cold. "Why?"

"I really don't think that's any of your business."

"If you're going to skip our lessons, it certainly is. Especially when I have to answer to the Triumvirate."

She flinched at the accusation but held his gaze. "I told you yesterday. Something's coming. I can feel it. Whatever mission the Triumvirate are sending Lucian on is related to my vision. I think the only way to understand what's coming is for me to go with him."

He rolled his eyes. "Oh, please. I already explained to you that your understanding will come from experiencing the vision again. Something we are slated to help you do today."

Effie straightened to her full height and glared at him. "I'm doing this, Kieran."

"Then I'm going with you."

She opened her mouth to argue further when his words registered. "Wait, what?"

He lifted a shoulder. "If you insist that you need to do this, then I will go with you. Anything related to helping you better understand your visions falls under my care."

More than a small part of her had been looking forward to some time away from Kieran and what had happened between them. For some much-needed perspective, if nothing else. Now he was going to tag along, and she'd be stuck with him and two Guardians.

Suddenly, her day was looking a lot less exciting, but she couldn't think of a valid reason to exclude him.

"Mother save me from insufferable men," she muttered, turning and stalking away from him.

"I heard that," he called after her.

"You were meant to."

CHAPTER 21

*L*ucian recapped his water flask before tossing it to Effie. She caught it, but just barely, her cheeks turning crimson as she fumbled with the heavy bag.

Refusing to meet Lucian's or Kieran's gaze, she looked instead at Kael, who was chuckling softly.

"Proud of yourself?" she growled.

His eyebrows shot up in surprise. "Me? What did I do?"

"Hobbled me for life," she grumbled.

Kael threw his head back and laughed. "You'll be fine in a day or two."

Kieran looked between them, his eyes narrowed with suspicion. "What's she talking about?"

"Kael has taken over her weapons training," Lucian answered.

Effie could feel the weight of her tutor's stare but would not look at him.

"That's your doing, I take it?" Kieran asked Lucian.

"The Triumvirate's, actually," Kael said, one of his dimples flashing.

There was entirely too much testosterone permeating the air for her liking. Effie turned to Lucian. "Should we get back to it?"

Something in her tone must have bothered him because Lucian frowned before giving a sharp nod.

They'd already spent hours scouring the jungle. When Effie asked what they were looking for, her only answer had been "anything out of place." Since she wasn't familiar with Bael, that wasn't particularly helpful. But then, what else could she expect from the Keepers or their Guardians?

Although their small group had yet to find anything that fell into that category, nervous energy continued to prick at her, leaving her on edge. She ran her hands up and down her bare arms in an attempt to alleviate some of her unease.

It was a humid day, the air thick with moisture. All four of them had removed their cloaks within a matter of minutes after leaving the portal. While Effie appreciated the sheer amount of tanned, sculpted muscle on display, she was more jealous that she could not follow suit. As a female, there were a couple of reasons she did not have the luxury of stripping out of her vest as the men had done, and so she was left with the thick leather clinging uncomfortably to her sweaty skin.

She might feel a bit better about it, if the men at least had to suffer as much as she did. As it was, her thin linen undergarment was soaked through, and did little to protect her from the chafing. Thankfully, she'd been able to peel off her blue tunic to remove at least one additional layer between her and the vest, but the way Kieran's eyes heated as she did made her want to tug it back on, oppressive heat be damned.

All in all, the day was shaping up to be one of the most unpleasant she'd had since leaving the Holbrookes. Between the tension simmering concerning her and Kieran, and her growing sense of unease and overall discomfort, she was in a foul mood.

The sky was completely obscured by the trees, washing the jungle in an eerie green glow as they picked up their packs and started working their way through the next uninvestigated area. Insects buzzed and leaves rustled as the creatures of the jungle went about their business, ignoring their visitors.

Effie lost track of time as she kicked at rocks and smacked at leaves that were as large as she was, not realizing the men were no longer in sight. It wasn't until the buzzing disappeared completely that she froze.

The hair on the back of her neck stood on end and Effie's heart began to race. Her hand moved to her hip, resting on the hilt of her dagger.

"Who's there?" she called out, her quavering voice underscoring her fear.

The snap of a branch was her only answer.

Effie spun around, eyes franticly scanning each bush, trying to find the source of the noise. She took a step back, and stumbled, falling down hard. Her teeth caught the inside of her cheek at the impact and the metallic taste of blood filled her mouth. Eyes tearing from the pain, she scrambled back, crying out in horror as the ground beneath her hands gave way. Her gravity shifted and before she could right herself, Effie toppled backwards into a yawning darkness.

She landed with a dull thud on top of something slimy and cold. It wasn't hard exactly, but not soft either. Gasping for breath, she blinked up into the gloom, barely able to make out the trees that were now far above her.

Too scared to move lest she fall again, Effie laid still, remaining motionless for several terrifying moments. Surely the others heard her scream and were seconds away from scolding her. She just needed to find a way to get out of this hole.

If only she could see.

Patting the area around her legs, Effie found the small pack that had become dislodged during her fall.

She sat up, trying hard not to think about the source of the rancid smell that filled her nose, or the sticky slime trickling down her back.

Opening the bag with trembling fingers, she searched for the flint and tinder she'd stuffed inside the night before leaving Helena's camp. Effie sent out a brief but heartfelt thanks for that moment of foresight. It took three attempts before a bright light flared.

A startled scream tore through her throat and Effie dropped her light. It flickered and died as it hit the ground.

But it didn't matter. Effie had seen all she needed to. It wasn't a hole she'd fallen into.

It was a grave.

Stomach churning, Effie gagged and pushed to her knees. The still decaying corpses rolled beneath her weight and she heaved again.

In the brief moment of light, she'd seen at least six disfigured bodies, each more horrific than the last. She had no idea how many might be in the hole with her and didn't care to know. One corpse was too many, especially if it was cradled against your back.

Another branch cracked and she could just make out the sound of shuffling steps over her frantic gasps of breath.

"In here, I'm in here," Effie screamed, relief that they'd found her causing the first of her tears to slip free.

More shuffling and then a body-shaped shadow eclipsed the few leaves she could still see.

When no voice called down to her, Effie knew she'd been horribly wrong. It wasn't help that had found her.

It was death.

CHAPTER 22

*L*ucian scanned the clearing, his face thunderous.

"I don't know how she managed to wander off," Kael muttered, his expression equally dark.

Lucian didn't bother to reply. His brother already knew he'd fucked up. Angry words would do little to help them find her, even if they did provide a means of venting some of the frustration boiling inside him. Although, at the end of the day, the weight of the failure was on his shoulders alone. As the one leading the mission, it was up to Lucian to ensure everyone returned in one piece.

Eyes narrowed, Lucian scanned the floor checking for prints.

Effie couldn't have gotten far, but there was no sign of her. They'd tracked her to the middle of a clearing that was within shouting distance of where they'd made camp for their midday meal before losing her trail. There was no reason they shouldn't have heard her if she'd been in trouble, and there was no sign of any struggle. It was like she'd up and vanished.

If they hadn't been in the middle of the damn jungle, Lucian would assume she might have stepped through a portal, except there were only three beings in Elysia with the knowledge and power to create a portal, and none of them had ever placed one here.

So, what then?

Lucian ran a hand along his jaw as he tried to make sense of what he was seeing, or rather, what he *wasn't* seeing. It couldn't be a coincidence that she'd disappeared in the exact area where they were scouting, which meant that he was missing something. It was either that or whatever she'd inadvertently triggered disappeared when she did.

But all magic left a trace. There should be *something* here.

"Do you think—"

Lucian cut Kieran off by holding up a hand. Closing his eyes, he focused on calming his breathing and centering himself.

As a Guardian, his power was nothing like the Chosen, whose gifts were linked to the Mother and her elemental branches. Since he was not of this realm, neither was his magic. His abilities were tied to the temporal threads that linked all living things together. Once seen, they could be manipulated. While he couldn't create anything new, he could transform anything that already existed. If someone else modified one of those threads, Lucian should be able to sense it and follow it to its source.

When Lucian opened his eyes, the world came alive. Golden energy swirled and pulsed around him, infusing the already vibrant jungle with its radiant glow. Everything from the towering trees to the tiniest insect had its own spark of life which was comprised of a tangle of threads connecting it to its surroundings. Lucian rarely allowed himself to view the world in its basest form, as it was too easy to accidentally tug on a string that could unravel everything. Only millennia of practice and iron-clad control gave him the confidence to do so now.

Even with his power unleashed, he almost missed it.

The dissonance.

The smudge of inky black staining on an otherwise brilliant strand.

Crouching down, Lucian let his fingers trail just above the strand until the palm of his hand hovered over the stain. Icy cold seeped into his skin and Lucian jerked his hand back.

"Luc?" Kael called. "You okay?"

Ignoring him, Lucian plucked at the damaged thread, slowly lifting it by an unaffected end until it was cradled in his hand. It allowed Lucian to inspect the damage without getting too close to the searing cold. As he watched, the stain shimmied up the strand causing the gold light to sputter and die, leaving only a withered gray fiber in its place. The closer the darkness got to his hand, the faster it moved, as if it was drawn to his own source energy and eager to make contact with his fingers.

Lucian dropped the thread, instinct warning him not to let it touch him.

He'd never come across anything like it. Not in Elysia or any other realm he'd walked.

His lip curled in disgust. He might not have the name for it, but there was no mistaking what was happening here. It was a magical parasite, stealing the energy of all it came into contact with to feed and power itself.

If not dealt with, that tiny stain would overtake the entire jungle, putting everyone and everything that called it home at risk.

Before Lucian could deal with the blight, he needed to follow it to its source. He knew without a doubt that's where he'd find Effie. Although the state he'd find her in was another matter entirely.

Still wholly focused on the one tainted strand, Lucian tracked it with his eyes. Woven as it was through so many others, sometimes he'd lose the thread only to pick it up again a few feet away. The longer he followed the shining tendril the less he lost track of it, which said more about the speed with which the blight was infecting the strands that surrounded it than his prowess.

"Mother save us," Kael breathed. The other Guardian must have tapped into his own power when Lucian came to an abrupt halt.

Lucian almost forgot to breathe as he took in the quivering darkness that had already claimed a half dozen trees and everything between them. His skin broke out into goosebumps at the sudden drop in temperature.

Letting go of his power, Lucian rapidly blinked to force his eyes to adjust. Nothing looked out of place, and yet . . . the sense of wrongness was undeniable. It scratched at his senses, urging him to retreat. He ignored the instinct and stood firm. Whatever the stain was doing, it was not visible to the naked eye, which must be how it snuck up on Effie.

Leaves rustled and the hair on Lucian's arms lifted. Another time, another place, it would have been unremarkable. Except that it was the first thing he'd heard—other than Kael and Kieran's muted voices—since following the thread.

Pulling his sword free, Lucian spun in the direction of the sound. Branches swayed and shifted as a grotesque figure stepped forward into the dappled light.

"Elder's holy balls," Kieran cried out.

Lucian shifted his stance, his blade already aimed at the being that appeared more corpse than man. It had clearly once been male, but the milky eyes that snaked with black were no longer seeing, and the flesh of its cheeks had rotted away giving it a rictus grin.

On its own, that was enough to make most grown men piss themselves, but for Lucian, the moment true fear struck his heart was when he noticed the bloody clumps of wheat colored hair dangling from the creature's outstretched fingers.

Rage, potent and pure, consumed him and Lucian roared.

The creature lunged, but Lucian was faster. His blade slid through the wrinkled gray skin of its neck as easily as melted butter. The head fell and rolled away, rancid black ichor spraying Lucian as the creature's body sank to the ground.

"What in the hell was that?" Kieran asked, his voice shaky and his usually tanned skin pale.

"A Shadow," Lucian answered.

"How did it get here?" Kael asked, his somber expression a stark contrast to his usual grin.

"Better question, why was it alone?" Lucian countered. "They are supposed to travel in packs."

"Who cares? That thing had Effie," Kieran said, already making his way toward the place the Shadow had come from.

"Wait," Lucian growled, gripping Kieran's arm.

The Keeper twisted out of his hold, teeth bared in a snarl. "She could be hurt."

"She might not be alone. Your rushing in could cause more harm than good."

Kieran glared at Lucian, his nostrils flaring and his chest rising and falling rapidly, but he stayed put.

Exchanging a look filled with years of understanding, Lucian and Kael crept forward, scanning the area for any sign of another Shadow. As far as he could tell, there weren't any. That didn't mean there wasn't danger.

Lucian took another tentative step forward, his body freezing as the ground beneath him turned soft and gave way. Throwing out an arm, he barely stopped Kael from toppling head-first into a sink hole.

"Where did that come from?" Kael asked, his eyes wide.

Lucian shook his head, about to respond when the first of the soft grunts reached him. Someone was down there. Kneeling, he peered over the edge of the hole, not wanting to alert a potential enemy that they'd arrived. All attempts at subtlety fled as Lucian's heart stuttered.

"What is it?" Kieran whispered, peering over his shoulder.

No response was necessary. He heard their shocked inhales of breath as the others processed what they were seeing.

The three men could only stand in stupefied horror and watch as Effie hacked at the Shadow whose bony fingers were wrapped around her slender throat. She'd somehow managed to take it down and was currently kneeling on his chest as her dagger sawed into the tendons of its throat. The hand around her neck spasmed, and Effie used the moment of freedom to pull out of its grasp. Using her free arm, she pinned his hand to the pile of rotting bodies beneath them and resumed her attempts at beheading . . . but her small blade was not up to the task of severing a head from its body.

"Die, damn you," she cried, her voice a hoarse croak.

Lucian made a swift mental calculation. The hole wasn't big enough for him to jump down and help her, he'd take up too much space and prevent either of them from being able to fight properly. That didn't mean he was willing to stand around doing nothing.

"Fledgling!"

Effie risked a glance up, her face smeared with blood and ichor. "Took you long enough!"

Lucian allowed himself a brief flash of teeth as he recognized her use of his earlier greeting. There wasn't time to do more than wave his weapon to make sure she understood his intent before dropping his sword into the pit below.

His blade sunk into one of the corpses just as Effie jumped off the Shadow, pressing her back against the wall. She scrambled toward the sword, losing her footing on the uneven ground as she struggled to pull it free.

Meanwhile, the Shadow had already pushed itself upright. It crawled to her, clawed hand outstretched and grasping at her ankles. She kicked its hands trying to keep her distance, but her focus was split between pulling out the blade and staying out of reach. Unfortunately, she was only successful at one of the tasks.

The Shadow pulled her down, hard. Lucian could hear the thud of impact as her head slammed into the bones of one of the corpses.

There wasn't enough space in the hole for Lucian or one of the others to jump down and help her, not without impeding their range of motion to fight. Instead, they were forced to watch helplessly as she twisted, clumsily swinging the freed blade up and into the Shadow.

"Its head! You have to cut off his head" Lucian shouted down.

"I! Fucking! Know!" she screamed as the Shadow lurched off her.

"That's it, stay angry," he whispered.

That spark of wildfire he was coming to associate with her would be the difference in how this fight ended.

Still holding onto the hilt, the sword slid out of the Shadow with a wet slurp. Chest heaving, Effie moved into a defensive stance, her eyes never straying from her target. The Shadow took one lumbering step forward and slipped on a body. Effie saw her opening and used all the power left in her shaking limbs to chop its head from its body.

She fell before the body did, her knees giving out from under her.

Lucian heard her whimper, heard the sobs of relief and shock that she'd never admit to once she was safely back in the citadel.

"It's all over, you're safe now."

"Just get me out of here," she panted.

"Are you okay?" Kieran called to her.

Effie slowly lifted her head, her matted curls sticking to her cheeks and neck. There wasn't an inch of her body that wasn't covered in gore. "What do you think?"

Lucian's lips twitched in the barest hint of a smile. She might not be okay, but Effie was going to be just fine.

CHAPTER 23

*E*ffie warily eyed the rope that Lucian tossed down. It wasn't that she didn't trust him to keep hold of the other end, but she could barely stand, let alone pull herself up along its length. She might as well try to sprout wings and fly.

"Just tie it around your hips and hold on. We'll do the rest."

She could have wept at the words. Her hands were still slick with grime, and the rope slipped from them into a pool of ichor and other things she didn't want to investigate too closely.

Swallowing back a wave of nausea, Effie grabbed the rope and quickly tied it around her hips. It took two tries to get the knot to hold, and portions of the rope were now as slippery as the rest of her.

"Give it a good tug to make sure it's secure," Lucian ordered.

Effie obeyed, even going so far as to let the rope carry some of her weight to make sure it wasn't going to slip or come untied again.

"Looks good. Hang on."

That was the only warning Effie got before she shot up. She used her feet to keep her body from slamming into the sides of the hole and clung to the rope with her hands. The men had her out of the hole in less than a minute.

She blinked up at three relieved looking faces. No one seemed to know what to say first.

Her face was starting to itch where the blood had dried. Peeling a piece of hair off her face, she grimaced. "You know, I don't think I want to go scouting with you next time."

Kieran blinked.

Kael tipped his head back and laughed.

Lucian just studied her, the bronze flecks in his eyes twinkling.

"Are you going to yell at me for wandering off now, or wait until we get back?"

"Would it do any good?" Lucian asked.

Effie crinkled her nose. "Probably not."

"Then why bother?"

Kieran moved closer, eyeing her for signs of injury. Other than a deep gash along the side of her right arm, and a few shallow scratches on her cheek and neck, she was mostly fine. She hadn't even felt the burning throb down her arm until Kieran's finger traced the skin alongside it.

Effie winced and gently pulled free of his grasp.

He frowned at her, his eyes dark with an emotion she didn't recognize.

She was lucky. Her familiarity with fighting the Shadows, along with Ronan's training, had kicked in as soon as the first Shadow dropped into the pit. She never saw what happened to the other one. He'd left in the middle of the battle and she'd been so thankful for the reprieve she hadn't given it a second thought.

Stiffening, she scanned their surroundings. "There was another one," she murmured, her voice dropping low.

"We took care of it," Lucian assured her.

"Oh. Good," Effie whispered in relief, the burst of renewed adrenaline leaving her in a rush.

The ichor burned where it made contact with her skin, and her muscles felt like pudding. It took more energy than she had left to remain standing.

"If you three aren't going to yell at me, then would you mind taking me home now?"

Before she finished speaking, Kael had an arm under her knees and was lifting her.

"Hey!" she half-heartedly protested.

"You guys go ahead. I will catch up," Lucian said, peering into the thick brush behind him.

Kieran begrudgingly stepped back, but his eyes never left her as Kael started walking in the opposite direction.

"My pack," she called over Kael's shoulder.

Lucian's dark eyes bored into hers for a long moment before he dropped into the pit.

Effie gasped.

"He'll be fine," Kael said softly, not breaking his stride.

"How will he get out on his own?"

Kael's lips quirked in a smile. "Won't be the first time he's had to climb his ass out of a grave. Won't be the last."

The dark certainty of the words coupled with his bloodthirsty smile sent a skitter of foreboding down her spine.

"I'd rather it be the last grave any of us have to deal with for a while, if it's all the same to you."

Green eyes dropped to her face. "I don't think you'll be going anywhere for a while."

Even though she'd suspected the same, the words still stung. "I was holding my own."

Kael's dimple flashed. "That you were, little warrior, but you're missing my meaning."

"How so?"

"The one thing you keep forgetting is that you are not disposable. You overlook your importance to the realm, and in doing so, fail to place any value on your safety. It makes you reckless and it puts you in danger."

Effie looked at a spot near his shoulder, the gentle rebuke, so kindly spoken, made her feel very small. She hadn't thought of it that way, but it was exactly what she'd been doing. Running headlong into one bad decision after another, with no thought to the consequences. If something happened to her, what did it matter? There was no one left to care.

"I've never been important before," she said so softly she wasn't sure he heard her.

After a few long strides, Kael dipped his head, his voice no louder than hers. "Maybe not in your own eyes, Effie, but you have *always* been important to those that truly see you. Perhaps it is time for you to truly see yourself?"

Tears pricked at her eyes and she squeezed them shut, not wanting him to see how his words affected her.

How can he say that? He's known me for all of a day, a dark, bitter voice echoed in her mind.

But he's been surrounded by those that can See so much more than what's in front of them, a quiet, but just as stubborn, voice answered.

"Did you learn what you had hoped?" Kieran asked, providing a welcome distraction from the ball of emotion lodged in her chest.

Effie cleared her throat, still not meeting anyone's gaze. "The only thing that was remotely similar to my vision was the fact that I—we—ran into Shadows."

She frowned, wondering what it meant that her vision hadn't been tied to Lucian's task after all. Had the pressing need to go with him just been a symptom of her desire to belong and not instinct guiding her?

"I guess I was wrong," she murmured, feeling foolish now on top of everything else.

"Or your vision has yet to pass," Kieran said.

Fear slithered through her at the thought of more of those creatures lurking about the jungle waiting for them . . . and the amount of bloodshed that would result.

"For all our sakes, I hope it never does."

Lucian caught up to them, her pack slung over his shoulder, and his sword back in the scabbard at his hip.

"All set?" Kael asked. The words sounded casual, but the look that passed between the Guardians was anything but.

"For now," Lucian replied, not bothering to slow down as he

passed them. "We should hurry; the Triumvirate need to know what we found."

He leveled his dark gaze on Kael who nodded and picked up the pace. Effie looked between them, her brow furrowed. *What else happened while we were separated?*

"Did you find what you were looking for?" she asked.

The tiny flutter in Kael's jaw told her they had.

Even though she thought she knew the answer, Effie asked, "What do you think it means?"

Her Guardian spared her a glance. "Nothing good, fledgling."

THEY MADE quick time now that they weren't inspecting every inch of the jungle. Lucian was the first to step beneath the stone arch that indicated the portal's location. Effie still wasn't sure how they knew where the portals were located, other than experience. There was nothing to indicate their presence, which seemed fairly irresponsible, all things considered. What if someone, or something, accidentally came through?

Kieran followed close behind him, leaving her and Kael to enter last.

"Think you can walk from here?" Kael asked, once they were back within one of the citadels many nondescript rooms.

Effie knew he'd gladly carry her wherever she wanted to go, but he was giving her the opportunity to avoid being gossip fodder. She nodded and he set her on her feet, his warm hand on her shoulder as he waited to ensure she was steady.

"I will take her to the healer," Kieran said. "You two are probably needed."

Kael looked to Lucian, who dipped his head in approval.

Turning back to them, Kael looked her over. "I think we'll skip training tomorrow," he said with a wink.

Effie rolled her eyes. "Who knew a Guardian could be so magnanimous?"

His laughter boomed through the hall as he and Lucian turned the corner and walked out of sight.

"Come on, then. Let's get you patched up."

Effie shot Kieran a thankful glance. They'd only made it a handful of steps before the first of the raucous cheers reached them.

"What the hell?" Kieran asked, his brows dipping low.

Effie shook her head. "Beats me. It's always quiet as a tomb around here."

They didn't have to wonder long.

Two men Effie hadn't seen before came barreling out of the twin doors at the far end of the hall. They were flushed, and the silver steins they held were sloshing liquid onto the floor.

"Is there some kind of party happening tonight?" Effie asked under her breath.

Kieran shrugged. "Nothing I'm aware of; the citadel is hardly known for its social gatherings."

Not sure whether to keep walking forward, Effie and Kieran remained where they were, watching the two stumbling men with no shortage of amusement. The taller of the two kept stepping on his robe, which caused his partner to crash into him. They'd already bounced off the walls at least twice.

"Should we offer our assistance?" Effie asked.

Kieran eyed her. "I'm not sure they'd welcome it. You are a mite bit . . . frightening at the moment, love."

Effie followed his gaze to her torn and bloodied clothes and limbs. "Right. Maybe we should head to the bathing chamber before the healers?"

Kieran snickered.

The two men reached them then, both offering wide grins and holding up their cups.

"May her reign never end!" the tall man cried.

"All hail the true Vessel!"

They clinked glasses and chugged, amber liquid spilling down their chins.

"Any clue what they're talking about?" Kieran asked, a bland smile fixed on his face.

"Sounds like Helena, but Mother knows why."

"I'm sorry, friends, we've been away for the day and seem to have missed the good news."

The shorter man's eyes rounded. "Why, it is only the best"—he hiccupped—"news of all time."

"Of all time you say?" Kieran said, tossing Effie a wink.

She hid her grin behind her hand.

The tall man nodded emphatically. "Oh yes. The Corruptor has been slain. The Chosen are saved."

Effie gasped. "Rowena's dead?"

The short man lifted Effie's tangled mass of hair away from her ear. "Dead as my dear granny," he shouted, as if she was hard of hearing.

The two men cackled and clinked their cups once more.

If Rowena was truly dead, then it was over. The news should have overjoyed her, but ice ran through her veins and Effie shivered.

For the first time when the now familiar tingles danced up her spine, Effie welcomed them.

"Kieran," she mumbled.

It was all she was able to manage before her knees gave out and she was lost to oblivion.

CHAPTER 24

*F*og swirled at her feet, and Effie looked around the wet walls of the cave. She knew this cavern.

She'd been here before.

Reaching out a trembling hand, she ran her fingers along the slimy service, her stomach twisting as her hand came back red.

Not water. Blood.

A small splash confirmed that her feet were already beneath the pooling liquid.

She slipped and slid as she ran, drops of thick red fluid spraying her with each pump of her legs.

Effie looked behind her, horror stealing her breath as the tidal wave loomed and surged toward her.

The need to get away overwhelmed her, and Effie raced ahead. The blood continued to rise, making it hard for her to continuing pushing forward. She trudged on, gagging as the coppery tang filled her mouth.

If she went under, she was dead.

The blood was now at her chest and Effie started to swim, trying to ignore the things that were brushing against her legs.

The fog lifted from the surface, and the first pale limb came into view.

"No!" she screamed.

One by one, more body parts floated to the surface.

Effie paddled away as best she could, but they were everywhere.

Even though she knew it was coming, her terrified screams echoed around her as she was pulled down into the crimson pool. It wasn't long before the red turned to black and all she could make out were the bodies of the dead as they surrounded her.

A head floated by her on the left and twisted on some invisible axis to stare at her.

Effie pressed her lips together, struggling not to scream. Not to drown in the blood of the fallen.

Black lines began to snake through its milky eyes. Its lips lifted in a horrific grin.

"Never safe," it hissed.

A brush at her shoulder had her spinning frantically around.

The scream she'd been trying so hard to fight was torn from her and Effie choked on the blood that filled her mouth.

Darrin's face, his beloved face, stared back at her. His skin was a mottled purple and white, his beautiful green eyes two black pits.

His hand lifted, his fingers weaving themselves through her hair as he tugged her closer.

Effie struggled to break free, but his grip was like iron.

"It's only just beginning," he breathed against her lips.

Even though there was hardly any breath left in her lungs, a sob broke free and a few bloody bubbles floated out.

Darrin's face contorted as if in pain and his fingers spasmed.

The next time he looked at her it was no longer the man she loved.

It was a monster and she was its meal.

Its mouth stretched into a wide, sinister grin and its tongue snaked out to lick up the side of her face.

"We're coming."

EFFIE WAS STILL SCREAMING when she came to.

"Effie. Effie, stop," Kieran murmured, his hands rubbing circles on her back.

The soft brush of skin against her body only served to remind her of the corpses bobbing in their own sea of blood.

She shrank away from his touch and scrambled away from him.

Hurt flashed across his face, but he gave her space, taking a seat across from her on the floor. She could feel his eyes roam over her, but she refused to look at him. Instead, she focused on breathing. Each ragged breath helped slow her racing heart but did nothing to ease the terror of her vision.

"What did you See?" Kieran asked, his low voice holding an authoritative edge she couldn't ignore.

Her mouth was dry, and her tongue darted out to wet her lips. Effie grimaced at the salty taste it left in her mouth. She really needed that bath.

"Shadows," she whispered.

"Like before?"

"Worse."

"How so?"

"I remember what they said."

"They spoke to you?"

Effie nodded, the tremors racking her body, growing in intensity.

Kieran pulled his tunic up over his head in one fluid move and held it out to her.

She stared at the dark green fabric without comprehension until he shook it at her.

"Take it," he demanded.

Once it was in her hands, she looked up at him.

"Put it on."

She did as she was told. The tunic slid down her body like a caress. It was still warm from being pressed against Kieran's body, and some of that keep seeped into her own trembling limbs, soothing a bit of the tension.

"Better?" Kieran asked.

"Yes, thank you."

"Tell me what they said."

Effie closed her eyes, a lone tear sliding down her cheek as Darrin's horrific visage reappeared in her mind. "It was a warning."

"Most visions are."

The bit of derision pulled her attention back to the present, helping her focus. "They said it wasn't over. That they were coming."

"What isn't over? Coming for who?"

Effie shook her head. "I don't know."

"Guess. It was your vision, your subconscious. What is it trying to tell you?"

She blinked back more tears as she replayed her vision once more, trying to suss out details she might have missed.

"The war, maybe? Those men—" she glanced around the hall, just now realizing they'd disappeared.

"No one here is a stranger to the visions. Once it took you, they went off to continue their celebration," Kieran answered, his intent gaze still locked on her face. "Now, what were you about to say?"

Effie's stomach hollowed as panic started to claw at her. "What if the vision was trying to tell me that the war isn't really over?"

"It's possible," Kieran acknowledged, although he didn't seem overly worried by the thought.

"Don't you think that's something the Triumvirate should know?"

He tilted his head and studied her. "Do you?"

"Yes!"

Kieran's eyes fell closed and she watched as his chest rose and fell in one, long breath. "Then you should tell them."

"I don't know where they are."

"I'm sure we can find someone who does, but first, let's get you cleaned up."

"I need to write it down first," Effie insisted, patting at her side in an attempt to grab her pack.

"Lucian still has it," Kieran answered.

"I need my journal," she said, her voice bordering on hysteria.

"I'll get it while you clean up," Kieran said firmly as he stood. "Come on. You'll feel better after you get into some fresh clothes."

Effie glared at him but accepted the hand he offered. "Why do I feel like you aren't taking me seriously?"

He shrugged. "Your emotions are high, it's been a long day, you're reading into things? I don't know, love, take your pick."

The condescendence rankled. "Fuck you, Kieran."

His eyes flashed and he shot her a one-sided grin. "Just say when."

"This is *so* not the time."

Smirking, he crossed his arms over his chest. "Distracted you long enough to help you feel more like yourself though, didn't it?"

Effie scowled, not caring that he was right. "I really do hate you."

"No, you don't."

"Yes, I do."

"Don't."

Effie glared at him; her voice furiously low. "Kieran, I swear on all that is holy, if you tell me one more time how I feel, I am going to throttle you."

"Men far more fearsome than you have tried and failed, love."

"They clearly lacked proper motivation."

His lips twitched, but the smile didn't come near his eyes. "They'd disagree with you."

"You are insufferable."

"So I've been told," he replied, completely unaffected. "Go. I'll find your journal and then we'll go to the Triumvirate so you can tell them what you think."

Eager to feel clean again—and get away from him—Effie nodded and stormed into bathing chamber.

One of these days the men around her were going to learn to start taking her seriously, or she was going to find them in their sleep and punch them in their balls. Then maybe they'd think twice before speaking to her as they did.

Dark satisfaction chased the thought, and Effie sank into the steaming water using thoughts of revenge to keep memories of her vision at bay.

CHAPTER 25

The only thing keeping Effie awake and upright was the pressing need to speak to the Triumvirate.

"I thought you said they were in here," she whispered, scanning the crowded room.

"They were supposed to be," Kieran replied, likewise twisting his head to try to find a sign of their hooded leaders.

Bodies pressed against them, pushing them into the center of the celebratory chaos. Effie hardly recognized any of the faces surrounding her, not that anyone stood still long enough to let her try.

"They aren't all Keepers, are they?" she asked.

Kieran jerked his chin in the negative. "Looks like they opened up the doors for the townsfolk to join in."

Effie could understand the desire to celebrate. Even if most of these people had been personally unaffected by the war raging in Elysia, to believe that the threat had been eliminated still had to bring sweet relief.

Too bad she was about to rob them of their short-lived respite.

Enjoy it while you can.

Effie tensed as a body flew into her back and an arm snaked around her waist.

"Have you heard?" Jo shouted in her ear.

Relaxing slightly, Effie turned around and forced herself to smile. "I did."

Jo's cheeks were flushed, and her eyes glazed. Clearly, she'd been celebrating for a while.

"Then why don't you look happier?" Jo asked, inspecting her more closely.

"Long day."

"Bad vision?" she guessed.

Effie nodded. "The worst."

Jo pat her shoulder. "We've all been there."

Wondering if this was her opportunity to find an ally, Effie opened her mouth to share her warning. Before she could speak, Kieran's hand grasped her wrist, pulling her attention. He shook his head no, his face cast in hard lines.

"Why can't I tell her?" Effie hissed, leaning closer to her tutor.

"It is not your place to spread unfounded fear. *If* the Triumvirate agree with your assessment, then they will be the ones to share the warning."

Effie wanted to argue, but it was a valid point, so she grumbled under her breath instead.

Jo smiled sympathetically. "Why don't you join me and the girls for a while? I'm sure we can help you unwind."

It was a tempting thought, but nothing would help her relax until she'd spoken with the Triumvirate.

"I can't, I'm sorry. I need to speak to Smoke or one of the Mirrors."

"Who?" Jo asked, her brows furrowed.

Effie blushed, realizing she'd slipped into her nicknames for the head Keepers.

"The Triumvirate," Effie said, raising her voice as if that had been the issue.

Jo laughed. "I must be tipsier than I thought. I could have sworn you said something else."

Effie gave her a bland smile and shrugged. "It happens."

"Well, you won't find them in here. Only one of them was here to begin with, and he left with two of the Guardians."

"Well where are the other two?" Effie asked, annoyance giving her voice an edge.

Jo shrugged. "No clue. Haven't seen any of them since."

Effie growled. *Perfect.* How like them to vanish just when she needed them the most.

"You can check the balcony," Jo suggested, pointing to a dark purple curtain. "That's the direction they left in earlier."

"Thank you," Effie said, already walking in that direction.

"See you in the morning?" Jo shouted over the din.

Effie gave her a noncommittal wave and focused on weaving her way through the mess of flailing limbs.

Kieran was close on her heels, his hand wrapped in the soft fabric of her tunic.

"You lied to your new friend back there," he said behind her, his breath tickling the back of her neck.

Effie's shoulders lifted defensively. "No, I didn't,"

Kieran made a clucking sound and shook his head. "And now you're lying to me."

Cheeks burning, she flung the curtain aside and moved into a dark alcove.

"Do the Triumvirate know that you've given them pet names?"

"Yes," she snapped.

"And do they actually respond to them?"

"Actually, they do. Keep pushing me, you'll get one of your own and I promise you won't like it."

Kieran laughed, his eyes glowing with the intensity of his smile.

He really is a beautiful bastard. It's unfortunate that he knows it too.

"Ah, Effie. You wound me."

She rolled her eyes.

"This way," he said, taking the lead across a short stone room and out into the glittering darkness.

Thousands of stars sparkled in a sky of deepest black. The moon

179

was hidden behind thick clouds, but a few scattered lanterns lit the way to the edge of the balcony where three robed figures stood looking out over the city below. There was no sign of the Guardians.

None of the revelry from inside reached them out here. The only sound on the balcony was the scraping of their boots against the cobbled stone.

As one, the three figures turned, facing Effie when she was halfway between them and the room they'd just vacated.

"I hate it when you do that," she muttered.

A sudden rustling of wind was her only answer. *They are definitely laughing at me.*

"I need to speak with you," she called out.

"Speak, Daughter, and we shall listen."

"I had another vision. This"—Effie gestured the way they'd came —"celebration is premature."

"The Corruptor is dead."

"I know that you were told that, but—"

"It has been confirmed."

"Fine, but that doesn't mean this is over."

"What isn't over?" one of the spectral voices demanded.

"Th-the war," she stuttered, aware of their scrutiny even though their faces were covered.

Silence stretched between them and Effie struggled not to fidget. She needed them to believe her before it was too late. A part of her wished Lucian was still here. He at least listened to her reasoning before dismissing her thoughts, maybe he could help her convince the others.

"That is not what has been foretold."

"Everything we've Seen suggests the opposite."

"Everything?" she asked, stunned.

If she was the only one to have a vision stating otherwise, there was no way they were going to take her word for it. She barely had a grasp on her visions as it was, how could she expect them to believe her now?

Their hoods dipped in a synchronized nod.

"Is it possible that something has changed? That perhaps this future was not a possibility before now," she asked, clinging to the hope.

"It is possible."

"But unlikely."

Her hands clenched into tight fists at her sides, her nails digging into her palms. There was very little Effie was sure of these days, but this was one thing she did not doubt. Her vision had been a warning. The Shadows were coming. Or perhaps since her visions were created out of what she was familiar with, if the threat wasn't specifically Shadows, then *something* was out there coming straight for them. Something dark and terrible that no one had ever seen before.

And when it got here, they were going to drown in the blood of the fallen.

The destruction would be absolute.

"Please," she said, her teeth grinding together in her desperation. She didn't know what to say to make them understand.

"Our assurance does not seem to move you. Why?"

Effie pressed her lips together, torn between believing in their experience or trusting her instinct. If she insisted on this, and was wrong, they'd never believe her again. She'd lose any credibility she might have, and their opinions of her were too important to risk losing.

Conflicted, she remained silent as her mind tried to find a solution that wouldn't end with her disgrace.

"You sought us out to share your concerns and now you won't voice them. Why?"

Effie knew it was Smoke who pressed her, the voice in her mind had taken on the deeper, more intimate cast.

The answer was simple, obvious even, but not one she'd willingly admit to: fear.

She was terrified because even though she was convinced she was right, there were still those lingering what-ifs floating through her mind. She'd been the laughingstock of her people before. Singled out, humiliated, cast aside. It was not a position she ever wanted to return to. Knowing what it meant to finally belong, the thought of having to resume hiding in the shadows to avoid the endless ridicule made her heart ache and her soul cry out.

"Daughter?"

The hint of concern she detected helped her find her voice.

"Can I show you?" she asked, recalling the first time the Keepers had come to her. How one of them, likely Smoke, had pressed his hand to her forehead and pulled the vision from her mind into his own.

Maybe if they saw it as she had, they'd be more inclined to believe her.

"Show them?" Kieran asked.

Effie jerked her head around, wondering why he sounded so incredulous. Surely this was something the Triumvirate did often enough.

"It is not something we do lightly."

"Why not?" she asked.

"Rifling through one's memories is dangerous."

"We cannot always control what we see."

"Most prefer we do not try, lest we see that which they'd remain hidden."

"You didn't think to mention that the last time?"

It wasn't that she had anything to hide necessarily, but the thought of someone stumbling across intimate moments or even the darker, secret memories she'd buried deep within her mind . . . it was unsettling to say the least.

"Last time?" Kieran parroted. "You've let them steal your thoughts before?"

"It's hardly stealing, Kieran. They were replaying my vision so as to better understand what I had Seen while I was still too new to understand it myself."

"Don't be naïve, Effie."

The vitriol in his tone was so unexpected that she blinked and took a step away. "Excuse me?"

"Do you really think, given open access to your mind, they aren't going to take everything they want?" His voice was low, his eyes narrowed on hers.

Effie shot a confused look at the Triumvirate, wondering why Kieran would make such awful accusations in their presence, and why they weren't correcting him.

"Why does my doing this bother you so much?"

"Everything they learn gets stored, shared, repeated. It is how they discover the patterns, discern the nuances within others' visions. What you're offering them . . ." he shook his head, looking disgusted, "you might as well walk back into that room and bare yourself for all to see. It'd be less of a violation, and less permanent."

"So, you're just trying to look out for me?" she asked in a carefully neutral tone.

"Well, somebody has to."

"Are you sure you aren't just jealous that I'm offering a part of myself to someone else? A piece you'll never have access to?"

Kieran's face paled as if she'd struck him. "Effie," he started, reaching out for her, but she stepped out of range.

"You're so certain you know me, Kieran, because of your dreams —as if those give you a sort of claim and special insight into who I am —but all you know is the story you created in your head about what those moments mean."

"That's not true," he said, his voice shaking.

"You don't know—you *can't* know—what those moments meant to *me*. What it felt like to live them and relive them. The pain, the joy, the love . . . those are mine and mine alone. For all that you See, you do not *know*." Her voice was low and throbbing with emotion.

She'd heard the Triumvirate say that exact thing to Helena once, but now she understood what they'd meant. A Keeper's visions would always be flawed by their biased interpretation of the events unfolding before them.

It made Effie even more certain she needed the Triumvirate to experience what she'd Seen. With their shared knowledge, they were the only ones who could know for sure if the threat of danger was real.

Anything else they'd discovered while searching, well, she'd just have to trust they wouldn't use them against her. And if they did . . . it wouldn't be the first time.

She turned away from Kieran and the hurt shining in his eyes. Purposefully, she closed the distance between herself and the Triumvirate.

"Do it."

They didn't insult her by asking if she was sure. Instead, the one she assumed was Smoke raised his arm, his spindly fingers unfurling to reveal the rune inked into his palm as he did.

Effie took a deep breath, bracing herself for his touch.

There was a brief moment of hesitation when Smoke's fingers sort of curled back in on themselves, as if he was the one who wasn't sure he wanted to see what she held within her. She lifted her eyes to where his would be—if he still had them.

"I trust you."

Her eyes fluttered closed as his feather-light touch brushed against her forehead. His skin was soft, but in the way of ancient paper that had been crinkled up and smoothed out over and over again. His long fingers slid through her still damp hair as his fingertips pressed down and anchored his hand on her head.

There was no warning, no way to prepare for the onslaught of images that flashed in her mind. She remembered the sense of disorientation from before, but this was different, more of a dam bursting and not a slow trickle. It wasn't just the visions that flashed in her mind. It was everything—her entire life—all at once.

Four-year-old Effie, sobbing in a closet after the other children had thrown rocks at her and laughed when she hadn't been able to use magic to protect herself.

Sixteen-year-old Effie being told she was good for nothing except spreading her legs.

Darrin as he caught on fire and told her he loved her.

Her grandmother's arms wrapping around her and pulling her close after a particularly long time apart.

Lucian's fierce expression when he'd found her in the tavern.

The feeling of Kieran's lips brushing against her neck.

Her fear.

Her insecurity.

Her desperation.

It was all there. Every flawed and uncomfortable piece of the puzzle that when put together encompassed the woman that she'd become.

And just when she thought there was nothing left, the blood-soaked walls of the cave and the floating corpses took center stage. There was nothing less terrifying about the vision when experienced in this fashion, and she could distantly feel her body start to tremble when the monster slid his wet tongue along her cheek.

Then it was over.

Effie had no idea how long it lasted, but her heart was pounding, and she was sucking in ragged breaths when Smoke lowered his hand. She didn't even realize she'd been crying until a knuckle brushed her cheek and wiped away a few salty tears.

She held still, waiting for their verdict.

"Our Daughter speaks true."

"The Corruptor is dead, but her legacy remains."

"We must warn the Chosen."

"When death comes for us, it will be merciless and absolute."

"Is there nothing we can do?" Effie asked, her voice breathless with relief that they'd believed her; that she hadn't been wrong.

"We will do what we've always done."

"We will keep watch."

"We will sound the alarm."

When they spoke next, Effie knew she was not the only one hearing their words.

"Elysia is under attack."

CHAPTER 26

*A*lmost a week had passed since the Triumvirate made their announcement. A week with no sign of the monsters that were lurking in the background, waiting to strike. Effie had expected more of an uproar in response to the news, but the Keepers had taken it in stride.

That was not to say that nothing had changed. Everyone took the threat seriously. The city was on high alert, many of the Keeper's canceling assignments to remain at the citadel or cutting short those that they were on to return home. No one wanted to be caught alone and unprotected when the monsters struck.

To that end, an unspoken curfew had also gone into effect, the city now shutting down with the sun.

All of which meant that the citadel was constantly packed with people. Effie couldn't go two steps without seeing someone, most of them strangers. It was a jarring change from how her first weeks had been. She missed the quiet calm from before. Her new home had been a sanctuary and now it was . . . restless.

Tension permeated the citadel. She could sense it in the whispered conversations that ceased as she passed, or the sideways glances cast her way when she'd walk into a room. Effie didn't blame them. She'd brought that chaos into their world.

Sighing, Effie eyed her mostly empty bowl of warm oats. It was the first time she'd been able to take an actual meal in the dining hall. Despite the influx of people, the mood was subdued. No one spoke above a hushed whisper and the easy laughter and warm smiles were a thing of the past.

It was unnerving, like the citadel was holding its breath, poised on the brink of something, and each one of its inhabitants was waiting for her to tell them what that something was. She could feel the weight of their expectations pressing against her. As the only Keeper who had Seen what was coming, she carried their anticipation like a yoke around her neck.

A soft chime sounded in the dining hall and Effie glanced up with a silent groan. Time to go.

The heavy door opened, and Effie wasn't surprised to see Lucian's dark gaze zero in on her. She gave him a small nod and stood up, carrying her dish to the bin holding the others.

Despite her protest that she didn't want to scout with the Guardians again after her run-in with the Shadows, the Triumvirate had requested that she continue to assist them, on the off chance it sparked something new with her visions.

Effie wasn't sure what it said about her that she was glad it hadn't. At least, not yet.

She was exhausted, emotionally and physically. Outside of the few moments she'd steal each day for a quick soak, Effie was constantly on the go and rarely alone. She'd wake before the sun to train with Kael, more determined than ever to ensure she could defend herself when the time came. Then, after a quick meal—usually consisting of her waving at Jo and the girls while stuffing a piece of toast into her mouth and hurrying off behind Lucian, Kael, or the towering blond giant named Nord—she would spend the rest of her day in the jungle.

On the bright side, her new assignment meant that her sessions with Kieran were on hold. If things between the two of them were a tangled mess before, they were beyond complicated since that night on the balcony.

Effie knew he meant well, but good intentions aside, his sense of entitlement where she was concerned had to stop. He wanted more than she could give him; more than she might ever be able to give him —or any man for that matter. It was a conversation that they'd need to have, but one she was in no hurry to initiate. There were bigger things to deal with at the moment.

"Are you avoiding me?"

Effie stumbled; his voice more jarring since she'd just been thinking about him.

"No?"

"Is that a question?" he asked, smirking.

"No," she replied more firmly, her own lips twitching up into a small smile. "Not a question and not avoiding you. I've been busy."

Kieran's eyes darted to the door and he nodded, his face unreadable. "Listen, I know you have to go, I just wanted to apologize while it still might make a difference."

It was a rare enough occurrence that Effie froze, turning her full attention on him.

His eyes closed briefly, and he sucked in a quick breath. When he spoke again, his words left him in a rush. "I never meant to seem like I wasn't on your side. I just worry about you and I only want what's best for you."

The words touched her, speaking to the little girl who'd rarely had anyone care enough to want to look out for her. Some of the ice around her heart thawed.

"I appreciate that, but, Kieran?"

He lifted a brow. "Yeah?"

"Stop assuming you know what's best for me."

A hint of pink tinged his cheeks and Kieran dipped his head. "I'll try."

"It's a start, I guess." She offered him a small smile. "I should go. Don't want to keep Sir Grumpy Pants waiting."

Kieran snorted. "Please tell me you call him that to his face."

189

Effie gave him a horrified look, which only spurred Kieran's laughter.

"I'll see you later, Kieran."

"Until then."

She gave him a small wave and turned to hurry out the door. Lucian was tapping his foot impatiently as she stepped out of the dining hall.

Effie stopped short at the look on his face. "Is something wrong?"

His eyes lifted at the sound of her voice and he shook his head no.

Effie frowned and studied the Guardian for a second before moving the rest of the way into the hall.

Lucian was barely approachable on the best of days, but today he seemed more dangerous somehow. A caged predator waiting for the door to open. Although tension radiated off him in waves, none of it was directed at her.

The thought should have helped her relax, but an uneasy Lucian shook her to the core. There are certain fundamental truths one builds their life on: the sun will rise tomorrow, fire burns, and Lucian is the most terrifying fucker around and he's not scared of anything. For any one of those truths to be disproven calls all others into question. Nothing good could come of Lucian being noticeably on edge.

"Just us today?" Effie asked, eyeing the empty hall.

"Kael will be meeting us later. He had some things to take care of this morning."

"Ah," she said, falling into step beside him.

Still on edge, she lowered her voice to just above a whisper. "Has there been any news?"

"No news. No sightings."

She let out a breath she'd hadn't been aware of holding. "I guess that's good."

Lucian grunted.

They walked a few more steps in silence, but his mood was making her stomach tie itself into knots.

"You're acting weird," she blurted.

Her Guardian stopped mid-step and looked at her. "Weird?"

Effie's face was on fire, but she nodded.

"How?"

"I don't know."

His brow lifted. "Interesting logic."

Waving her hand at his face she tried to explain. "You're always kind of scary and broody, but today you're a lot broody. Or maybe distracted?" Effie let out a frustrated breath and shook her head. "I don't know how to explain it. You're just not acting like yourself."

One side of his mouth lifted. "Kind of scary?"

Effie sighed and crossed her arms. "That is the part you'd pick up on."

"You've never seemed remotely scared of me."

"Guess I'm good at hiding it," she said, turning away to start walking again.

Lucian followed, his long stride taking him past her so he could hold the door open to the portal room. Effie still thought the name was a bit of a misnomer. There were no shimmering pools of power, or really any clue at all that portals were anchored to the nondescript stone room. She'd dreamt more than once about accidentally stepping through a portal and not being able to find her way back.

Effie moved toward the left wall since it was the portal they'd used the day before.

Lucian stopped her by grasping the back of her cloak and giving it a sharp tug.

"That one," he said, pointing to the opposite wall.

"Really?" she asked, surprised because it was the only portal they'd never used.

Lucian nodded, his dark eyes filled with shadows that made her shiver.

Tentatively, she placed her hand on his arm. "Are you sure nothing's wrong?"

His eyes dropped to where she touched him, when they lifted again the metallic flecks near his pupils seemed to glow. "Of course something's wrong," he growled, his hands flexing and unflexing as if he was trying to grasp his weapon. "Our enemies are out there, and we are no closer to finding them today than we've been all week."

"Right," she murmured, still not believing that was all that was weighing on the warrior.

"Let's go."

Dropping her hand, Effie followed him, her breath still catching in her throat as she walked toward the wall. Even though she'd done it several times now, her brain never quite understood that she wasn't about to bash her face into the stones. She didn't take another easy breath until her boot crunched over fallen leaves.

The jungle was darker today, heavy clouds obscuring the patches of sky visible through the treetops. Effie shivered and pulled her cloak tighter around her body, squinting up at the sky as a gust of wind caused the branches above her to shake.

Something soft and cold brushed her cheek. Glancing around, Effie noticed tiny white flakes swirling through the air.

"Is that . . . snow?" she asked, her fingers lifting to her cheek.

Lucian nodded, clearly unimpressed with her observation skills.

"In the jungle? Where are we?"

"Northern border."

Fear shot through Effie's body, turning her blood to ice. "As in, the one near Vyruul?"

"You know of another border to the north?"

"Smart-ass."

His quirked brow told her what he thought of that insult.

"Is it really a good idea to be sneaking around so close to Rowena's home?"

"Greyspire was decimated and the Corruptor is dead."

"Oh," Effie replied softly, not even mildly appeased by his reminder.

She fell silent as she moved through the forest at Lucian's side. He seemed to know where he was going, but everything looked the same to her. Especially once the jungle was blanketed in white, the snowfall heavier as they moved closer to the border. It should have looked like something from one of the fairy stories her grandmother had told her, but Effie couldn't shake the feeling that the ghosts of Rowena's victims haunted this place, their restless spirits lingering even after the threat of her reign was extinguished.

A branch snapped and Effie let out a garbled scream, her dagger drawn and thrust out in front of her as she spun around. She would have felt foolish if Lucian's sword wasn't also leveled in the direction of the noise.

"Mother's tits," Effie swore when a familiar blond head poked out.

Seeing their blades, Kieran lifted his hands. "Hello to you too."

"What are you doing here?" Lucian demanded.

"Offering my services."

Heart still racing, Effie sheathed her blade. Lucian was slower to lower his.

"How is sneaking up on us being helpful?" she asked, still shaken.

"I didn't mean to startle you. I would have called out, but I wasn't sure if the footprints in the snow back there were yours."

"Who else would they belong to?"

"How did you even know we'd be here?" Lucian asked.

That was probably the better question to start with.

"I had a dream."

The hair on the back of Effie's neck lifted. Effie and Lucian spoke at the same time.

"Why didn't you say anything earlier?" Effie asked.

While Lucian asked, "What did you See?"

Kieran shook his head, his lips pinched with worry. "I wasn't sure when it would come to pass, until other events fell into place."

"What other events?"

"Speak, Keeper," Lucian said, his deep voice sounding like growling thunder in the relative quiet of the snow-covered jungle.

Kieran paled, his eyes the only color in his face. "Shattered glass, bloody footprints, voices when no one's there, a pale hand pulling back a dark hood."

Effie blinked at her tutor. She'd never heard him make any reference to his dreams, outside of the ones that she starred in.

193

"These were the events that have already come to pass?" Lucian asked.

Thank the Mother one of them was better at dealing with a Keeper's visions. Effie was still trying to wrap her head around the fact that Kieran's dream had led him to them here.

Kieran licked his lips and nodded. "A glass shattered in the dining hall shortly after you left. Someone stepped on it, their slippers too thin to offer protection from the sharp fragments. Their blood smeared across the floor . . ." he trailed off, shaking himself out of his trance. "Anyway, that's when I put it together."

"And your dream showed you us? Here?" Effie asked.

Kieran nodded, looking like he was about to be sick. "What was left of you."

Her breath left her in a whoosh.

"Did you see what happened?" Lucian asked.

"No, just the aftermath."

Lucian and Effie exchanged looks; his of grim determination, hers a bone-deep terror.

"That's why I had to come after you. I thought if someone else was here, if I could warn you, maybe it would make the difference."

Lucian gave a terse nod, his eyes scanning their surroundings like he expected someone to jump out from behind one of the trees at any second.

"Maybe we should head back?" Effie suggested.

She didn't expect Lucian to agree, but she didn't anticipate the look of disapproval he shot her way either.

"It's not that crazy to wait and fight another day if the deck is stacked against you," she insisted, feeling the need to defend herself.

"I'm a Guardian, Effie. I do not run away from my duty. Ever."

He stared at her, as if the intensity of his gaze could drive the point home. Maybe it did. Effie looked away while something that felt suspiciously like shame worked its way through her.

No matter how far she'd come from the girl who used to cower behind her hair, she was still far from a hero. She'd fought in a few battles, even defeated a few enemies, but at the end of the day, when it really mattered most, her instinct was to run and hide, not stand and fight.

The crunch of footsteps in the snow was her only sign that Lucian had resumed his trek further into Vyruul. Effie was quick to follow, not eager to get left behind.

As Kieran moved into position beside her, he brushed his knuckles against her forearm in a silent offer of comfort. She ignored it, not ready to accept solace of any kind just yet.

The three of them walked until Effie could only assume they'd officially crossed the border. The scent of pine was filling the air and there wasn't a thick, ropey vine to be found. The sky had grown dark, their signal that it was time to head back. No matter what Lucian said about running, they never stayed out after dark. The jungle was too dangerous to risk it.

Goosebumps scattered along her arms as another gust of wind tossed her cloak up into the air.

This time, there was no crack of a branch to alert them of an intruder.

Lucian was in front, ahead of her and Kieran, but still within her line of sight. Kieran was on her left, but too far away for her to touch. She may as well have been on her own.

The tickle along the side of her neck was no stray piece of hair. The path it took was too deliberate. Effie stopped breathing; her body posed on the brink of flight.

"Where are you running off to in such a hurry, dearie?" a voice rasped just behind her. If death had a voice, this was most assuredly it. Rough and gritty like sand, but as insubstantial as a speck of dust tossed about in the wind.

Her mouth went dry. She couldn't answer if she tried.

"Pretty girl," the voice said near her left ear, "you will make a tasty treat."

Effie shuddered, a strangled whimper the only sound she could manage. The monsters she'd faced in battle had always been more animal than human. The only tormentors she'd ever had to deal with that could actually speak were the ones she'd never learned to fight.

They were the ones that still haunted her dreams and made her feel as small and helpless as the little girl who used to hide in the back of her closet.

The ring of steel filled the air and Effie's eyes fluttered closed with relief. She was not a little girl anymore, and she was not alone.

"Unhand her," Lucian ordered, his voice filled with the promise of violence.

"Not so fast," death answered, its hand snaking up to grasp her by the throat. "The girl is mine."

"Over my dead body," Kieran said, twirling his weapon in his hand as he slid into a fighting stance.

"That can be arranged."

CHAPTER 27

The start of battle always brings a wave of cool calculation. Even amidst the chaos of war, the world can slow to the point that each individual moment plays out for an eternity. And so it was in this instant as the vein in Effie's neck visibly pulsed with her terror.

Lucian saw the tiny flutter and he felt his rage ignited. Death walked among them now, but it would not be theirs.

It took less than a heartbeat for the Guardian to assess their opponent.

This being was not like his brothers that they'd slain. It was sentient. A creature with its own mind and purpose, not one driven by the whims of another. With Rowena dead, there was no reason it should still be alive at all. But there was no mistaking those milky white eyes snaked with black.

It was wearing armor, or pieces of it. Metal chest plate and gauntlets on its forearms. Its skin was decaying, pieces of its gray flesh already rotted away, including most of its nose and a good portion of its cheeks.

He'd been a soldier once, or at least he had been before he was taken. Was any of that honor still in there, or was it lost along with any semblance of the man he'd once been?

Kieran moved into position beside him and together—without even a shared look between them—the two men took their first steps onto the battlefield.

The Shadow's hand grasped tighter, beads of bright red blood blooming where its jagged nails cut into her tender skin.

Effie squeaked and tried to pull out of the creature's hold, but it only served to press her closer to the beast behind her.

Lucian snarled. Between one breath and the next, he called forth his power, wanting to see what lay beneath the surface. This was not an enemy he'd fought before, and even the smallest tendril of information could make a difference.

The snow shone with the brilliance of the golden light as the forest's essence was revealed. It was blinding, and for one endless second, Lucian saw nothing else.

Thankfully, instinct pulled his eyes away from the light and back toward his enemy. Lucian recognized that inky stain, only this time it wasn't a smudge. It was a pulsing pillar of darkness. The Shadow was corruption incarnate. A taint that must be destroyed before it could infect anything else.

Lucian released his power. It would do no good here. Even seeing the threads of life flowing through the creature, they were twisted and there was no telling what would happen if he pulled them. It was not the time to find out; not with Effie trapped in the Shadow's embrace.

"Distract him," Lucian murmured, his voice barely more than a whisper.

Kieran straightened and took a swaggering step forward. Lucian recognized the courtly persona. It was one Kieran used whenever he wanted to establish dominance. Lucian would have laughed, except he knew firsthand how fucking annoying it was. He'd asked for a distraction, and if the Shadow really was a creature with its own mind, it could do the trick.

"Didn't your mother ever teach you the proper way to court a lady?" Kieran asked, his voice a cultured sneer.

The Shadow's eyes darted to Kieran. "I take what is mine."

"The lady is not yours."

The creature ran his nose up the side of Effie's neck and cheek. Her face twisted in a grimace and Effie gasped for breath. She was starting to hyperventilate.

"I'm the one holding her."

Kieran moved closer, standing directly between Lucian and the Shadow, pulling his entire focus.

Lucian took a silent step back, angling his body to the tree line. If he could get behind the Shadow, he could take him unaware.

The creature let out a groan of satisfaction and lifted his face from Effie's neck back to Kieran. "I love the smell of fear."

Effie's throat bobbed, but she did not cry out. Lucian could practically see her mental battle for control. She was winning, but not for much longer.

Lucian took a few more steps and then froze.

"I know what you're doing, princeling. It won't work."

"We're just having a conversation," Kieran said easily.

"You think to trick me." The monster threw his head back and laughed, his stringy hair sliding along the back of his armor.

Kieran tilted his head, his face expressionless. "And that makes you laugh because . . ."

The Shadow's head snapped up and his smile turned into a feral grin. "Because you are the ones who are trapped."

In a single move, he released Effie, shoving her into Kieran and twisting to face Lucian. He staggered as she barreled into him, but they did not fall. Kieran caught Effie, helping her right herself before pushing her behind him.

"Guardian, you disappoint me."

"I wish I cared."

A dry rattling cough that could have been a laugh filled the air.

"It doesn't matter. You'll be dead soon, and I'll be feasting on your bones."

One after another, more Shadows slid into view.

Six.

Eight.

A dozen.

It didn't take a Keeper's prophecy to see how this would play out.

Lucian mentally shrugged. He'd lived a long time. Today was as good as any to die. It didn't mean he'd make it easy for them.

He ran his hand along his blade, subtly changing it from a solid piece of metal to something molten and other. An in-between form where it was still metal and still capable of slicing through flesh like liquid butter. But changed just enough that it was also able to flow around and into its target, searing and burning through anything it touched. Technically there was no word to describe this in-between state, but Kael had once referred to it as the death mist, and Lucian thought that was as accurate as anything else.

Today it would hopefully live up to its name.

Lucian didn't wait for the smug bastard in front of him to speak again. Spinning, he swung his blade around his body, beheading two of the creatures that had thought to sneak up on him. When he was facing the one who'd held Effie again, he slashed hoping to collect a third head.

He was not so lucky, but the creature's right arm did fall to the floor in a spurt of black ichor and cries of outrage.

The Shadow looked down at his arm and back up to Lucian. "You'll pay for that, Guardian."

Lucian shrugged. "Doubt it."

The Shadow bared its teeth and lifted its remaining arm, a ball of purple fire growing in its hand.

Effie cried out, but Lucian kept his eyes trained on the enemy in front of him, trusting that Kieran could keep her safe a while longer.

"Lucian, it's Shadow Fire!" she screamed. "Don't let it touch you!"

The Shadow hurled a ball of purple flame at him, but Lucian dodged and sprung forward, severing its other arm from its body. He should have ended it instead of drawing out the battle, but he wanted to make the fucker pay for putting that note of fear in his charge's voice.

The creature wailed. "You rutting bastard!"

Lucian pressed forward, his voice low and ugly. "Sorry you can't play with your balls anymore."

"This isn't over," the Shadow hissed.

"It is for you," Lucian said, swinging his blade true. The Shadow's knees hit the floor and his head toppled off rolling a few feet away.

Lucian spit on the creature's dead body before turning his attention back to the others.

Seven of the walking corpses remained. Five of them stood in a loose circle, cackling maniacally while Effie and Kieran each fought one of their brothers. Two more were dead at their feet.

The ball of Shadow Fire had already consumed the trees behind him, and it continued to rage and burn as it crawled across the snowy ground. From what he knew of it, the purple flames would continue to burn until no fuel remained.

It looked as though only three of the remaining Shadows also had the ability to call on the corrupted elements, although thankfully none of them seemed to be tied to Fire. The Water user lobbed balls of acid at Kieran's feet, forcing him to leap comically to the side while mid-fight. The other two controlled Earth, and they worked together to make the ground quake and roll.

Effie struggled to keep her balance. Her face was pale and dirt-smeared, but her eyes never left her enemy as she met him blow for blow.

Pride flowed through him at the sight of her. She may not have always been a warrior, but she'd become one.

Confident that they were holding their own, Lucian shifted his focus to the nearest creature.

"Let's dance," Lucian crooned.

"So eager to court death, Guardian?" the Shadow hissed as it ambled closer.

A familiar face peered out around the base of a nearby tree. Lucian's smile stretched wide. They might have fewer numbers, but they were no longer outmatched.

The Shadow tilted its head. "You smile at the thought of death?"

"Just yours," Lucian said, swinging his blade.

This one was faster than his brothers. He easily dodged the attack. *Air blessed.*

The Shadow ran forward, slamming his fist into Lucian's stomach.

Lucian laughed. "That all you got?"

"I will rip your innards out and make you eat them. I will—"

There was a wet gurgle as Kael ripped the Shadow's throat out.

"I'm sorry, I didn't get that," Kael said as the monster fell.

"Good to see you, brother," Lucian said.

"Thanks for saving some of them for me."

As one, the two Guardians turned back to the battlefield. Two of the Shadows stepped back, planning to escape. Lucian and Kael lunged for them.

The ground moved, and Lucian slid across the now muddy surface, but his aim was steady. His blade cut through the Shadow's legs, just above its knees.

He shifted his weight, planning on springing up and moving on to the next of the creatures. But one was already waiting for him, a sinister grin on its face.

It was the corrupted Water user. Acid dripped from its fingers, the ground hissing everywhere a drop made contact.

"Have you ever heard the sizzle of flesh as it burns from the body?" the creature hissed, its eyes closing as if in ecstasy.

Lucian was fast, but the creature was faster.

A ball of the green liquid splashed down and the air was filled with screams.

EFFIE SLID her blade out of the monster, sliding its length along her leg to clean it before turning to the next.

Time held no meaning on the battlefield. It slowed or sped up as it wished, each moment lasting forever only to be completely replaced by the next. It was survival in its purest form. The ability to see only what is right in front of you until you are safe enough to address the next threat.

Effie scanned the forest, assessing the needs. There were three remaining Shadows, each engaged in battle with one of her friends.

She wasn't surprised to see that Kael had arrived. Kael's weapon of choice was his hands, he moved faster than her eyes could track as he tore apart his opponent like it was a ragdoll and not a power-infused monster.

Kieran was engaged with the last of the Earth wielders, and Lucian . . .

Effie's mouth opened in a silent scream.

Lucian was crab-walking away from the Shadow that stood over him, green acid dripping from his fingers. Solely focused on the monster above him, he wasn't aware of the threat behind him.

The purple flames devoured the trees until a wall of dancing flame stretched as far as she could see.

A wall that Lucian was scrambling straight for.

Another battle—another man—and a death so brutal she'd never survive it a second time filled her mind.

"Lucian, no!" she screamed, her body flying as she ran to him.

The air was knocked out of her lungs as an arm like steel wrapped around her hips and pulled her back.

"Not so fast."

Effie didn't check to see who grabbed her. Friend or foe, it made no difference. She threw her elbow back and simultaneously lifted her foot up. There was a grunt and she was free, running once again.

"Effie!"

She didn't falter. Screaming, filling the forest with the sound of her battle cry, Effie threw herself at the Shadow that continued to corral Lucian back against the Shadow Fire.

She may as well have flung herself at a brick wall. She bounced off and hit the ground hard and the smell of burning flesh filled the air as the acid splashed over her. But her blade jutted out of the monster's chest.

The monster turned its head to face her, its sadistic grin growing wider. Acid rained down upon her as the Shadow threw itself on top of her prone body.

"You wanted my attention so badly, little girl. It's yours."

The acrid smell of burning flesh filled the air, and Effie didn't even recognize the screams that were torn from her throat as the Shadow bit down on the side of her neck.

Pulling.

Chewing.

Tearing.

Everything hurt. Her body was on fire.

But Lucian . . . at least the Guardian was alive.

He glared down at her, his eyes a black so dark she could get lost in them.

He was yelling at her, but she didn't hear a word he said. She was too focused on the fact that this time she'd be the one who burned.

CHAPTER 28

*K*ieran dropped to his knees, letting the Shadow Kael had thrown fly over his head and into the wall of purple flame. He laughed and stood to face him.

They watched as the corrupted Fire consumed it.

"Lucian, no!" Effie screamed.

Kieran's heart dropped in his stomach before he even turned around.

Effie was sprinting over to Lucian as he was trying to scramble away from the monster that stood above him.

Kieran needed only a second to figure out what had triggered that sound of horrified desperation in her.

The purple flames were less than a body length away from Lucian, and once they made contact with his skin, he'd be consumed by them. She was lost to the memory of a previous battle—one where the flames had won.

Kael tried to stop her, grasping her about the waist to keep her out of harm's way.

She dropped him to his knees with two unexpected and efficient strikes, the first to his gut, and the second to his manhood. Kieran winced in sympathy.

Effie was like a blinding streak as she pumped her arms and legs and launched herself into the air. Her blade slid through the Shadow's chest, but the momentum propelled her forward, her small body no match for the monster's brute strength. She bounced off him and landed on the ground with enough force Kieran felt his own teeth clack together.

Lucian was finally able to push to his feet and Kieran was moving, both men zeroing in on the Shadow that threw himself on top of Effie.

His stomach rolled as she screamed. He wasn't going to get to her in time, but Lucian could.

The Guardian grabbed the Shadow by the back of his neck, tearing him away from Effie's spasming body. Green acid, red blood, and black ichor pooled away from her in some macabre imitation of a rainbow. The Shadow had torn out a piece of her shoulder where the muscle met her neck. Kieran could see the bone jutting out through the wound.

It was too much.

He heaved, dropping to his knees as his stomach emptied itself.

Lucian's face was twisted in rage. Kieran flinched from the heat of it even though it wasn't directed at him. He swung that blurred sword of his, decapitating the monster in one clean move before spinning around and looming over Effie.

"What the hell were you thinking, you little fool?" he shouted down at her.

Kieran crawled over to where her body lay, his lip curling back in disgust. "Can't you see she's injured, you fucking asshole?"

Shock flickered across the Guardian's face. He hadn't known, hadn't had a chance to see what the monster had done to her.

Kael joined them, his hand cupped over his crotch. "Is it bad?"

Kieran looked down at Effie just as she smiled, and her eyes fluttered closed. It was so peaceful. So out of place here in the aftermath of their battle. Wordlessly, he looked back up at the Guardian.

Kael paled, his skin chalky and gray.

"You have one job!" Kieran shouted as he tore a piece of his tunic off to press against the wound in an attempt to stop the bleeding. "You were supposed to keep her safe. She should not be the one worried about saving *you*."

Grief clouded Lucian's eyes, but any trace of emotion vanished as he knelt down and took her limp body in his arms.

"Who knew someone so tiny could be so fierce?"

Kieran didn't think Lucian knew he'd said it out loud.

Sorrow tinged Kael's face as he stared down at the woman cradled in Lucian's arms. "She's a brave one, our little warrior."

"Elder's rotting teeth, you two act as though she's dead and gone. Let's get her back to the citadel before you kill her with your premature mourning."

His bravado was forced. Effie didn't look good. In fact, Kieran had seen fresh corpses that looked better than she did. Some of the Shadow's acid had eaten away a good chunk of her heavy mass of hair, but what was left was matted and tinged red from her blood. Her skin was leeched of color, except for the deep purple smudges below her eyes and the gray cast of her lips. And her limp, boneless limbs did not resemble anything of the animated woman they belonged to.

If not for the wet rattle of her breaths, he would have thought she was dead.

Effie's death had never been part of his dreams, but the future could be altered with a single choice. There was no knowing what the catalyst of change would be.

So even though he'd seen a different future, Kieran was no longer sure all of his dreams would come true.

CHAPTER 29

*E*ffie was aware of nothing before the hushed voices reached her ears. She couldn't make out the words, just a general sense of worry.

"We've got to stop meeting like this," she croaked as the walls of the healing wing swam into view. Kieran and Kael were nearby, both still in their battle-stained clothes. She couldn't have been out for too long if they hadn't bothered changing. The room was bathed in soft amber, which meant that it was early evening. She'd only been unconscious for a few hours, at most.

"Take it easy, little one," Kael murmured, squeezing her hand. "You lost a lot of blood. The healers cleaned the wound and patched you up, but there wasn't anything they could do about that."

"I still don't understand why not," Kieran muttered from his perch across the room.

Kael rolled his eyes, sounding like a harassed teacher as he explained—probably not for the first time—"We've already been over this. While healing is a gift that stems from the Water, branch, blood itself is only partially comprised of water. Healers cannot manipulate life's essence; thus, they cannot do anything about blood loss. Now shut up, or I'm kicking you out."

Kael looked back down at her and winked, but some of the usual sparkle was missing from his eyes. He looked worn out. Effie didn't imagine she looked much better.

"What happened?" she asked, licking her cracked lips.

Kael's smile was sad. "You were very brave."

"She was very stupid," Lucian corrected from somewhere out of sight.

"If you're going to be an asshole, then you should leave," Kieran said.

Effie's lips twitched. "Looks like things are back to normal."

Her eyes felt heavy, but she fought the urge to close them.

Kael's smile warmed a fraction, but still didn't touch his eyes as he brushed a piece of hair off her forehead. "As much as they can be."

Effie tried to lift her hand to his face. "Why do you look so sad?"

"You scared me, little warrior."

"I scared you? How?"

"I thought we'd lost you." The hand near her face brushed along the sensitive skin connecting her neck and top of her shoulder. "You'll have a scar. The healers couldn't do anything about the damage the acid had already caused."

Something Ronan said came back to her, and Effie smiled again. "A real warrior carries their scars with pride. It's a reminder that they fought and lived."

"As they should," Kael said with a smile.

Lucian and Kieran remained suspiciously silent.

Twisting her head, she found their grim faces. "I'm sorry if I scared you as well."

"You have no reason to apologize," Kieran said, his eyes lingering on Kael's face before returning to hers. "It is good to see you looking well again."

She lifted her eyes back to Lucian. His arms were crossed, and his brows were low over his eyes.

Effie tried not to let her hurt show when it became clear he had nothing to say to her. "Has anyone sent word to Helena about the Shadows and how they . . ." she trailed off.

"Are now walking, talking corpses?" Kieran offered.

Effie nodded.

"No, we were waiting to see for ourselves that you would wake."

Her cheeks heated and she looked away, embarrassed that she'd kept them from their duty.

"I'll write to her. She's probably annoyed I haven't sent her anything yet."

"We'll make sure it finds its way to her."

Effie nodded and pushed herself into more of a seated position. "So, what now?"

"What do you mean?" Kieran asked.

"Now that we know what's out there, what do we do?"

"We cleanse the land," Lucian said, as if it was obvious.

"How will we know where to find them?" she asked.

"Their corruption leaves a stain. It will be easy enough to track now that we know what to look for," Kael answered.

"Do you know how to cleanse it?" she asked, looking between the three men.

"Not yet," Lucian said.

"Helena might. She's done it before."

Lucian dipped his chin. "It would be helpful to know what she did."

"I can ask when I send my letter."

Pushing away from the wall, Lucian headed to the door. "I'll bring you some paper."

Her eyes tracked his movement across the room and out the door. "He's angry with me," she whispered.

"He's angry with himself," Kael corrected.

"As he should be. The bastard almost got her killed."

Effie hadn't stopped to think. When she'd seen Lucian heading toward the Shadow Fire, she'd just reacted. It didn't matter what happened to her. She wasn't important in the grand scheme of things. Not compared to one of the Guardians.

Frowning, she stared at the door, her emotions a jumbled mess inside of her.

211

"He'll get over it," Kael said, pushing to his feet. "Someone should tell the Triumvirate that you're awake. I'll see you later, little warrior."

Effie squeezed his hand. "Thanks, Kael."

He winked at her and slipped out of the room.

Turning to Kieran, Effie froze at the chill against the back of her neck. Her hand reached up, surprised to feel skin instead of the heavy weight of her curls.

"What happened to my hair?" she asked, more stunned than upset.

Kieran cleared his throat. "The acid burned most of it away along the left side. We, um . . . we cut it for you."

Fingering the shorn curls, Effie humphed.

"Do you want to see?" Kieran asked.

Curious, she nodded. For as long as she could remember, her hair had been a wall to hide behind. Something to protect her from the sneers and stares of those that belittled her.

Kieran grabbed a mirror from the table and moved to stand beside her. He held it up and a woman she almost didn't recognize stared back at her.

Without the bulk of hair, the angles of her face were sharper. She no longer looked quite so childlike, even with the smattering of freckles along her nose and cheeks, or with her wide eyes.

Instead of falling down to the base of her spine, her hair now fell just to the bottom of her jaw. Smiling, she pulled a curl back behind her ear and pushed the mirror away.

"I think I like it."

Kieran returned her grin, his gaze warm. "It suits you."

There was a sharp knock on the door and Lucian walked in holding out some parchment and writing tools for her. He placed them on the foot of her bed. "Whenever you're ready."

"Thank you."

He glanced up at her, his expression unreadable. "You should get some rest."

"I'm not tired."

A muscle in his jaw twitched, but he didn't fight her. Instead, he looked at Kieran. "Take care of her. You know how stubborn she can be when it comes to taking care of herself."

Kieran nodded. "That I do."

"I'm right here, you know."

Without another glance, Lucian left the room.

Effie threw a pillow at the door.

"What was that for?"

"He's a pain in my ass."

Kieran snorted.

"Seriously, the way he's acting you'd think I'm the one who tried to kill him, not save him. He's infuriating."

Her display of temper only seemed to amuse Kieran.

"So are you," she said with a scowl.

"Me? What did I do?"

"You know what you did."

He lifted his brow, arms crossed over his chest. "I've been a perfect gentleman."

"But for how long?"

Kieran leaned down and kissed the tip of her nose. "Too long."

"Rogue."

Kieran winked. "Brat."

Effie chuckled and tried to make herself more comfortable. Her body ached and she couldn't keep the grimace from her face.

"They left you some tea for the pain."

She wrinkled her nose. "I don't want medicine. It's just going to make me sleepy. I'd rather have some wine. It will dull the edge but let me stay mostly alert."

"I can make that happen."

"Excellent."

"Be right back."

Once she was alone, Effie eyed the ivory scraps of paper near her feet.

Wetting the nib of the quill, she began writing.

KIRI,

FROWNING, Effie bit her lip and crossed out the title. Knowing Helena would get a kick out of it—having corrected Effie's formal use of her title instead of her name more than once—she started again:

~~*Kiri,*~~
  Helena,

I HOPE this letter finds you well. I apologize that it has taken me so long to write to you. To be honest, I started more than once, but wasn't sure what I could tell you that wouldn't bore you to tears. Somehow, I don't think you'll be very interested in hearing about my daily sessions with my tutor (which is how I spent the bulk of my days until recently).
  But I digress. I've had a vision—a warning. The war is <u>not</u> over.
  Rowena may be dead (congratulations, by the way. I can't wait to hear about how you managed it, even though I wish I could have been there to see it for myself) but the remnants of her corruption linger. The Shadows are still alive, and they have evolved. They can talk and seem to have regained the use of their individual power.
  There's no telling what else is out there, but according to Lucian (my Guardian—think Ronan on his worst day after a night of drinking and you might have an idea of what he's like) Rowena's corrupted Spirit magic is still strong within them. Worse, and perhaps more importantly, the corruption is also affecting the land.
  I haven't experienced it myself but based on the way it was described to me, it sounds like what we experienced in the Forest of Whispers. Lucian said the land must be cleansed, but no one knows how.
  If it's not too much trouble, I think we could use your help. I'm sure that you are too busy to come yourself, but even a letter explaining how

we can cleanse it would be appreciated. I fear what could happen if it grows unchecked . . .

At the very least, I thought you should know what's out there. Sooner or later it will find you, and I didn't want you to be caught unaware.

Please tell the others that I miss them, and I hope they are taking a much-needed break after all that they must have endured. That includes you.

UNTIL WE MEET AGAIN, may the Mother watch over you,

YOUR FRIEND,

EFFIE

CHAPTER 30

*E*ffie giggled as she stumbled down the hall. Kieran had left her hours ago with the order to get some rest, but she was feeling restless, and not ready to see what might find her in her dreams. After finding a proper pair of pants and a tunic and vest not stained with blood and gore, she polished off the rest of the bottle of wine he'd brought her and went on a mission to find another one.

She hoisted the bottle of pale pink alcohol higher and grinned. It wasn't wine, but it would do. Giving the hall a furtive scan, Effie uncorked the bottle and took a quick gulp before tucking her prize back under her arm and making her way back to her room. There wasn't any reason she could think of why anyone would care if she drank herself silly—she more than earned it after the day she'd had—but she also didn't want to risk someone trying to take it from her.

"What are you doing out of bed?"

Effie froze. *Mother's heaving tits.* Spinning around, she tried to hide the bottle behind her back.

But this was Lucian and he missed nothing.

His eyes narrowed and he glared at her. "Blood loss and alcohol, Effie? Good choice."

She returned his glare with one of her own. "I'm a grown woman. I can do whatever I want."

It would have sounded better if she hadn't hiccupped.

"Hand it over."

"No, it's mine."

"Effie, don't make me come over there and take it."

Her stomach warmed at the thought. The idea of Lucian stalking toward her and crowding her body with his was exactly what she wanted.

Effie waved the bottle over her head. "You want it? Come and get it."

She spun away and started to run, but she only made it a handful of teetering steps before he was on her.

"You're acting like a child," he snarled, snatching the bottle out of her hands and throwing it down the hall. It shattered and Effie pouted.

"Now look what you've done."

Lucian had managed to twist her around when he grabbed the bottle, and her back was pressed against one of the walls. There was barely an inch separating their bodies. She could see his nostrils flare with each angry breath he took.

"You're supposed to be sleeping."

"Who shoved that stick up your ass?" she asked.

If she'd been in her right mind, she never would have said it. She would have been horrified at the thought alone, but all Effie was feeling right now was that deliciously warm tingle working its way through her body.

Lucian's eyes narrowed. "How much have you had to drink?"

Effie shrugged. *Just the better part of a bottle of wine . . . and a few sips of pink deliciousness.*

"Damn it, Effie."

"Damn it, Effie," she parroted in her best I-am-Lucian-hear-me-roar impression.

Lucian pinched the bridge of his nose and groaned. "Millennia spent wandering the realms and you are going to be the thing that finally kills me."

Hurt stabbed at her and Effie blinked back angry tears. She knew she'd mouthed off to him, but she couldn't be such an annoyance to have deserved a comment like that. Not when she risked her own life trying to save his.

"You're a real ass, you know that? It was a long day. Mother's tits, it's been a long week, and all I wanted was something to take the edge off. Why do *you*"—she poked him—"get to tell *me* what I'm allowed to do or not do?"

He glanced down at her finger and then back up at her face. "You have a habit of poking me."

"You have a habit of being a bossy asshole."

Lucian snickered. "You enjoy swearing."

"When the occasion calls for it." She narrowed her eyes as a new thought occurred. "Are you going to tell me it's not ladylike? Because so help me—"

Lucian pressed his fingers to her lips. "Shh. Stand down, fledgling."

His voice had lost its edge and Effie couldn't think past the warm pressure of his fingers pressed against her lips. The impulse to nip them was hard to resist, but he moved before she could give in to it.

He leaned down until his eyes were level with hers. "Believe it or not, it is not my life's mission to make you miserable."

Effie's instinct was to snort and roll her eyes, but she was transfixed by the sincerity shining in Lucian's dark gaze, so she remained still.

"What, no comeback?" he asked, his warm breath fanning over her face.

There was something about his playful smirk that made her think he was actually a bit disappointed. When you were built like he was, it was probably a pretty rare occurrence that someone actually stood up to you.

Effie quirked a brow. "I was waiting to see where you were trying to go with that emotionally stunted excuse for an apology."

"Is that what it was?" he asked, his voice still a low rumble.

"Wasn't it?" she teased.

He chuckled and looked away, shaking his head. "What am I going to do with you?"

"You could try kissing me." The words were out of her mouth before she realized she'd said them out loud.

Heat bloomed in her cheeks as Lucian's head snapped back to her. It was the first time she'd ever seen him look stunned.

"What did you say?"

"Um," she mumbled, licking her lips nervously.

There was no getting out of it.

The words were out there now, and she couldn't take them back. More importantly, she didn't want to.

She didn't know where the suggestion had come from. She hadn't ever consciously thought of Lucian as more than the person who knew how to get under her skin better than anyone else. But now that the image had taken hold of her mind, she couldn't let it go. Crowded as he was around her, she was more aware of herself as a woman than she'd ever been. For once she didn't feel small or insignificant . . . and she really, really liked it.

Heart pounding, Effie forced herself not to look away. "I said, you could kiss me," she murmured in a throaty tone she didn't recognize.

"Effie," he breathed, her name sounding like a strangled groan. Lucian dropped his head until his forehead rested on hers. "We can't."

He sounded tormented.

Effie lifted her hand and rested it against the scruff of his cheek, pressing lightly until he met her gaze. "Says who?"

"I'm a Guardian, and you are very drunk . . ."

Effie grinned. "You know how I feel about stupid rules."

Lifting her chin, she guided his face down to hers and brushed her lips against his. It was the first time she'd ever been the aggressor, and the feeling of power rolling through her was as intoxicating as the wine.

Lucian practically vibrated with tension as her lips moved over his. For one terrible second, Effie thought he wasn't going to kiss her back.

But he did.

Mother, how he did.

He growled low in his throat, his hands coming up to cradle either side of her face as he pressed against her. The heat of his body along the front of her and the cool stone at her back only fueled her desire.

His lips were hot and hard against hers, a silent demand she was more than happy to answer.

Effie's knees went weak as his tongue slid against hers. Liquid heat pooled in her belly, and she lifted to her tiptoes to try to get closer to the source of her pleasure. The unconscious move caused her chest to rub against him, and the delicious friction made her moan.

Lucian froze, his breath leaving him in ragged bursts.

"Effie . . ."

"Shh, don't stop," she whispered, trying to kiss him again.

He turned his face away. "Effie, don't."

"You're trying to tell me what to do again," she teased, trailing kisses along his neck.

She felt his throat bob beneath her lips.

"I'd be taking advantage of you."

Effie pulled back with a laugh. "Taking advantage of me? How is that possible when it's what I want?"

He wouldn't look at her. "You're drunk. You don't know what you want."

Ice replaced the desire in her veins.

"And you do?" she snapped, running her hands along her arms to alleviate some of the chill.

He glanced at her and quickly looked away, but not before she saw the barely banked heat there. He wasn't as unaffected as he pretended to be. It should have made a difference, but the sting of his rejection was intensified by the alcohol that she'd consumed. The only truth that mattered was she'd offered herself to him, and he'd turned her down.

Old pains resurfaced and she stumbled away from him.

Simple, ungifted Effie. Not good enough to love. Not good enough to fuck.

Never, ever enough.

"You know what, Lucian? Forget it. You don't want me? Fine. I'll find someone who does."

"What's that supposed to mean?" He made to grab at her wrist as she turned to walk away from him.

She knocked his hand away with a feral snarl. "Don't you dare touch me. Not when you've made it so apparently clear how much the thought repulses you."

"Effie, you're acting like a child."

That phrase. That damned phrase.

Eyes narrowed and voice dripping with venom, she spat, "You may see me as a child Lucian, but I know someone who is more than aware that I'm a grown woman and who would be *thrilled* with the opportunity to prove it."

She stormed away, ignoring Lucian's shouts. The need to prove that she was enough—to anybody—had taken over. The only thing that mattered in her drunken haze was the need to feel loved again. Even if only for one night.

And Effie knew just the man to help her.

CHAPTER 31

*K*ieran sat on his bed, fingers running over the soft fabric of his blanket distractedly as he thought about the blonde beauty curled up in the healing chamber a couple floors above.

An unguarded Effie was a luxury Kieran hadn't realized he'd been craving. She'd laughed more than she had since arriving to the citadel, her giggles infectious as the wine worked its special brand of magic on her. With each sip, her tension and inhibitions ebbed, allowing him to catch a glimpse at the woman she kept hidden beneath her prickly exterior. It was what he'd been waiting for. How he'd always imagined spending time with her would be.

Fisting the blankets in his hands, Kieran let out a soft groan. He could easily become addicted to the sound of her laugh. When he'd left her, Effie's cheeks had been a delicious rosy pink, and her eyes hooded. There wasn't a trace of the mistrust or the shadows of her past hidden in her eyes. She was there with him, fully in the moment.

He hoped when the morning came she still looked at him with the same open expression.

Kieran's head shot up as the door opened, revealing a disheveled Effie. She slammed the door closed behind her, pressing her back against it.

Recognition shot through him. This was it. She was here, in his room. Finally, the dream that had changed the entire course of his life was finally about to come true.

"Effie," he breathed.

Having relived the dreams more times than he could count, Kieran knew what would come next in perfect detail. His smile grew when her bright eyes found him.

"Kieran."

It was just as he pictured. Her flaxen curls skimming her jaw, her eyes even more luminous without the fringe of her hair to hide behind. The brush of freckles across her slightly upturned nose and cheeks. The sharp arch of her brows, and the deep berry color of her lips.

Chuckling to himself, Kieran finally knew why her cheeks were flushed and her eyes glassy. She *was* drunk. Because of him and the bottle of wine he'd snuck up to her. He hadn't put together the clues before now. Not even the change in her hair had registered.

Anticipation already had his heart pounding in his chest, his body primed and eager for what would come next.

"Are you all right?" he asked.

Effie swallowed and gave a sharp nod. Her sweet voice was huskier than usual as she replied, "I wasn't sure I would find you here."

Grinning he asked, "Where else would I be?"

He felt a bit like an actor on stage, finally giving the performance he'd been practicing for his entire life. He knew each word, but the meanings felt different this time. Maybe because it was actually real.

She lifted one shoulder in a careless shrug. "I don't know. Around." She waved her hand to emphasize the word. "You are always disappearing."

"I can't tell if you're relieved to find me here or disappointed."

Effie snorted. "Me either."

Kieran chuckled. "And yet you sought me out anyway. Why?"

Her cheeks darkened, and she finally tore her gaze from him, staring resolutely over his shoulder. "I'm here to take you up on your offer."

He studied her with hooded eyes, his lips curling up in a seductive smile. "You'll have to be more specific, love."

A muscle ticked in her jaw. "You know which one I refer to," she ground out.

"Indulge me."

Her eyes darted to his. "Why are you making this so difficult? Isn't it enough that I'm humiliating myself by coming here in the first place, or does it not count unless I drop to my knees and crawl to you?"

Kieran allowed himself a moment to savor the unintentionally sensual picture she painted. He took a few more steps so that he was standing directly in front of her.

"Call me old-fashioned, but I don't find myself particularly eager to bed an unwilling woman. A man does have his pride."

Effie huffed out a breath. "So do I. I won't beg you to take me, Kieran."

He let out a soft snarl, his already aroused body reacting to the words. "What if I want you to beg?"

Her breath hitched, and her eyes darkened. She was not immune to them either. "I won't," she whispered, but the words were unsure.

Kieran grinned. "By the time I'm through with you, love, you will be," he promised, weaving his fingers into the feathery softness of her curls and slamming his lips to hers.

She gasped beneath him before her lips softened and began to move against his.

Kieran groaned, loving the feel of her surrender.

Thank you. Kieran didn't know who he was thanking, only that the years of loneliness and exile were worth every miserable second because finally Effie was going to be his.

He was never going to let her go again.

EFFIE GIRL, what did you get yourself into?

Kieran was taking his time, tasting and exploring her. It was getting hard to remember why she was here. The rough scrape of his hands as they slid up the sides of her body and pulled her tighter against him was exactly what she hadn't known she'd been waiting for.

The press of his hard body, the thrum of his heartbeat against hers, the feel of his hands roaming all over her . . . each detail warred with the others for her attention. She was consumed by the joy of being worshiped by a lover, and a skilled one, it would seem.

Effie wrapped her arms around his neck, her nails digging into his shoulders as she clung to him.

"Effie," he groaned, trailing nibbling kisses along her jaw and down her neck.

The heat of his mouth against her cool skin made her shiver.

She wasn't ready for the kiss to end, so she cupped his cheek and pulled his face back to hers. His chest rumbled with laughter, but he did not deny her. Kieran's hands continued their slow exploration, one finally coming to rest on her breast. Effie had never been so aware of a single part of her body. Who knew so much pleasure could come from being touched there?

A soft sound escaped her throat and she pressed into him. His other hand traced the edge of her bustier where the leather met the skin. Gooseflesh raced along her body in response to the whisper of a touch. His fingers worked their way down the fastenings, plucking each one free as he pressed another soft kiss against her lips.

She was overwhelmed, her mind torn between enjoying what he was doing and slight panic at the thought he was about to see her naked. There was a quick rush of cool air when the last fastening was free and her bustier dropped to the floor. The only thing separating her skin from his gaze was a sheer linen undershirt. Her body was quick to respond to the realization, her nipples pebbling and her stomach clenching.

Shivering, she pressed her thighs together, trying to relieve some of the unexpected ache.

Kieran's eyes had dropped down to her body when he'd unwrapped her. As they lifted back to her face, the sheer longing in his expression stole her breath.

She couldn't believe that she was the reason he looked like that;

that someone would actually stare at her with that much unadulterated need.

He gently bit her lip as he tugged her arms down to her sides. His hands skimmed her body, moving up and down twice before she realized he was slowly inching up the soft fabric of her undershirt.

Her eyes never left his face, entranced by what she saw there.

"Beautiful," he murmured.

His touch was feather-light as he explored her newly exposed flesh. He dipped down, cupping each of her breasts and brushing the tips of his fingers along her swollen peaks. She groaned when he took one of them in his mouth, the damp heat sending waves of pleasure through the rest of her body.

He nipped her and the slight sting of pain was enough to pull her out of her sexual haze. She was in over her head. When she'd come here, she'd known peripherally that this might happen, but it was another thing entirely to actually be experiencing it. For her emotions to tangle themselves up inside her as she learned what it was like to be truly desired by a man.

This wasn't a game, or something to prove any longer. These feelings were real. It was all real.

"Kieran."

He pulled back to look up at her, his face flushed with desire. "What is it, love?" he asked in a deep rasp.

"I don't know what to do."

She hadn't meant to make the admission out loud. She was torn. If she stayed . . . if this went further, there was no turning back. But it felt so damned good . . .

"It's okay, I do."

He'd misunderstood her words, but it didn't matter. Either way, he'd made the decision for her.

His arms banded about her waist, lifting her like she weighed no more than a sack of feathers. She wrapped herself around him, burying her face in his neck and enjoying the spicy smell of him.

"Do you trust me?" he whispered against the top of her head.

I'm not even sure I trust myself right now.

"Yes," she finally answered.

Her back touched the mattress as he laid her on top of his bed. For a heartbeat, she couldn't see his face, just the outline of his body as he stretched above her. He could have been anyone . . .

Trembling, Effie lifted her hand up to him. "Please . . ."

What was she asking for? And who was she asking?

Not even she knew the answer.

In that long, drawn-out moment, one thing became crystal clear. She shouldn't be here. Not like this. Lucian had been right; she was drunk. To go down this road with Kieran would mean something different to him than it did to her. It wouldn't be fair to either of them.

He leaned over, his face coming back into view. "I told you I'd make you beg. And we're only just getting started, love."

Effie froze. "I have to go."

Kieran blinked; his confusion almost comical. "What?"

Pushing him off of her, she slid her legs over the side of his bed and scrambled to find her undershirt on his floor.

"I'm sorry, I shouldn't have come here. It was a mistake."

"A mistake?" he asked in a low, angry tone. It was nothing like the seductive purr he'd used only moments before.

She threw on her shirt, her haste making her clumsy. It took two tries to get her arms through the holes. She refused to look at him as she picked up her leather bustier from the ground and used it to shield her body from him.

"I'm sorry," she whispered, barely containing her tears of shame.

She risked a glance at his face, and quickly looked away.

He was shocked, and she felt like the worst kind of fool.

As she turned toward the door, Kieran whispered, "This wasn't what was supposed to happen. I-I Saw it."

So, this was the dream he'd Seen. The reason he'd been so certain that she would be his.

Humiliation tore through her. Knowing that ending up here had been inevitable made it so much worse. Like she'd been destined to make an ass of herself, first with Lucian and then with Kieran. Destined to be the Mother's walking mistake.

"Forgive me," she sobbed, running from the room.

She didn't stop until she reached her own, slamming the door behind her with a crash. Sliding down its wooden surface until she was a crumpled heap on the floor, she finally gave in to her tears.

What have I done?

She'd just made a fool of herself with not just one of the men in her life, but two. And there would be consequences to face with each of them.

If she ever found the courage to face either of them again.

Groaning, Effie buried her face in her hands. Mother save her, she wasn't even sure she was going to look at herself in the mirror again after the little performance she just put on. She'd barely been on her own for a month and had already turned into someone she didn't even recognize.

This wasn't her. She wasn't careless with other people's feelings, or quick to jump into anyone's bed. What in the Mother's name had she been trying to prove?

Disgusted with herself, Effie curled up into a ball and cried herself to sleep.

CHAPTER 32

The dawn came, and with it, a pounding headache. Or maybe that was the door. Effie opened one eye only long enough to grab the pillow from beneath her head and hurl it at the offending piece of wood. The feathered sack flew wide and landed without a sound on the floor.

Effie glared at it. *Traitor.* Temples throbbing, she fell back.

Three more loud bangs shook the door.

"Go away," she groaned, pulling the covers up and over her head.

"If you felt fine enough to pickle yourself with drink last night, you're well enough to train with me today."

Kael. Knowing who was at the door made her no more inclined to get up and answer it.

"I have no problem coming in there if you don't get your ass up and open this door."

Effie froze. *He wouldn't.*

"I will!" he called, making her wonder if she'd spoken out loud.

Not wanting to find out, Effie pushed herself into a sitting position with a pitiful whimper. All things considered her body felt fine. It was her head—and her pride—that were wounded.

She wished the night before was a hazy, distant blur, but it wasn't.

231

As the night faded, so had the warm glow of the alcohol. In the morning, all that was left was shame. If she saw her Guardian or her tutor this day, she was turning and running the other way, pride be damned.

No one, not even the Mother Herself, could force her to have that reckoning in the state she was in.

Not today.

Maybe not ever.

"Effie," a warning growl sounded.

She glanced down to ascertain her state of dress, pleased to see when she'd crawled into bed she'd also managed to get herself properly attired. With the way things had ended up the night before, she wouldn't have been the least bit surprised to see that she'd ended up with pants hanging over her head, and her leather vest tied around her legs like some kind of diaper.

The rattle of the door was her last warning.

Effie scrambled up and forward, pulling the door open with a baleful stare.

She couldn't even muster up the energy to tell him to fuck off.

Kael didn't bother trying to hide his amusement. "Had fun, did you?"

Squinting, she glared up at him. "Is this what fun looks like to you?"

He ruffled her wild curls. "Maybe not currently. But last night must have been one for the books."

You have no idea. Effie froze in panic, her eyes shooting up to his. *Or do you?* Had Lucian told him what had transpired between them last night? She didn't think Kieran would have said anything to the smirking Guardian, but Lucian . . .

"Let's get some food in you. It will help."

The mention of food sent her stomach roiling. "I don't think that's a good idea."

He gave her a sympathetic look. "One of Liza's homebrews, then."

"Liza?"

"The cook." Kael nudged her. "Come on."

"Kael, I can't go out in public like this. I'm a fright."

Effie was guessing, but she didn't have to look in a mirror to know that her curls were standing up in every direction, or that her face was probably blotchy and tear-stained. Tilting her head, she took a tentative sniff and winced at the smell of alcohol radiating off of her skin. *Mother's tits, how much did I drink?*

"I take it this is your first hangover."

"Elder's balls, there's a name for this?"

Kael snickered. "Little one, for as long as there's been booze, there have been men to overindulge. If it makes you feel better, we've all been there and survived."

Effie shook her head in wonder. "Why in the Mother's name would anyone willingly succumb to this more than the once?"

Her friend's eyes brightened with memories. "The morning might hurt, but the night's revelries are worth the ache."

Scowling up at one of the floating balls of light, Effie wholeheartedly disagreed. This was hell, but a fitting punishment given the mess she'd made of things.

Sensing something in her silence, Kael looked back at her. "I take it that was not your experience."

Effie blushed from the tips of her ears down to her toes. She couldn't meet his gaze as she mumbled, "Not quite."

He brushed a finger beneath her chin. "Whatever you think you did, there's nothing so bad that you cannot make amends."

Cheeks burning, she shook her head. "Some things you can never take back."

Kael hummed. "Words or actions?" he inquired after a long stretch of silence.

Effie contemplated the question, frowning as she replied, "Both?"

"Are you asking me?" he chuckled.

Scrubbing both her hands over her face, Effie groaned. "I don't know."

"But you remember what happened?"

"Unfortunately."

"Do you want to tell me about it? I could offer a fresh perspective."

"Absolutely not," she said, finally meeting his eyes again.

Kael's gaze roamed over her face. "Then I will say just one more thing and not mention it again."

Effie remained quiet as she waited for him to chastise her, practically willing him to say aloud the things she had said to herself the night before. Maybe it would purge some of this awful ache inside of her.

"I have seen how he looks this morning, and it is true that harm has been done, but not the unforgivable kind. Show that you are sorry. Make your peace, and it will be forgotten."

Effie blinked up in confusion. *Which he?* Two pairs of haunted, angry eyes floated through her mind.

Nothing in any realm would pry the question from her lips. Instead, she nodded.

It was not what she'd been expecting, but it was sound advice all the same. She could not take back what she'd said or done, but she could try to make amends. Perhaps she could salvage at least some of her dignity, if not the friendships themselves.

Not that friendship had been on her mind the night before.

Effie forcibly pulled herself away from that dangerous line of thought. The only way she'd been able to tame her tears the night before had been once she'd stopped allowing herself to think about the sting of Lucian's rejection . . . or the feel of demanding lips moving over hers. She didn't let herself think about the differences between their kisses. Not how one touched her with the reverence of a man seeking salvation as he pressed her against the wall, or how the other had practically ignited her with the intensity of his passion as he undressed her.

And she definitely didn't think about how the man who'd died to save her—whose last words were ones of love for her—had never once touched her with the kind of all-consuming need both of the others had.

Nope. Not once.

Her misery must have shown on her face. Kael nudged her with his shoulder.

"Come, little warrior. We will feed you, and then we will train. I think you will find that by the time we are through, all is not as hopeless as it seems."

She scoffed but did not argue. The hope that he was somehow right was too potent to ignore.

Effie trailed along behind Kael, lost to the thoughts she kept trying to ignore. He held the door open for her and she stumbled in, her eyes immediately pulled to the right.

She froze, the air leaving her lungs as she fought the impulse to run.

Lucian was there, his dark gaze boring into her as if demanding she spill each and every one of her secrets. Only Kael's steady presence at her side kept her from shrinking back out of the room.

As Effie stared wordlessly at her Guardian, a prickling at her neck had her eyes dart to the left. Harsh buzzing filled her ears as Kieran's accusing gaze found hers.

Mother save her. Both of them? She was ill-prepared to deal with one of them, let alone both at the same time.

The scrape of wood against stone pulled her eyes back to the right. Lucian stalked toward them; his expression carefully neutral.

Hysterical laughter bubbled up, and Effie's hand shot out squeezing Kael's forearm.

He looked at her with concern. "Effie?"

"Please don't leave me," she begged.

Maybe Lucian wouldn't kill her if there were witnesses.

"I'm surprised to see you out of bed this early. How are you feeling?" Lucian asked.

Out of everything he could have said, polite formality was not what she expected.

"G-good morning," she stuttered.

She'd braced herself for cruel words, not kindness. The lack of them caught her off guard, leaving her defenseless.

There was not a trace of last night's anger—or passion—on the Guardian's face. There was nothing at all to hint at the so-called harm Kael had alluded to. If she couldn't recall—with heartbreaking clarity

—each breath-stealing kiss and every ugly word she'd said to him, Effie would have thought she imagined the whole thing.

"Are you well?" he inquired again.

Effie didn't know how to answer that. She felt like wolf shit. Her heart was a conflicted, battered thing inside her chest. The amount of shame and embarrassment that filled her right now should be impossible for a woman her size, and if that wasn't enough, her stomach was about one surprise away from having her doubling over and emptying it on Lucian's polished boots. Wouldn't that be the perfect end to the morning?

"I'm alive," she answered finally, her voice sounding like she'd swallowed shards of glass.

Lucian's lips twitched. "I'm glad to hear it."

"As am I. I think."

Kael chuckled.

"I find that no matter the malady, sleep is always a fitting remedy."

Effie's mouth opened and closed. *What in the Mother's name is going on here? Who is this man, and what has he done with Lucian?* There is absolutely no way in hell that this limpid, pleasantry exchanging man was her Guardian. He was being far too amiable and lacked all of the scowling, simmering violence that called to her.

She didn't trust it. Not for a second.

Kieran's cultured laugh rang out and Effie's eyes closed.

No. Please no . . .

His lips were twisted in a cruel smile as he joined them, and Effie knew before the first syllable fell from his lips that her punishment was finally starting.

"Unfortunately for Effie, she hardly slept a wink last night. Isn't that right, love?"

The temperature in the room dropped to arctic levels and Effie shivered, her eyes lifting up to Lucian's face. He was too well-trained to show how the words affected him, but Effie caught the throb of a vein in his throat and the slight tightening around his mouth. He didn't look at her, but she knew his words were for her.

"At least she found her way back to her room."

Kieran's laugh was filled with innuendo. "And with all of her clothes too."

The vein in Lucian's neck was throbbing faster now. She couldn't bear to see what he thought of her, so she didn't lift her eyes up any further. It was one thing to have words thrown in your face, it was another to learn they'd been acted upon. Just as it was twenty-times more painful to have your shameful actions spoken about as if they were a source of public amusement.

Effie's heart dropped to her knees. If there had been any flicker of hope that Kieran respected her enough not to humiliate her in front of the Guardians, it died a slow and painful death then and there. She bit the inside of her cheek, using the pain to keep herself from sinking into a pit of despair.

Beside her, Kael's warm hand wrapped around hers, offering silent support.

The tears she'd fought so hard to keep in check, spilled down her cheeks.

"Better that clarity comes too late than not at all," she whispered.

Unmoved by her tears, Kieran landed the final verbal blow. "Thankfully not before I learned the exact shade of those perky—"

"Enough!" a familiar voice roared from behind her. A warm hand grasped her upper arm and gently, but firmly, tugged her back.

She was too stunned to resist, blinking up at Ronan's glowering face as it twisted in disgust. There wasn't even time for her to wonder when he'd arrived. She was too busy being thankful his disgust was not aimed at her. She didn't think she'd survive disappointing him as well.

Ice blue eyes promised death as they found Kieran's. "Finish that sentence and I'll geld you."

Kieran's throat bobbed, but he kept his mouth shut.

Ronan turned to Lucian next, his lip curled in a sneer. "And you . . "

Lucian's dark gaze was searing as it dropped to her and then to where Ronan still held her. "Let her go," he said, his voice a dark growl.

Ronan's cheeks were flushed with anger, until they were the same shade of red as his braid.

"So now you want to protect her? What kind of man allows such slander of one under his protection?"

Lucian's eye twitched, but he didn't back down. Not even Ronan, in all his fuming glory, intimidated her Guardian.

"If you want to keep your hand, *Shield*, you will remove it from my charge this instant."

"You know who I am? Good. Then you'll know that I mean it when I say if I find out you've been allowing this abuse to go on unchecked, it's me you'll be answering to. All of you."

Effie swallowed, still too stunned by his appearance to fully take in what was happening. She glanced around at the others.

Kieran's ears were pink, but he wasn't looking at Ronan. He was staring at Lucian with a look so dark Effie wanted to hide behind Ronan's towering frame. She'd never seen that kind of hatred, not even when she'd worked for the Holbrookes as their ungifted servant.

Kael was a silent sentinel as he watched the exchange. He placed a hand on Lucian's shoulder, as if telling him to stand down.

Lucian ignored him, looking instead to Effie. His dark eye glittered, the metallic flecks all but snuffed out as he waited. He didn't speak or give any indication of what he was waiting for, but he didn't need to. She already knew. If she hinted in any way that she didn't want to go with Ronan, Lucian would destroy him.

It was then that she finally understood. Of all the power and strength these men collectively possessed, only one of them should truly be feared.

But never by her.

While Ronan, Kael, and Lucian were all warriors with countless kills between them, there was a hint of madness blazing in Lucian's umber eyes that bespoke a primal resolve the other's lacked. As he stood there, staring down at her, a part of his mask was stripped away, lying bare a piece of his soul.

Guardian was not just a title; it was Lucian's defining purpose. There was nothing that would get between him and that duty. With a single, penetrating look, Lucian told her that he would protect her with his dying breath, no matter what she'd done or the potential fallout of his actions. Things were far from resolved between them. She owed him another apology at the very least, but for now the weight of her mistakes abated enough for her to draw in an easy breath and shift her focus to the man beside her.

"You picked a hell of a morning to arrive," she muttered, pulling Ronan's icy glare to her.

His expression softened and he lifted a scarred hand to brush away the last of her tears. "It would seem you left a few things out in your letter," Ronan said.

She could feel the other three men staring at her, but she ignored them. "I don't recall writing that letter to *you*."

Ronan smirked, holding out a hand for her to take. "Perks of the job."

She placed her hand in his, allowing him to lead her from the hall as if he'd done it a thousand times before. The flood of relief she felt at their escape was impossible to ignore. She could have kissed Ronan she was so grateful, except kisses were what had gotten her into this mess in the first place, so she settled for a teasing question instead.

"Do you know where you're going?"

"Not remotely." Despite the words, he walked with a confident swagger back toward the central archive. "Now that it's just the two of us, you going to tell me what that was about?" Ronan asked.

Effie grimaced. "I'm never drinking again."

His booming laugh bounced off the walls. "Oh, Effie. I can only imagine the trouble you've gotten into. At least you're keeping them on their toes."

"That's one way to look at it."

"Fine, keep your secrets for now. I'll pull them from you eventually."

Effie had no doubt that he would. She'd seen the way he'd looked at Kieran and Lucian. Not wanting to think about how that would play out, she asked, "How did you even get here?"

Ronan held out a dark purple stone. "You asked for help. Here

I am."

"You've been to the citadel before and were able to use the Kaelpas stone to get here directly? Why do I find that unlikely?"

Ronan grinned. "One of the hooded fuckers was waiting for us in the jungle. He brought us here."

Effie shook her head at his irreverence, biting back a smile. "Us? So, the rest of the Circle is here as well?"

"Am I not good enough for you?" he asked, quirking his brow.

Effie grinned. "I mean no offense, but I asked Helena for help."

Ronan feigned being wounded. "Helena and Von are taking some much-needed time for themselves. She was unavailable, but I did not get the impression from your letter that you could wait."

Effie squeezed his hand. "Thank you for coming. You assumed correctly."

A slight feminine cough met her words as they turned into the circular room.

Effie looked up, catching sight of a woman whose mass of black hair was a tangle of curls and braids. Small charms twinkled like stars in the dark cloud of her mane as Reyna, leader of the Night Stalkers, moved closer. Her face was clear of the swirling paint she wore when heading into battle, and her leaf-green eyes crinkled as she smiled warmly.

"Nice to see you again, Keeper."

Effie bowed. "You as well, Lady Reyna."

The Night Stalkers lived in the Forest of Whispers, a sprawling forest that bordered Bael along its Southern end. They were one of the Forsaken tribes; those that had been forgotten by the Chosen for not living by the way of the Mother. Living amongst the trees, and using shadows to cloak themselves, the Night Stalkers were the protectors of the forest—and they were deadly assassins.

If Helena couldn't be here, Reyna and Ronan were far from a consolation prize.

Three hooded figures glided into the room.

Reyna and Ronan lost their smiles and Effie sighed.

So much for getting reacquainted.

CHAPTER 33

"*We* *are glad to see that our daughter's warning reached you.*"

Ronan's eyes narrowed at the use of their psychic voices, but his voice was steady as he replied. "Effie is part of the Kiri's court. We will always come when aid is requested."

Effie flushed with pleasure. Helena had said the same the last time they spoke, but to hear Ronan reinforce the words helped settle something inside her that had been unmoored since arriving in the citadel.

"*We fear that this new threat is just beginning.*"

"That is what her letter said."

"*The Corruptor's magic has left a stain on the land.*"

"*The stain must be cleansed.*"

"*Before the perversion of life goes unchecked.*"

"How do we find the stains?"

"*We are still seeking an answer.*"

"There's no mention of this in any of the prophecies?" Ronan asked with thinly veiled disbelief.

The Triumvirate's answer was silence.

Understanding how unique and biased prophecies could be, Effie thought it wasn't so much that there wasn't a prophecy as perhaps a sign that had been misunderstood. They were likely still in the process of working through the Hall of Prophecies searching for a pattern or clue they'd originally missed.

"You mentioned the Shadows are sentient now?" Ronan asked, turning to Effie.

Effie nodded, revulsion and fear snaking through her at the reminder. "Yes, whatever tethered them to Rowena snapped when she died, but did not undo her magic entirely."

Ronan frowned and exchanged a glance with Reyna. "Does that sounds familiar to you?"

"Sounds like her Generals," Reyna murmured.

Effie flinched. Rowena's Generals were the members of her corrupted Circle. The men whose power was left intact after she bound them to her so that she could unleash them on Elysia. They were the only Shadows with access to elemental magic. They were responsible for the death of Darrin and her grandmother.

Taking a shaky breath, Effie forced herself to pay attention to the conversation and not get lost in her grief.

"But the Generals were destroyed," Ronan pointed out.

"As were the Shadows that were nearby when she died."

Ronan and Reyna exchanged a look.

Reyna spoke first. "Serena mentioned that packs had escaped. Perhaps they were too far away when she died to be affected."

Ronan nodded. "They regained their independence, but their power was too corrupted for them to fully return to themselves."

Effie shuddered. Those creatures could be anywhere. Worse, the farther away they got, the further their infection spread.

"We need to get the word out. If the Shadows have already attacked here, they will have struck other villages as well. We should be able to track them if we can trace their path," Ronan murmured, his gaze calculating.

"I can dispatch the Night Stalkers," Reyna offered.

Ronan nodded and lifted his eyes back to the Triumvirate. "I would like to see the attack site."

They dipped their heads in a nod.

"What do you hope to find there?" Effie asked, a sense of foreboding taking hold of her at his request.

"A sense of the corruption; to see if we can recognize the feel of it to warn the others what to look for," Reyna answered for him.

Pinpricks shot up her arms and Effie rubbed her hands up and down trying to alleviate the sensation.

"Daughter?" Smoke inquired.

Effie shook her head, unable to speak as a wave of nausea caused her to stumble.

"Effie?" Ronan asked, his hand snaking out to grab her as her knees buckled.

She was already screaming before the vision fully pulled her under.

Tendrils of darkness wrapped themselves around her body, slithering across her skin until they covered every inch of her. She burned, but not with the heat of fire. It was the searing pain of absolute cold.

This was the absence of heat . . . of life.

Effie clamped her mouth closed, her only defense against the darkness that had her suspended in the air.

Eyes wide, she scanned what used to be a thriving rain forest. The trees were skeletal, their branches dangling like withered limbs beside the corpse of their once beautiful trunks.

The sky above swirled with clouds, lightning flickering deep within the foggy depths, as more of the tendrils shot out from the clouds moving straight toward her.

Effie tried to move, but she was caught fast. Her eyes wide with terror as she struggled to breathe.

One of the tendrils took the shape of a hand, its blackened fingers caressing her cheeks before grasping her and squeezing hard. It was forcing her mouth open.

She fought as best she could but she was defenseless against the strength of its grasp.

More of the smoky tendrils converged before her, turning first into a ball of swirling darkness, and then into the shape of a man. There were no distinguishing features, but there was no missing the sinister smile, or the glide of a tongue across its mouth.

Without warning, it sealed its ice-cold lips over hers and pumped her full of the darkness contained within.

Effie's body spasmed at the invasion, unable to breathe as she was filled with tendril after tendril of corruption.

She was screaming, begging for it to stop, but the voice grew fainter until it was no more than a ragged whisper as the relentless invasion continued.

When the creature made of nightmares finally finished, the horrible reality became clear.

There was not just one walking nightmare, but two.

She was one of them.

EFFIE HEAVED, her body trying to purge her of the darkness that still felt like it was slithering inside of her. Wiping her mouth with the back of her hand, she pushed herself up, gasping for breath, her body ice cold.

Ronan's arms were banded around her as he helped her into a seated position. He knew better than to ask if she was alright.

Reyna's hand was pressed against her ankle, one more anchor to this reality. She let the heat of their touch warm her, even though she still shook with the imagined cold.

"What did you See?" Ronan asked, speaking near her ear.

Effie shook her head, not ready to give voice to the vision.

"Journal," she mumbled, wanting to write it down instead of saying it out loud.

"Daughter." Smoke folded to his knees beside her, the move so graceful it could have been slow-motion.

She flinched when he lifted his hand.

"Let me help you."

After a tense silence, she jerked her head in a nod. Gently, he rested his hand against her head. This time, Effie felt nothing but blissful emptiness as he replayed her vision.

She barely breathed as she waited for his reaction.

The Keeper jolted as if struck by lightning, falling back as her vision ended.

The Mirrors raced forward, hands outstretched to lift their brother off the ground.

Ronan and Reyna exchanged a worried glance over her head.

The Triumvirate never showed a reaction or acted with any kind of haste. Something was terribly, terribly wrong.

Effie licked her cracked lips, her racing heart feeling like it was about to fly out of her chest.

"What . . . what does it mean?" she finally asked when the silence became unbearable.

The Triumvirate were silent, as if they were too shocked to speak. Finally, Smoke's voice filled her mind.

"It was the first marker. Darkness rises."

Reyna's sharp inhale told Effie he hadn't spoken to her alone.

Holding out a hand to help her stand, the Triumvirate spoke as one. *"The Shadow Years are upon us."*

FROM HIS HIDING place in the hallway, Kieran turned away from the Triumvirate and their guests to slide back into the relative safety of the dark. Smoldering anger and small flickers of guilt wormed their way through him. He silenced the guilt and focused instead on the anger, letting it fuel him.

Effie had betrayed him.

It had taken only one look at the haunted eyes of the Guardian when she'd stepped foot into the dining hall to realize what had happened; why she'd fled from him.

Rage unlike anything he'd ever felt took over, and the need to mark her as his became his driving need.

He knew he'd hurt her when he implied she'd spent the night in his arms. If things had gone the way they were supposed to, she would have. And she wouldn't have felt any embarrassment about the fact, either.

She should have been overjoyed at the thought, but instead of joy, she'd felt guilt and she'd run. Because of *him*.

Kieran let out a low snarl at the thought of the Guardian trying to claim what was his.

Effie would forgive his harsh words.

She was his. The girl from his dreams.

The one he'd left everything behind to find.

He would not lose her now.

He just needed to prove that he was her future. The only one that mattered.

With a soft whistle, Kieran peeled himself away from the wall and made his way to the unmarked door.

Pushing it open, he wandered into the Hall of Prophecy, letting the door close behind him with a soft click.

FROM THE AUTHOR

If you enjoyed this book, please consider writing a short review
and posting it on Amazon, Bookbub, Goodreads and/or
anywhere else you share your love of books.

Reviews are very helpful to other readers and are greatly
appreciated by authors
(especially this one!)

When you post a review, send me an email and let me know! I
might feature part, or all, of it on social media.

XOXO

meg@megannewrites.com

ACKNOWLEDGMENTS

I have a small army to thank after getting through this one. Firstly, to **my readers**, I really hope you enjoyed the first glimpse into Effie's journey. There's been something special about this character since she appeared in Reign and I knew she needed her own series. Thank you for all of the messages and emails letting me know your thoughts. I appreciate all of you so, so much.

To **my husband**, thank you for being my alpha reader, for letting me run into your office to shout random plot points at you like you are having the same internal debates I am, and for always being there with a hug or an emergency unicorn when things get messy. I love you.

Mom and Dad, thank you for being my de facto storage facility while I am out of the country. You make it easy to chase my dream, and I am so lucky to have you.

To my sprint gals (gang? Did we ever pick out a crew name?) **Melissa, Heather, Chanda** quite simply this book wouldn't exist without you. You make work feel like hanging out with some of my best friends. I appreciate all of the advice and encouragement. And quite frankly, I'd probably go two or three days without putting on a clean shirt if I knew you wouldn't notice on our Skype chats. **Kel, Raye, Jess** you are more than friends you are heroes. Thank you for putting me back together when I felt like I was coming apart. **Analisa, Dom** thank you for helping make my book shine. I am so blessed to have found you. I swear you both have halos.

And lastly the best little spoon in the world, Henry, and my future Instagram star, Karma. You two will never read this, but your unconditional love make my heart melt. Thank you for keeping me company while I write all the words. Our snuggle breaks are one of the best parts of my day.

ABOUT THE AUTHOR

Meg Anne has always had stories running on a loop in her head. They started off as daydreams about how the evil queen (aka Mom) had her slaving away doing chores; and more recently shifted into creating backgrounds about the people stuck beside her during rush hour. The stories have always been there; they were just waiting for her to tell them.

Like any true SoCal native, Meg enjoys staying inside curled up with a good book and her cat Henry... or maybe that's just her. You can convince Meg to buy just about anything if it's covered in glitter or rhinestones, or make her laugh by sharing your favorite bad joke. She also accepts bribes in the form of baked goods and Mexican food.

Meg loves to write about sassy heroines and the men that love them. She is best known for her adult fantasy romance series The Chosen, which can be found on Amazon.

ALSO BY MEG ANNE

THE CHOSEN UNIVERSE

THE CHOSEN

Mother of Shadows

Reign of Ash

Crown of Embers

Queen of Light

THE KEEPERS

The Keeper's Legacy

The Keeper's Retribution (Coming 2019)

The Keeper's Vow (Coming 2019)

OTHER WORKS

CURSED HEARTS

CO-WRITTEN WITH JESSICA WAYNE

Star-Crossed

Amria

Supernova

ANTHOLOGIES

25 Days of Christmas

Tales of Vixen Falls

Of Thrones and Crowns

The Monster Ball Year 2 (Coming 2019)

59226239R00158

Made in the USA
Middletown, DE
10 August 2019